D1414405

LAWLESS DESERT

C.M. CURTIS

PUBLISHING
kwympublishing.com
info@kwympublishing.com

1st Edition
Cover Design/Page Layout by KWYM Publishing, LLC

ISBN-13: 978-1508677390
ISBN-10: 1508677395

DEDICATION

This book is dedicated to Martin Durrant.

Contents

FOREWORD

There really was a town named Pick-Em-Up Arizona, though very little is known about it now. In fact, there seems to be no one alive today who even knows its exact location. The extent of the available information about the town is a little about the believed origin of the name Pick-Em-Up, the fact that it was located between Charleston (now a ghost town) and Tombstone, and that it consisted chiefly of saloons and brothels—more than enough information for a fiction writer.

CHAPTER 1

Martin Chambliss figured there were at least five Apaches out there, maybe more. There was no way to tell for sure. Earlier in the day Rodriguez had killed one, and Randall, the soldier, had wounded another. Now Randall and Rodriguez were both dead.

Chambliss himself had killed two Apaches on the day they had attacked the stage. It had happened very suddenly. The driver had been the first to die, and then the rancher from Tucson, and then the young man—occupation unknown—who was going to meet his fiancée to marry her. Gratefully there had been no women on the stage, just the five men and the driver. And now Chambliss was the only one left, and he knew the Apaches knew it.

So far no one had been taken alive to be tortured to death as he had been told the Apaches liked to do. But everything he had heard told Chambliss that the Indians would expend great effort to keep from killing him outright for that very reason. Well, he wasn't dead yet, and he wasn't caught yet, and bleak as his circumstances may appear, formidable though the enemy may be, he had enough confidence in his own abilities to at least give him a hope of survival.

Chambliss had never fought Apaches before. Almost everything he had known about them—before yesterday—he had acquired second hand. But he had lived among other Indians. He had, in fact, grown up among them and had skills of his own. And the Apaches had already gotten a pretty good taste of the accuracy of his shooting.

They had rifles. He had seen some of them, and they fired the occasional bullet, but mostly they had shot arrows, telling Chambliss their supply of ammunition was low. This was definitely in his favor; however, he knew better than to base too much optimism on the fact. These Indians were very good with their bows and arrows; they had demonstrated that amply over the past two days. And as for bullets, well, it only took one to kill a man.

He took a sip from the water bag, grateful that it was winter in this Arizona desert. The summers, he had been told, were brutal. There were other problems to think about, too, and one of them was food—he had none. He glanced at the two dead bodies lying against one wall of the cave and felt a deep sorrow. They had been good men, both of them. Randall, the soldier, had been an experienced Indian fighter. He knew the Apache well and had respected their fighting abilities, and in a short time Chambliss had learned a lot from him.

Randall had said the Apache did not like to fight at night, but they would sometimes do it. Night was coming on. They had not attacked last night or the night before. Would they choose to do so tonight? Chambliss believed they would. The shallow cave, with its partial stone barricade, had been a good thing up to now. In truth, it was little more than an indentation in the rock, but it provided protection from attack from above and on three sides. Randall, who knew the area, had led them to it after the initial attack on the stage, and the three men had been able to defend it and hold off the Indians. But Chambliss felt that tonight it would become a trap, therefore he must leave it before they came for him. He could not fight them all.

Though his knowledge of the Apache had all been recently acquired, much of it had been acquired firsthand, and he could see they had things in common with tribes that he knew well. To underestimate them would be fatal. His greatest advantage, he believed, would lie in the fact that they would underestimate him. He was a white man, and there were some things that white men simply did not do as well as Indians—or so they would believe. But in the area where he came from, Martin Chambliss had been a woodsman and hunter and tracker of considerable renown. It had often been said of him that he knew Indian ways as well as any Indian.

The Apaches out there could not possibly know these things about him. They would expect him to stay in the cave and continue trying to hold them off, hoping they would eventually tire of the game and leave. He had no intention of doing that.

He took stock of his provisions. When the five men had boarded the stage in El Paso, they had been aware that Apaches were raiding in the area. It was because of this that there were no women or children on the stage and the men were all well armed. But the rifles they carried were all of different calibers, and most of the men had come prepared for a brief fight rather than a long standoff. Chambliss had only two cartridges left. He checked the weapons and the pockets of his two dead companions and found that Rodriguez was completely out of bullets and that Randall had only one cartridge left for the rifle he had brought to the cave.

Their weapons being of no use to him now, Chambliss took Rodriguez's rifle and wedged the barrel under a protruding rock, bending it. Then he held it by the barrel, swung it against the rock, and broke off the stock.

When he had checked the dead men's pockets, he had found Randall to be carrying five cartridges of a caliber that was not compatible with any of the rifles the three men had carried away from the stagecoach. Chambliss now loaded Randall's last bullet into the chamber of his rifle, and then, one by one, he pried the lead slugs out of the brass casings of the five useless cartridges and poured the powder into the end of the barrel. These things he did mostly by feel while crouched behind the stone barricade, knowing he must keep a constant watch and never relax his vigilance. His eyes continuously scanned the terrain that was visible to him from his position, particularly the bare area that any enemy would have to cross in order to reach the opening.

With a sharp stone he dug into the floor of the cave until he found clay about a foot down. He dug some out and mixed it with a little water from the water bag the men had managed to bring with them when they'd abandoned the stagecoach. Using a stick, he tamped the clay as far into the barrel as he could and then carefully cleaned the opening so there would appear to be nothing unusual about the weapon. This rifle was now a bomb. At some point, he would offer it as a gift to the Apaches.

Chambliss, like most outdoorsmen, possessed keen eyesight as well as the ability to study and memorize terrain so as to be aware of any change. Just before dusk, he noticed a small bush that was out of place and he shot it. There was a grunt and a shuffling sound, then nothing more.

One less Apache to worry about. Hopefully they would think twice before trying to sneak up on him again.

When darkness came, he blacked his face and hands with charcoal from an old campfire inside the cave. Because they were dark in color, he had earlier removed Randall's army blouse and pants from the man's body and he put them on now over his own clothes. He was wearing moccasins because he always wore moccasins. He had worn them all his life and did not feel comfortable using any other kind of footgear. And he had long ago grown immune to the stares and comments of people who disapproved.

He shouldered the water bag and picked up his rifle. He had made a sling for the plugged rifle out of Rodriguez's belt, and he now slung it over his other shoulder, patted the sheath knife he always wore on his belt, and slipped out of the cave. The moon had not yet shown its face, and the night was very dark.

He thought he had a pretty good idea where the Apaches had left their horses; he and his companions had passed through the area during their retreat to the cave. It was a grassy meadow with a small spring at one end. In this Arizona desert, there weren't a lot of grassy meadows, and springs were few and far between. This one, Randall had told him, would be dry during the long, hot summer months, but right now it was a good place to picket horses, perhaps the only one for miles around.

Having grown up among Indians and learned their ways from his childhood, Chambliss possessed the ability to move silently, and now this ability served him well. He found the meadow without difficulty. Peering over the rim of the hill, he was able to make out the dim shapes of several horses on picket ropes, and he could hear them cropping the grass. Had the Apaches left someone with the horses? Had they believed it would be necessary? He doubted it.

He could not waste time trying to make sure. By now they likely would have discovered he was missing from the cave and would be searching for him. Would they expect him to go to the place where they had left their horses? Again, he doubted it.

Soundlessly, he moved down into the meadow, his head and eyes in constant motion, keenly alert. Moving quickly around the meadow, he found the picket ropes and, one by one, cut the throats of the horses, leaving only one alive for himself.

One huge advantage the Apaches had over him was that they knew this area, while he was new here. But least now he was mounted and they were afoot. Hung around the neck of one of the horses he had found a hide bag that contained some dried meat, a small amount of loose flour, and some piñon nuts. He ate some of this food as he rode, grateful to be putting something in his stomach after so long a time.

Most white men were not comfortable riding bareback, but Chambliss had first learned to ride that way as a small boy, and in his life he had ridden as often without a saddle as with one. He did so now, riding in the darkness, not following any trail but orienting himself by the stars, and when the morning sun finally sank the horizon, it was at his back. Had he lost them? Was he safe now? He knew that to assume so could be dangerous. "Never underestimate an Apache," Randall had told him. "They're smarter than we are. The only reason we ever win a fight is because there are more of us and we're better equipped."

Chambliss learned this firsthand when, just before noon, the horse he was riding grunted and its forelegs buckled. As he slid off the horse, the rolling report of the rifle shot caught up with the lead slug that had killed the animal.

Everything he owned now was hanging on his body or in his hands: The water bag, the small Apache food bag, and the two rifles. He dropped the plugged rifle—his gift to the Apaches—on the ground beside the dead horse and left it there as he slipped into the brush. Once undercover he quickly changed his direction. A short time later he came to a trail and decided to follow it.

There was one thing he did not know about Apaches, something he had never thought to ask, and now he wished he had: Were they runners? The Indians Chambliss had grown up with were consummate woodsmen. They traveled mostly on foot and could run all day without stopping to rest, carrying their food and water with them and frequently consuming small amounts as they ran. Chambliss could do the same as well as the best of them.

He started off now, moving toward the northwest, his long legs taking easy, loping strides, his tall, slender, muscular body settling into a rhythm that he could keep up all day long.

The day had warmed up, and he took a sip of water on the run and stopped to quickly remove the soldier's clothing that he had put on over his own. Afterward, he slipped over a rise in the land, then stopped and flattened himself on the other side, peering over the top. As he watched, he saw three Apaches running toward his downed horse. They were not tall men, but they were big chested, and he could tell by their smooth, easy stride that they were runners.

The first one to reach the dead horse saw the discarded rifle, picked it up, checked the breach, and, finding that it was loaded, held it triumphantly in the air for his companions to see. Two of the Apaches carried bows and quivers of arrows. None of them now were carrying rifles, which told Chambliss that the bullet that had killed his horse was their last one and they had discarded or cached the now-useless rifle that had fired it.

It was time to move on and he did. A short time later, glancing back, he saw the Indians come over the rise from which he had observed them. He picked up the pace a little. There would be no more stopping now. The Apaches would not stop until they captured or killed him or they could no longer run. And he would not stop until they captured or killed him or he could no longer run.

Once again he knew he must count on them underestimating him. He was a white man, and they were Apache. They would believe that no white man could outrun them. If they believed this, it was his hope that they would expend energy in an all-out effort to run him down. He would conserve his strength. He would save it for the end. But this would mean allowing them to get closer.

It was sometime around noon when the trail he was following passed between two low bluffs and curved around behind one of them. It only took him a few seconds to climb to the top of the bluff and take a bead on chest of the lead Indian.

They spotted the movement and started to dive into the brush, but too late. He had already squeezed the trigger. The Indian was thrown backward, landing on his back in the trail. He rolled onto his side, made a few convulsive movements, and was still.

Chambliss wasted no time. In seconds he was back on the trail and expended some of his strength in a burst of speed to regain the lead he had maintained for several hours, afterward settling back into his comfortable pace.

It was early afternoon when he decided it was time for his next ploy. His rifle was empty now; useless to him except as a club, and he wanted to discard it. But before he did he wanted to even the odds. At a point where the trail began a slow upward rise, he pretended to be laboring, slowing down, and finally coming to a stop. He turned to face the Apaches, resting his hands on his thighs—the picture of exhaustion. Their cries of elation came to him from across the valley, but then he turned, and showing them renewed strength, continued on up the rise. He glanced over his shoulder and saw one of the Apaches holding the plugged rifle to his shoulder. The gun had exploded, and the Indian was on the ground before the report reached Chambliss' ears. He turned to look, and even from the distance he could see that part of the man's head was missing.

The last remaining Apache went to his friend, briefly knelt beside him, then leaped to his feet and, with a burst of speed powered by rage, fairly flew across the narrow valley. Chambliss discarded his empty rifle and matched his speed with that of the Apache. He swept up the grade and over the rise, allowing the weight of his body and his momentum to carry him down the other side in long leaping strides.

They ran on through the day, hour after hour. There were no more strategies to employ, no more tricks. They would run until one of them lacked the strength to continue. If Chambliss tired first, the Apache would shorten the distance between them and put an arrow in his back. If it was the Apache whose legs faltered, Chambliss would leave him behind.

The sun was directly ahead of him now, descending toward the horizon. He looked back frequently, expecting the Apache to put on a burst of speed at any time. The Indian certainly now understood that this white man was no ordinary white man. He could move silently in the night like an Indian, and if the race was not ended before darkness came, the Apache might never see him again.

Just before dusk the Apache began closing the gap. This was the time for which Chambliss had been hoarding his strength all day. As he quickened his pace he uncorked the water bag and took a final swallow, taking care not to drink too much. He didn't want a lot of water sloshing around in his stomach. He had been eating the dried meat, the flour, and the piñon nuts in small amounts throughout the day. There was a little meat left, and as he ran he removed it from the bag and put it in his pocket, discarding the bag. He took another swallow from the water bag and turned it over, allowing the remaining water to run out, and then he dropped it on the trail. He wanted no excess weight of any kind to slow him down.

He checked behind him again. The Apache was putting everything he had into this final sprint. He held his bow in one hand and an arrow in the other. Just a little closer and he would nock the arrow, pull back the bow string, and release.

Chambliss knew he had to be careful now. He had to watch the Apache closely and at the same time watch the trail ahead. One misstep, one stumble, would mean death. He let the Apache draw closer, took a quick backward look, and saw the Indian nock the arrow. Chambliss put on a burst of speed and widened the gap. It wasn't hard to do; he still felt good, and it forced the Indian to do the same, expending his strength—and he had been running all day without food or water.

Several times Chambliss repeated this action. Each time, the Apache nocked the arrow and raised the bow, and, each time, the white man pulled out of range. But finally, Chambliss heard what he had been listening for. With darkness approaching, the Apache had decided to put everything he had into one final, heroic effort, and Chambliss heard his grunts of agony.

He forced his body into a hard sprint. It was time to show the Apache that he had lost. It was time to take the heart out of the Indian. He filled his lungs and gave the war cry of the Ojibwe. He increased the length of his stride and pulled away from the Apache almost as if the man were standing still. It felt good. His body was responding as it always had. He was young and in his prime and he had been putting food and water in his stomach throughout the day. He ran up to the top of a hill, stopped, and turned to look behind him. The Apache was stopped in the middle of the trail, far behind.

Chambliss gave the Ojibwe war cry again, and he and the Apache gazed at each other across the distance for a few moments. Then the Indian turned and began a slow trot back down the trail.

CHAPTER 2

As soon as the Apache was out of sight, Chambliss turned and resumed running, wanting to put plenty of space between him and the Indian in the event the man should attempt some form of trickery. He left the trail and ran until darkness made running dangerous and then walked for several hours, making as little sound as possible, confident the Apache could not track him on such a black night as this. Finally he began searching for a safe place to rest.

He found a place where no one could sneak up on him, and though he slept well, his mind was alert to every sound. At dawn he came instantly awake. He got up and checked his surroundings and then took stock of himself. He had recovered from yesterday's run. There was a little stiffness in his leg muscles, but there was no soreness. And though he was hungry and extremely thirsty, he felt very much alive and energized. He ate the last of the Apaches' dried meat, and after another survey of his surroundings, he started on his way again.

He needed water. He could last for days without food, but he would have to find water soon. This may present a problem, owing to the fact that he was in unfamiliar territory. There may be springs nearby, but he did not know how to find them.

In his native region, in the forests of Michigan and Wisconsin, he knew how to survive. But in those forests, water was plentiful. He also knew which plants were edible and was skilled in the art of making snares and deadfalls in order to obtain meat. But this Arizona desert was very different from anything he had experienced before.

In his mind there was still a need for caution. He was in Apache country and he was alone. He needed to get to Tucson, his original destination. The person he was coming to see lived near there. Chambliss knew he was not out of danger. He had escaped the Apaches, but he was very much lost in a hostile and unfamiliar land.

As he considered these matters in his mind, his eyes were

constantly moving, alert to his surroundings, both near and distant. Now they caught a hint of dust in the air toward the west. Whatever was creating the dust was coming in his direction. He decided to investigate, and an hour later found himself on a hilltop observing a distant group of riders. They were keeping to an established trail and were white men, and ten minutes later he was waiting by the side of the trail as they approached.

He had hoped they would be soldiers, but they were not. From every description he had read and every picture he had seen, he could tell they were riders of the range, complete with Stetsons and chaparreras. They were all well armed, each man possessing a carbine and a pistol, and seeing him, they reined in.

The lead rider looked Chambliss up and down, taking in his sweat-stained clothes, his moccasins, and his lack of hat, weapons, or canteen. He had no provisions or anything in which to carry them. He did not even own a blanket. And he was sure he had not sweated away all the charcoal he had used to blacken his face before leaving the cave night before last. He must look a sight.

The rider shook his head in manifest disgust, and then, as if he had every right to interrogate, he said, "Who are you?"

Resenting the rider's tone, Chambliss was slow to answer. Finally he said, "Name's Chambliss, what's yours?"

Ignoring the question, the rider said, "What's your story?"

"I was on the stage to Tucson. We were attacked by Apaches."

The rider's brow furrowed. He turned to an older, gray-haired man next to him, and the two exchanged a skeptical look. He said, "That's a long way from here. What'd you do? Ride your horse to death runnin' away from the fight?"

It was clear to Chambliss that this man would not believe the truth, so he said nothing. When it became obvious he was not going to answer, the rider showed his irritation. He looked again at Chambliss' moccasins and said, "Steal those off a dead Apache?"

Chambliss stolidly maintained silence.

An ugly expression came over the rider's face, and he said in an ominous tone, "Well, mister, you've got some explainin' to do. We'll take you along with us, and I promise you'll do it." He turned to the man next to him and said, "Whitey, you're going to have to ride double."

"Aw, Pete, don't make me ride double with this jasper."

The man called Pete said nothing. He spurred his horse forward, and the rest of the group followed except for Whitey, who looked at Chambliss and grumbled, "Climb on."

Whitey held out his hand, and Chambliss used it to swing up behind the saddle.

Whitey said, "You ride the same horse with a man, you ought to know his name. Mine's Jim White, known to most folks as Whitey."

"Good to meet you, Whitey, and thanks for the loan of the back end of your horse."

As they followed the other riders, Whitey said, "Chambliss, out here we don't ask a man a load of questions. It ain't considered polite. But I'll tell you right now, there's some holes in your story big enough to throw a mule through. So sooner or later you're going to need to do some communicatin'."

"If I do," said Chambliss, "it won't be to Pete."

His only view of Whitey was the back of his head, but he thought he saw it nodding.

———————➤

A man who is accustomed to riding can stay in the saddle all day long and not feel it, but riding on the back of horse's withers is another thing entirely, and Chambliss was glad when the trail rounded a hill and revealed to his eyes a green valley in the distance, with its house and barn and corrals and outbuildings.

Whitey had offered him water from his canteen, and Chambliss had gratefully accepted it. But his stomach had been seriously neglected, and he looked forward to a real meal. After the horses were unsaddled, rubbed down, and led to pasture, the men walked up and started filtering into the cook shack to eat. Chambliss followed them. He could smell the savory aroma of food, and his awakening stomach began growling in anticipation. He was disappointed in this, however, when Pete said, "You're comin' with me to meet the boss."

"What for?" asked Chambliss. "I don't plan on staying here."

"We found you on our range. You got to talk to the boss."

"You didn't find me, I found you."

"Come on," said Pete gruffly.

"I'll come too," said Whitey.

"No need," said Pete.

"I'll come anyway."

Pete scowled but said nothing more.

The main house was a long, low building that formed almost one complete side of the quadrangle that was formed by the house, bunkhouse, tack shed, blacksmith's shed, cook shack, and miscellaneous other buildings.

The front room of the main house was spacious and open, and as Chambliss looked around, he realized that the boss must have a wife. Everywhere were the markings of a woman's taste, but done in such a way as to not appear overly frilly or feminine. A man could be comfortable here too.

He heard the swish of skirts coming from down a hallway and assumed he was about to meet the wife of the boss. She came through the open doorway, and Chambliss involuntarily sucked in his breath when he saw her. She was a slender, full-figured, dark-haired woman with a creamy complexion and large brown eyes. Those eyes sought Whitey first and then Pete, who inclined his head toward Chambliss and said, "We caught this ranny on our range. Says he was in the stagecoach that was hit by the Apaches."

Her eyes reached Chambliss' face at the instant of this pronouncement, and her surprise was as momentary as the blink of an eye. Recovering quickly, she said, "I had understood that all the men on the stage were killed."

"Only them that stayed and fought," said Pete with an unmistakable tone of disdain.

She glanced at Pete, and Chambliss saw a faint expression of impatience—or something more—fleetingly touch her features. "Why don't we let the gentleman tell his story?"

Pete gave a derisive snort.

The woman said, "What is your name?"

"Chambliss."

"Would you like to tell us what happened, Mr. Chambliss?"

"No."

Her eyebrows elevated. "No? You don't wish to share your experience with us?"

"Why should I? I'm being treated like a criminal by people who have no military or legal authority."

Pete pulled his pistol and put the muzzle against Chambliss' ribs. "Beggin' your pardon, ma'am, why don't I take him out to the barn and show him our authority. After a while, we'll come back in and he'll be happy to talk."

"No, Pete. Put your gun away. He's right. We have no authority to treat him like a prisoner or a criminal, and he doesn't have to tell us anything he doesn't want to." Turning to face Chambliss, she said, "You have my apology, Mr. Chambliss, and I for one would be very much interested in hearing your story if you should choose to tell it. And if you do not, you are free to go."

"Your apology is accepted, ma'am. But you owe me another."

Pete flinched and growled, "Well, I'll knock . . ."

"No, Pete. And what apology would that be, Mr. Chambliss?" She folded her arms on her chest.

"Well, ma'am, where I come from we still put a lot of stock in good manners, and we especially believe in treating visitors with courtesy. So far the only one who has shown any kind of courtesy toward me is Mr. White here, who, after picking me up in the middle of the desert, offered me his canteen. I was brought here, and knowing I had been in the desert for days without food, I was not offered a bite to eat, even though everyone else went directly to dinner. But the worst offense of all is to be brought to meet a beautiful woman without being given a chance to wash up or shave or even comb my hair. And so far, no one has even told me your name. I've heard about western hospitality, but I have to say I'm not impressed."

There was a glint of mirth in her eyes as she extended her hand and said, "Guilty on all counts, Mr. Chambliss, and you have my most sincere apology. My name is Jane Quilter, and I am the owner of the Diamond J Ranch. You've already met my foreman, Pete Oxley, and Mr. White, who . . ."

Pete interrupted, unable to contain his outrage. "Ma'am, are you going to let a no-account drifter talk to you that way and then apologize to him?"

She turned and all mirth left her eyes. "Pete, because of you the reputation of this ranch has suffered today. This man should have been offered water and food and our best hospitality. So far as I can see, he's done nothing wrong except having escaped being murdered by Apaches. And if that's a crime, then I hope that I shall become a criminal if ever I am attacked by Indians. Now do as I say."

Chambliss did not like the look he saw in Pete's eyes at that moment, but if Jane Quilter noticed it, she gave no indication. Whitey had stood, silently observing these proceedings, and Chambliss suspected he was a man of deep insight, one who kept his cards close to the vest.

———————

Fried potatoes with onions, beef steak, hot biscuits, beans, and fresh tomato slices never tasted better to any man than they tasted to Chambliss on that day. The meal left him feeling lethargic and sleepy, and he was reminded of how little rest he had gotten the past few days and nights since the Apache attack. But he greatly looked forward to his next interview with Jane Quilter, so he borrowed a razor from Whitey, shaved and washed up as best he could, returned the razor, and said to Whitey, "The boss said she wanted to see me after I ate."

Whitey nodded. "I'll go with you."

On the way over to the house Whitey said, "I was watching the way you looked at Miss Quilter in there a while ago. I'll advise you, mister that she's already taken. And if she weren't, she's too high class for fellers like you or me." He stopped and looked into Chambliss' eyes. "Do you understand what I'm tellin' you?"

Chambliss nodded. "I understand."

They were almost to the door when Pete Oxley, who had been sitting sullenly in a chair on the front porch, got up and joined them and they all went inside.

Jane Quilter could be seen in an adjacent room, sitting at a large mahogany desk, bent over some papers. She got up and came out, waving the three men to seats. Chambliss noticed that Whitey sat nearest her, facing Pete and Chambliss. The older man was obviously very protective of Jane, and of this Chambliss approved.

Jane said, "Well, Mr. Chambliss. Do you have a first name?"

"Horace."

She smiled. It seemed to Chambliss that she almost laughed. "Do you mind if I call you Horace?"

He smiled back at her. "No."

"Then you may call me Jane."

He gave a nod.

"Now," she began, "would you like to tell us your story?"

"No."

Her eyebrows went up. "I believe now, Mr. Chambliss, you're the one who's being impolite. May I ask . . . ?"

He interrupted her. "I'd be happy to tell my story to you and Mr. White, but not while he is in the room." He inclined his head toward Pete. Pete's face reddened. He rose to his feet. "Well, I'll . . ."

"Pete," said Jane. "You are only getting what you deserve. You were rude to Mr. . . . to Horace. You offered him no water or food. You insulted him in my presence. Now, we would like to hear his story, and if he won't tell it with you in the room, then I'll have to ask you to leave."

Pete faced her, his lower lip quivering with anger. "Ma'am, I'm the foreman of this ranch, and I'll not be treated this way."

Chambliss saw Whitey stiffen at this disrespect, but he said nothing. Now Jane stood up and faced Pete. "Yes, you are the foreman of this ranch, and if you want to remain the foreman of this ranch, you will obey my orders without question. Is that understood?"

Pete spun on his heel and walked out of the room. Jane sat down and took a few moments to compose herself, during which she exchanged a long and significant look with Whitey. She turned back to Chambliss and looked at him, and he liked what he saw in her eyes.

He told the story as accurately as possible, and when he was finished, Whitey said, "That is the biggest bunch of double-distilled dishwater I ever heard. I had you figured for a different sort of man, Chambliss." He turned to Jane Quilter and said, "Ma'am, I'll see he gets to town tomorrow, and he can find his own way from there."

She said gently, "No, Whitey, I can tell when a man's lying. I believe him."

"Ma'am, no one outruns an Apache. A real fast white man, if he's mighty scared, might outrun one for a short distance, but an Apache can run all day long."

"According to Horace, the Apache following him did run all day long."

"And that's my point, ma'am. We're not made like them. They're a special sort of human, different from us. They think different and act different. I don't think an Apache could ever learn to write a book or build a wagon. We're better than them in that way, but no white man outruns an Apache—or sneaks past them and kills their horses."

She looked at the floor for a time, and then she said, "Horace, would you mind waiting outside? I'd like to speak with Whitey in private."

After Chambliss left, Jane said, "I appreciate your opinion, Whitey, and I hope you won't be upset with me, but I'm going to offer Horace a job here at the ranch."

"Ma'am, I think you're makin' a mistake. I understand that you trust him. I trusted him a little, too, in the beginning. But that story just don't hold water. He's an easterner. He knows nothin' about Indians, and he knows nothin' about the desert . . ."

"There are Indians in the east, too."

Grudgingly he nodded his head. "Yes, ma'am, but not Apaches."

"Maybe they're not so different."

"Miss Jane, you go ahead and do whatever you think best. You know I trust you. But I hope you don't mind if I keep a close eye on that Chambliss—a mighty close eye."

She smiled. "I'm glad to have you as a friend, Whitey."

He blushed. "Ma'am, don't say things like that. You know I can't . . ."

"Can't what?" she teased. "Take a compliment?"

"Yes, ma'am. Call me a homely, ornery, grizzle-tailed old maverick, and I'll be a lot more comfortable."

"Why, Whitey, I just think people haven't said enough nice things about you in your life. Maybe that's my job."

He grew sober, and she knew he wanted to say something difficult. "Ma'am, you may not think it's my place, but I think you need to be a little careful with that . . . with Chambliss. You're a kind woman. Sometimes you're a little too kind and that can give a man ideas. I wouldn't want a no-account bum like him gettin' ideas. I might wind up havin' to shoot him."

"Have I done something wrong, Whitey?"

"No, ma'am. I'm not sayin' that. It's just that you're young and maybe there are some things you don't know a lot about yet. A certain kind of man, in the presence of woman as fine as you—why, he don't need much subsidizin'. And this one . . . well, it seems to me he started right off bein' a little forward. I can yank him up short by the ears, and he'll catch on just fine, but not if you . . ." He stopped. He seemed at a loss for words.

"Not if I encourage him," she supplied.

"Yes, ma'am."

She smiled. "Thank you, Whitey. I'll be more careful."

He stood and started to leave the room, but she stopped him. "Whitey, I imagine Horace will need to go to town to buy a hat and some riding boots and a few other things, since he lost everything on the stage. I have a letter that needs to go out, and we need a few supplies. Take some of the boys and ride into town tomorrow. You can leave first thing in the morning. And, Whitey, Horace will probably need a little guidance from you.

"Guidance?"

"You know, advice on the kind of clothes he'll need for ranch work. Boots, a hat, things like that. Let him buy them on my account, and I'll take it out of his pay."

Whitey nodded. "Yes, ma'am."

With the exception of Pete Oxley and a particular few of his friends who were openly hostile, the men in the bunkhouse were neither friendly nor unfriendly to Chambliss, and he understood this well. He knew it would take time to be accepted, more so because he was not a westerner. These men considered him to be a tenderfoot, and when it came to ranching in the Arizona desert, he was.

Next morning after the men had saddled their horses, Jane beckoned to Chambliss and Whitey from the front porch of the house. She gave Whitey a folded paper. "This is a list of supplies I need."

"Yes, ma'am."

Handing Chambliss an envelope, she said, "While Whitey is getting the supplies, you can mail this."

"Yes, ma'am."

Whitey came near voicing his disapproval of this, but Jane stopped him with a look.

To the people of the Diamond J, going to town meant going to the small town of Sahuarita, fifteen miles south of Tucson. The town, Whitey informed Chambliss, did not have a post office, but letters left at the stage office would be taken to the one in Tucson.

It was a three-hour ride across the desert to get to Sahuarita, and

Chambliss enjoyed the ride. It was springtime, and all the desert flowers were in bloom. There had been rains recently, and Whitey told him the desert was "as green as you ever see it." It was not comparable to the green of the forests of Wisconsin that Chambliss had so recently left behind, but the desert was certainly beautiful in its own way.

"I went back east once," Whitey told him. "Back to Missouri. Trees everywhere. Couldn't see a thing for the trees. Out here, from just about anywhere, you can see way off." He pointed. "Climb up on that bluff there, and you'll see twenty miles in every direction."

It was true, thought Chambliss. It was a wide-open country with a big sky above it that stretched the eye and the imagination.

Sahuarita wasn't much of a town, but Chambliss liked it. It had its own kind of charm.

"Stage office is over there." Whitey pointed, and Chambliss rode that way, stopping at the hitching rack while Whitey stopped at the general store. There was something he wanted to do, and he didn't want Whitey to see him do it, so took his time climbing down from the saddle and tying up the horse, watching to make sure Whitey went inside. He then went around the side of the building to the back, where he carefully opened the letter Jane had given him, and began to read it. So engrossed was he in the letter that he failed to be vigilant. He spun around just as Whitey came around the corner.

When the old man saw the opened letter in Chambliss' hands, his face took on an expression of intense disgust. He strode up to Chambliss, snatched the letter from him, and said, "That's about as low as a man can get." He wheeled and walked back around the corner.

Chambliss had lost his baggage when the stagecoach was attacked, but he had been carrying his money in a money belt beneath his waistband, and he still had it on him. Before going back around to the street, he removed some cash and stuffed it into his pocket. Afterward, he went out to the general store, and with no guidance from Whitey or anyone else, found the things he needed and made his purchases.

He didn't like the feel of the high-heeled riding boots on his feet—his moccasins felt so much better—but he understood the need for them and assumed he would grow accustomed. The hat was another thing. He liked it immediately.

He bought a used revolver and a holster with a cartridge belt. He was good enough with a pistol but had always preferred a rifle. He could not find a rifle for sale in Sahuarita that met his standards, so he decided to borrow one from the ranch until he could make the trip to Tucson to buy one of his own. He purchased a few other miscellaneous items that he would need and afterward went over to the saloon. He downed a beer and then remembered something he had intended to do. As he was leaving the saloon, Whitey was coming in, but the old man pushed past him without speaking.

Chambliss went to the stage office and found the agent. "What can I do for you, young man?" the agent asked.

"I wanted to talk to you about the stage that was attacked by Apaches five days ago."

"Yes?"

"I was on that stage."

There was disbelief in the agent's eyes. He said, "I assume you know all about what happened? Apaches attacked the stage and killed everyone."

"You say they killed everyone, but were all the bodies found?"

"The army sent a patrol out from Fort Lowell. They said the stagecoach was burned up. There were bodies around it. Scalped and mutilated."

"But not all the passengers were accounted for, were they?"

"They usually aren't. Apaches like to take some of 'em to torture."

Chambliss was beginning to think this was pointless. He turned to leave, saying, "My name is Chambliss. I'm at the Diamond J."

"Pretty tricky thing to get away from Apaches," said the agent. "I expect the army will be wantin' to talk to you."

"Diamond J," repeated Chambliss. He had no real expectation that anyone would want to talk to him. Nor did he care. He had only come in out of a sense of obligation.

He went out, then went back in and said, "Where's a good place to get a meal?"

The agent pointed and said, "Down the street, other side. Mexican place."

Several of the Diamond J riders were already there, sitting at the long, narrow plank table, wolfing their food. Chambliss looked at the menu board on the wall and recognized none of the words. The menu was obviously in Spanish. He asked the Diamond J rider nearest him, a man named Hal, what was good.

"It's all good. Depends on what you want."

Chambliss looked back at the menu board and said, "What's an enchilada?"

Hal said with a completely straight face, "That's a roast beef sandwich." The other men watched intently, their expressions completely neutral.

Chambliss continued, "What are tamales?"

"Pork chops."

"Salsa picante?"

"Gravy."

It went on like this until Chambliss had gone through the menu, making mental notes. When the pretty, young Mexican girl came to take his order and he asked for the pork chops with gravy, she looked at him blankly. One of the Diamond J riders stepped in, helpfully speaking to her in Spanish. She smiled and nodded and went back to the kitchen.

"Thanks," said Chambliss.

"Don't mention it."

There was very little conversation around the table while Chambliss waited for his meal. The Diamond J riders seemed to be taking a long time to eat their food. They chewed slowly, glancing occasionally at each other with blank expressions.

When his food came, Chambliss looked at it and said, "Doesn't look like any pork chops I ever saw."

"They make 'em a little different out here," said Hal. "They taste pretty good, though."

"What's this?" Chambliss asked, holding up a shiny-skinned, tapered, dark green vegetable by its curved stem.

"Why, that's a Mexican pickle," said Hal. "Those are real good. I can sometimes eat ten or fifteen of them at a time. Eat 'em like they was strawberries."

Chambliss had begun to suspect something was afoot, but he was willing to try this new food. And he did. He took a big fork-full of his tamale with salsa and nodded appreciatively, but by the end of ten seconds his eyes were watering, his nose was running, and his mouth felt like it had been shoveled full of hot coals.

"Maybe you're not used to Mex food," said Hal. "Take a big bite of that pickle there. That'll cool things right off."

When Chambliss had begun to show all the signs of asphyxiation, with the notable exception that his complexion, rather than being blue, was a high tone of red, the Diamond J men erupted into chaotic approbation of Hal's achievement, and the cowboy received numerous congratulatory slaps on the back.

And when Chambliss was able to breathe again and joined in their laughter, he too became the recipient of a few amiable back slaps, and he realized that he had taken the first step toward acceptance by this rough crew of men.

This was a good thing because on the ride back to the Diamond J, Whitey ignored him completely, acting as though he did not exist. The men who had been in the restaurant, however, maintained a continuous flow of hilarity during the ride and upon their arrival back at the ranch, they rehearsed the incident in exaggerated fashion to those who had had the misfortune of not being present. Hal was indeed the man of the hour, and Chambliss was far more popular than he had been when they had set out that morning.

Whitey asked one of the men to tend to his horse and went directly to the main house. And Chambliss knew why. It wasn't long before the old man came to the bunkhouse and with a scornful air indicated to Chambliss that the boss wanted to see him. Without speaking, Chambliss tramped out, crossed the yard, and knocked on the door.

C.M. CURTIS

CHAPTER 3

Jane was waiting, sitting in an overstuffed leather chair. Chambliss stood across the room, facing her, his hat in his hands. For a few moments neither of them said anything. Each seemed to be waiting for the other to speak first. Finally she said, "So you read the letter?"

"Yes. Twice. It was . . ." He hesitated. "It was a nice letter."

"I meant every word of it.

She rose from her seat and said, "It's so good to see you again, Martin."

"Good to see you too, Jane."

She came to him and they embraced. He felt her shudder as he held her, and when he kissed her there were tears on her cheeks.

"I've missed you terribly," she said. She laid her head on his shoulder, her face against his chest. Her shoulders shook with sobbing. "I thought I had lost you forever," she whispered.

"I'm here now."

They sat on the divan and held each other, not speaking; she with her head on his chest, he with his face in her hair, breathing in its familiar and long-missed fragrance. Presently she said, "I love you, Martin."

"I love you too, Jane."

She closed her eyes, and a single sob shook her slender shoulders. She said, "You have no idea what it means to me to hear that. After that awful quarrel we had, I felt as though you hated me. I'm so sorry for the things I said."

"No," he said. "It was my fault. I . . ."

"No, Martin, I was a spoiled child. You said so yourself. And you were right. It has only been a few months, but I've grown a lot since coming out here. I'm no longer that spoiled girl who said those hateful things and then ran away. When they brought you to me yesterday, I could not have been more surprised, or more thrilled, to see you."

"You did a good job of hiding it."

"I was so happy to see you, I wanted to fly to you and throw my arms around you."

"You hid that pretty well, too"

"I've gotten good at hiding my feelings. Out here you do that." She took a moment to dry her eyes, and as she did, her lips formed a little feminine smile that he knew well. She asked, "What did you think when you saw me?"

"I had no idea this was your ranch. I just kind of wandered on to it, not knowing where I was. I wasn't as good as you at hiding my surprise, but when you greeted me like a stranger, I knew that for some reason you didn't want anyone to know we knew each other, so I pretended."

She seemed a little disappointed at this answer. She said, "You did fine. I'm sure no one suspects."

"It was hard to do. I wanted to clear the room. I wanted to tell everyone to leave so I could hold you in my arms and kiss you and forbid you to ever leave my sight again."

Her expression turned tender. "Martin, do you really mean that?"

"Jane, why do you suppose I came all this way?"

Her eyes grew moist again, and there was a silence as they held each other. After a moment, she pulled away, smirking. "I suppose you think you're clever, calling yourself Horace. Don't tell me you're still jealous."

Chambliss grinned. "Should I be?"

She grew sober. "No. Not then, and not now. There's never been anyone but you."

"Nice to know," he said softly.

I wrote you a letter," she said. "But by my calculations, it probably arrived after you left Wisconsin. Martin, I hardly slept at all last night for thinking about how close you came to being killed by the Apaches. Your story was true, wasn't it?"

"Yes."

"I'm the only one who believes it, you know."

"Yes, I know that."

"I know you so much better than these people do. If they knew you the way I do, they would not doubt you."

"It doesn't matter. Nothing matters now that we're together.

Now, tell me what's wrong. Why don't you want people to know who I am?"

Her countenance grew troubled. "Martin, I need your help. In the short time I've been here, I've come to love this ranch. I love it partly because of all that my grandfather sacrificed to build it and partly because of what it is. You know, it's as much a horse ranch as a cattle ranch. Grandfather bought some of the finest stud horses and mares in three territories, and now, Diamond J's horses are sought after. We get pretty high prices for some of them. But since I've been running the ranch, we've been losing a lot of stock. Pete tells me the Apaches are running them off. I know Apaches will sometimes do that, but . . .'"

"You don't trust Pete, do you?"

"No."

"Then fire him."

"I tried. He just laughed at me."

The color rose to his face. His jaw muscles tightened, and he stood up, "Then I'll do it. I'll do it right now."

"No." She stopped him. "Sit down, Martin, and listen to me. Pete is a gunman. He has a reputation. If you try to fire him, there will be a gunfight, and one of you will be killed. If that were you, my life would be ruined. You must take care of yourself—for my sake."

He sat down and drew a deep breath, "I'm not afraid of Pete."

"I know that, but you're accustomed to different ways. You need to learn their ways before you take any chances. But there's more than that," she continued. "If Pete is involved in this, he's not alone. We have to know who he's working with if we want to stop the rustling. Just firing him or even killing him wouldn't be enough."

He sat in contemplation for a few moments, then said, "What about Whitey? Do you trust him?"

"I would trust Whitey with my life. He was devoted to my grandfather, and he is devoted to me. In his younger day he was probably a match for Pete, but not now."

"Does he know you suspect Pete?"

"Yes."

"So, what's your plan?" asked Chambliss.

"Until you came, I didn't have one. My plan now is for you to become a member of the crew and try to learn everything you can. We need more information, and you're the only one who can get it."

He nodded. "All right. Tell me everything you can about the crew."

"A lot of them are good men, men who worked for my grandfather before he died."

"Even Pete?"

"Pete came along not long before that. Somehow he gained grandfather's trust, and when the previous foreman died—and he died mysteriously—grandfather made Pete the foreman. Pete has since brought in quite a few of his friends. I hired them before I started to suspect something was wrong. I have hired no one since then, except for you. And now Whitey wants me to fire you."

Chambliss grinned. "Because I read the letter."

"The letter that I wrote for you."

"It was clever of you to address it to Lester Howard."

She smiled. "I knew you would know it was for you as soon as you saw the name."

"When I saw it I was afraid it would be bad news. I was afraid you would be repeating the things you said to me before you left Wisconsin."

She reached up and touched him tenderly on the face. "Please forget those things, Martin. I was angry. I didn't mean them."

"I'm sure you did—at the time."

"I thought I did. I thought I would never want to see you again. I thought I could live without you. I was wrong on both counts."

He said, "We were both wrong. Let's forget all that." There was a pause and he asked, "What do we do about Whitey?"

"I'll tell him the truth," she replied.

"Please don't. I know you trust him, but if I'm going to do this, I don't want to have to worry about who is loyal and who is not. Sometimes it's the people who are the most trusted who turn out to be traitors."

She dropped her eyes. "All right, Martin. I'll do as you say, though I will feel like I'm betraying a friend. When I came here I knew nothing about running a ranch. I'm still just learning. Whitey is my advisor. He's the one who helps me and counsels me. I would be lost without him."

"How will you explain to him why you didn't fire me for opening the letter?"

"I'll simply tell him that you apologized, that you were very sorry, and I intend to keep you on."

"He won't like it."

"No, but he does what I say. He's the one man here on this ranch besides you that I know for sure I can trust."

"It's going to be tough," he said, "seeing you every day and not being able to hold you in my arms."

"Yes, it will be unbearable, but from this moment on, even when we think we're alone, we can't act as though there were anything between us. If we do, it could put you in danger."

"I would risk the greatest danger in the world just to be with you like this."

"But I would not let you. So, for now, we'll simply have to endure."

She closed her eyes and laid her head on his chest again. And so they remained for a while until she said, "You've stayed too long. People will become suspicious."

Reluctantly they pulled away from each other. He stood up and drew her up to him and kissed her again. "I don't know if I'll be able to stand it," he said.

She closed her eyes and put her head on his chest and said, "Life is so hard sometimes, so unfair."

They separated, and he walked to the door with leaden feet.

Whitey was standing across the plaza, waiting. Jane beckoned him inside and told him, "I didn't fire him, Whitey."

"But, ma'am," protested Whitey. "What he did was . . ."

She stopped him. "I know. You're just going to have to trust me in this. He was very apologetic, and I told him I would give him another chance."

Whitey was shaking his head, looking at the floor, holding his hat in his hands. "Miss Jane, you know I'll do whatever you say, but I don't have to like it."

"Thank you, Whitey."

He turned and left the house.

The next day Chambliss began learning the work of a cowpuncher. He had arrived during the latter part of spring roundup, and he and the other riders were sent to the farthest corners of the ranch to haze the cattle out of every brush-filled pocket on the range. He was struggling to grow accustomed to the high-heeled riding boots he had purchased in Sahuarita. They felt confining and stiff, and he could not feel the ground as he walked. However, he appreciated their usefulness. The pointed toe made it easy to slip the boot into the stirrup, and the high heel kept the foot from slipping too far through. The high tops of the boots, along with the chaps he had purchased, protected his legs from the thorny desert brush. All of this notwithstanding, he found his moccasins infinitely more comfortable.

From the very beginning Chambliss was able to spot the riders who were loyal to Pete Oxley. They were standoffish around him, and, he observed, they were not completely accepted by the other men. There appeared to be two factions in this crew, which confirmed what Jane had told him.

The story of his first encounter with Mexican food had become a campfire favorite among the Diamond J riders, and it was often reenacted. At these times, Chambliss was generally asked to describe his thoughts and sensations when the effect of the hot chili pepper had reached its peak in his unaccustomed mouth. To the delight of the listeners, Chambliss used terms like, "the hottest fires of hell," "a mouth like a blacksmith's forge," and "molten lead being poured down my throat."

Chambliss enjoyed these recitations as much as the other men did, prompting Hal Dean, the author of the prank, to comment on one occasion, "I like a man who can laugh at hisself."

Chambliss responded, "Keep that in mind, Hal, because one of these days I'll pay you back."

One afternoon, Chambliss and several other punchers rode into the Diamond J headquarters ahead of the dust of a rather large group of riders they had been observing for some time. They waited, everyone armed and prepared, until a man stationed on the barn roof shouted, "It's the army."

"They'll be comin' to talk to you, Chambliss," said Pete Oxley. "To hear your cock-and-bull story about how you outran the Apaches." He turned and tramped toward the bunkhouse. Chambliss went to the front porch of the house, sat in a chair, and waited. Whitey was also seated on the porch some distance away, but he did not speak to Chambliss or even look at him. Hal Dean came and sat beside Whitey.

There were eight of them, plus two Apache scouts. The only one to dismount was the officer in charge, who introduced himself as

Captain Roderick, and said to Whitey, "I'd like to pay my respects to Miss Quilter, and then I need to speak to a man named Chambliss, if he's here."

"Over there," said Whitey, pointing to Chambliss. The disdain in his voice was clear and intentional.

Jane stepped out onto the porch at that moment, looking stunning in a green dress with simple white lace around the throat and wrists. Chambliss felt a surge of pride and not a little amusement as he watched the ill-concealed reactions of the men in uniform.

Captain Roderick swept off his hat, gave a slight bow, and said, "Jane, you're looking lovely today, as always."

"Thank you, Captain. To what do we owe the honor of your presence, and will you be able to stay for some refreshments?"

"Unfortunately, I'm here on army business. I need to speak with Mr. Chambliss, but, as for the refreshments, I would be most grateful." He turned to face his men. "Sergeant, the men may dismount and water their horses."

Jane caught Chambliss' eye and motioned him inside. Then, seeing Whitey and Hal, she said, "We still have some of those Sonora lemons, and Josefina is making lemonade. Why don't you two join us?"

Hal seemed uncomfortable with the suggestion and said, "I better get back over to . . ."

"Nonsense," she said. "Come in and have some lemonade."

The four men and their elegant hostess went into the house, where the entire group sat down at Jane's request.

It soon became clear to Chambliss that Jane and Captain Roderick knew each other fairly well. Moreover it was quite obvious that Roderick had feelings for Jane. Josefina, Jane's Mexican cook, whom Chambliss had not met before, brought in the lemonade, and they all sipped for a few minutes while Jane and the captain talked about the weather and other trivialities. Presently Roderick turned to Chambliss and said, "The stage agent in Sahuarita says you told him you were on the stage that was attacked by Apaches. I'd like to have you meet my Apache scouts and tell us all exactly what took place."

Chambliss nodded.

Out on the porch, Roderick turned to face Jane. "There's a dance in Tucson in two weeks. I was wondering if you would go with me."

"Todd," she said, "I'm honored that you would ask me again, and

I had a wonderful time last time, but I have to tell you something. Before I left Wisconsin, there was a young man that I was very close to. We had an understanding. We quarreled before I left, and I told him I never wanted to see him again, but being out here, I've learned that my feelings for him haven't changed at all. I recently wrote to him, and we have renewed our understanding."

Clearly disappointed, Roderick said, "I can't tell you how sorry I am to hear that, Jane. But I'm happy for you, and let me say he's a very lucky fellow."

"Thank you, Todd."

The two Apache scouts were sitting apart from the rest of the group, impassively observing. The captain motioned to them, and they crossed to stand nearby. "Now," he said. "Mr. Chambliss, would you mind telling us how it all happened?"

Chambliss told the story from the beginning of the Apache attack up to the point where he was found by the Diamond J riders and taken to the ranch. He told it as he remembered it, without embellishment or self-deprecation. When he was finished, Roderick said, "We went out there and buried all the bodies."

"Did you find the two in the cave?" asked Chambliss.

Roderick jerked his head toward the two scouts. "Those are Apaches, Chambliss. Of course they found the two bodies in the cave."

Thoroughly disgusted, Whitey snorted and walked away. Hal had an odd look on his face. He looked directly at Chambliss for a moment and then followed Whitey.

There was a sound, and Chambliss' eyes shifted toward it. He noticed that the two Apaches did the same. None of the white men appeared to have heard it yet.

A man on horseback came riding into the fortlike enclosure of the Diamond J. He was a big man, and he rode a big horse. He wore a blue cavalry shirt, but none of his other attire matched the uniform. His hat was of leather, with a flat top and wide brim, and it had clearly been with him for many long seasons. His pants were of faded denim, and he wore the typical Apache high-topped moccasins. He carried a long knife in a scabbard slung around his neck, a colt dragoon in his waistband, and a Winchester across the pommel of his saddle. His long hair was brown mingled with gray, and his beard, stained with the dribble of a thousand cuds of tobacco, hung down to the middle of his chest. He rode with an easy sort of arrogance, and there was something about him that made everyone except the two Apaches pay attention.

"This is Clay Lamb," Roderick said to Chambliss. "One of our scouts."

Chambliss gave Lamb the faintest of nods and received nothing back except a piercing gaze. Lamb was definitely taking his measure. And the fact that the first thing he looked at was Chambliss' feet was not lost on Chambliss. The two Apaches had done the same thing.

"Mr. Chambliss was just telling us the story of how he outran the Apaches," Roderick told Clay Lamb, and Chambliss picked up the faintest tinge of sarcasm in the statement. Up to now he had found nothing about Roderick to make him dislike the man, but if Roderick was going to accuse him of being a liar, no matter how subtly, that was another matter altogether.

Roderick said, "Mr. Chambliss, would you repeat your story for Mr. Lamb?"

"No," replied Chambliss.

There was a momentary silence, during which Roderick seemed surprised at the retort. It was time, Chambliss had decided, to hoist his colors. Where he came from, a man's reputation meant everything, and even the slightest insinuation that he was a liar was not taken lightly. He said to Roderick, "I told you exactly what happened. If you want him to know, you tell him."

Roderick made a wry smile and gave a brief nod. "All right." He turned to Lamb and began reciting the story as he had heard Chambliss tell it. As he spoke, Chambliss went to the bunkhouse, pulled off his riding boots, and from the war bag he had purchased in Sahuarita, took out his moccasins. He put them on, liking their familiar feel. Then he went back out and walked directly past the two Apache scouts, intentionally leaving the prints of his moccasins in the dust in front of them. If they didn't recognize them as the same ones they had seen on their visit to the scene of the stagecoach attack, they were no kind of trackers.

Turning his back to the group, he walked to the porch and sat in a chair. Roderick and Lamb were in earnest conference. Lamb said a few words to the Apaches and received a few in reply. He turned to look at Roderick and gave a nod, nothing more. Roderick walked over to Chambliss, and Chambliss saw a new respect in the soldier's eyes. Roderick sat in the chair next to him and said, "Quite a thing."

Chambliss nodded.

Pointing to the moccasins, Roderick said, "Been wearing those long?"

"All my life."

Some of the soldiers were talking among themselves, unaware of what had just happened, but aside from them, no one said anything for a few moments. Roderick broke the silence, saying, "I could maybe use a man like you as a scout."

Chambliss glanced at Jane's face and saw alarm. He said, "Thanks for the offer, Captain, but I'm working for the Diamond J."

That evening marked the end of Chambliss' acceptance among the crew of the Diamond J. When the soldiers left and he went to the bunkhouse, he immediately noticed the change in attitude and knew why it had come about. Whitey and Hal had been talking.

He lay awake in his bunk long after the other men had fallen asleep. If it were not for Jane he would leave this ranch. He had no desire to work and live with men who thought him a liar. But Jane was here and she needed him. And for her, he would put up with whatever he had to.

After the soldiers left, Jane went to the kitchen where Josefina was cleaning up. Josefina said, "I saw him. He's just like you described him."

Jane smiled but said nothing. She and Josefina had become close friends during the time Jane had been at the Diamond J. They were about the same age, and surprisingly, despite vastly different backgrounds, they had much in common.

Josefina had grown up in Arizona and gone to school there and spoke English as well as she did Spanish. She was loquacious, clever, and perceptive, and the two young women sometimes talked and laughed long into the night.

After Jane's grandfather had died, his cook, an elderly Mexican woman who had been with him for fifteen years, decided to move to California to live with her daughter. Consequently, when Jane arrived at the Diamond J, there was no cook. She did not see this as a major problem; she was perfectly capable of cooking for herself. But

Whitey strenuously advised her against that, saying, "The men will have to respect you if you are going to boss them. You're going to have a hard enough time as it is, earnin' that respect, and it'll never happen if you have flour on your nose and dough on your elbows."

So Jane put out the word she was looking for a cook. That same week, Josefina showed up at her door, and the two young women became instant friends. Jane did not even bother asking Josefina about her qualifications. Far more than a cook, she needed a friend. She was surrounded by men, and she was lonely for female companionship. Moreover, she was grieving over the recent breaking of her engagement to Martin Chambliss, the man she had loved since her childhood, and she needed someone to talk to about it. She immediately perceived Josefina to be a sensitive and compassionate person, and she didn't care if the young woman couldn't boil an egg; she hired her.

Josefina finished drying the lemonade glasses and sat at the table opposite Jane. She said, "Things will be better soon. Just wait and see."

"I hope so, Josie. It's so hard to be patient."

Josefina silently regarded Jane. After a few moments, she said, "You have never told me how the two of you met. Was it terribly romantic?"

Jane chuckled. "Not at all. We've known each other since we were children. We're from the same town and we went to school together."

"Tell me about him. What is he like?"

"His father was a drunkard, and his mother ran off when Martin—that's his real name—was just small. There are a lot of Indians in that area, and Martin's house was very near one of their villages. He spent most of his time there. Sometimes he would stay away from home for weeks at a time. I doubt his father even noticed. He pretty much grew up with the Indian boys. He was practically one of them; in fact, they made him a tribe member when he was old enough—some sort of manhood ritual, I believe. Anyway, he gained quite a reputation among the whites, as well as the Indians in the area."

"You said you went to school together."

"His father spent most of his time drinking and mostly ignored Martin, but he did insist that Martin attend school—probably the only good thing he ever did for him."

She stopped speaking, and there was a silence. Presently, she said, "How am I going to stand it, Josie?"

Josefina was pensive for a moment, then she brightened, giggled girlishly, and said, "We have to start planning your wedding. That will keep your mind occupied. We will make it the biggest fiesta the Diamond J has ever seen."

Jane smiled. "No. There was a time when I wanted that, but now . . . I just want to be his wife."

Josefina frowned. "Tell him to be careful of Pete Oxley and his men. Heaven help him if he pushes them into a fight."

"No, Josie. Heaven help them."

CHAPTER 4

The following morning Chambliss and three other riders, one of them Hal Dean, were sent by Pete Oxley to the northernmost edge of the ranch to round up any cattle they could find there. When they got there, Hal instructed Chambliss to ride into a rugged, hilly area and work it out. "It'll take you several days to do the job right," said Hal coldly. "See that you do. There's a line shack there, and it has food and coffee and blankets. You can spend nights there. There's a brush corral that we built around a spring. Keep the cows in it until you're finished. Don't try to find us when you're done; just drive the herd back to headquarters."

Chambliss had heard about this part of the range. It was the one place where none of the riders wanted to be sent—a rattlesnake infested hell filled with catclaw and chaparral and jumping cactus. It was brutal work for man and horse, and Chambliss knew exactly why Hal had sent him there.

It took him four days to haze out the bulk of the cattle that had taken refuge in that maze of canyons and draws, and at the end he had less than twenty head to show for his efforts. He drove the last of them into the brush corral on that last night, and early the following morning he started the drive back home. It was late afternoon when he came over a rise expecting to see the picturesque scene of ranch headquarters below. He reined in suddenly, stared for a moment, and then spurred his horse into a run.

Every building had been burned to the ground: the ranch house, the barn, the bunkhouse, the cook shack, and all the outbuildings. All the livestock were gone. A man was there, sitting on his horse and gazing at a long row of fresh graves. Another man was picking through the ashes of the cook shack.

The basic picture was clear, and Chambliss did not waste time asking questions he already knew the answers to. He rode into the yard and shouted, "Were any women killed?" The man on horseback was a tall, angular man with a long, mournful face. He sat astride a striking roan stallion. He pointed to the man in the ashes and said, "Talk to him." He spurred the stallion and rode away.

The other man turned a haggard face up to Chambliss, and Chambliss recognized him as the crippled Diamond J cook, an old man named Art. Chambliss repeated the question, almost screaming it.

Art said, "No, but if you're thinkin' of Miss Quilter, they carried her off, along with Josefina, that Mexican gal that cooked for her."

The words hit Chambliss like a fist in the gut. He forced himself to remain calm. "Has anyone gone after them?"

"Hal Dean and a few of the hands that were left alive chased 'em. The rustlers were waitin' for 'em. They ambushed 'em and shot 'em up pretty good. They were all killed or wounded and their horses shot or run off. Hal was creased on the head. Didn't wake up 'til the next day. I went out in a wagon and brought back the live ones and the dead ones." He pointed to three graves at the end of the row that looked a little more recent.

"Didn't anyone tell the army?"

"The army rode out yesterday."

Chambliss' first impulse was to spur his horse out of the yard and fly in pursuit of Jane, but he knew he would accomplish nothing by doing that. He would need information and supplies.

"How long ago did it happen?"

"Three days."

He was outraged. "Why did it take so long for the army to get on the trail?"

"They were all out on patrol. Chasin' Apaches."

Chambliss struggled to keep a clear head. The men who had taken Jane had a three day lead on him. He looked at the row of graves and was appalled by their number. There were nine of them.

"Were there any survivors?" he asked.

"Only four, after the ones that went after them got ambushed. All the survivors are wounded. One of 'em is old Whitey. They shot him in the chest, but he's a tough old coot. He might pull through yet."

"Who's the man on the stallion?" Chambliss pointed at the tall rider who could still be seen in the distance, riding away.

"Slim Ewart. He owns Antler. It's a little spread, west of here.

They're the closest neighbors to us. We took Whitey over there, so Slim's wife, Sally, could take care of him."

"It was Pete Oxley and his friends who did this, wasn't it?" said Chambliss.

"Pete Oxley and his friends, along with some others I'd never seen before. There was a fight in the bunkhouse the night before. Roundup was over, and all the hands were back except for you and Hal and a couple others. The bad feelings between the old hands and Pete's boys blew up. There wasn't any gunplay, but it got pretty bloody. I guess that was what touched off the powder keg."

Art spied something in the wreckage and reached down and pulled it out. It was a cast-iron skillet. He brightened. "This was brand-new. Bought it last time I went to Tucson. Guess it's seasoned now." He looked back at Chambliss, and his countenance seemed to sag back into the tragic present. He said, "Whitey tried to stop 'em from takin' Miss Jane, but . . ."

Nothing more needed to be said. Whitey had been shot trying to protect Jane.

"They hit so fast the boys weren't hardly able to fight back. I was pinned down in the cook shack and couldn't get to a gun. Some of the boys were not even armed when they got shot down. It was . . ." His voice trailed off. He seemed to be unable to find words to describe the horror of the massacre.

"How was it they didn't kill you?"

"Me?" Art looked down at the ground and murmured, "I thought they were going to. I had to leave the cook shack when they fired it, and I just stood there out in the open, waitin' to die. But Pete just laughed at me. Guess they figured I wasn't worth the trouble of pullin' a trigger."

Chambliss had no time for compassion. He said, "Did they go south?"

"Yes. And you can bet they're deep into Sonora by now. That Captain Roderick took some men and followed, but the army can't cross the border."

"I can."

"You?" Art made no comment, but his skepticism was obvious.

Chambliss said, "Where would they cross the border?"

"They'd go through Skeleton Canyon. The Mexicans call it Guadalupe Canyon. Rustlers always use it. Dangerous place. That's about all I can tell you."

Chambliss heard a sound and waited. Presently, Hal Dean rode into the yard. He wore a bandage around his head, upon which his hat was laid. His left arm was also bandaged. His face was pale. He rode up and said to Chambliss in an unfriendly tone, "Where've you been hidin' out?"

"What are you talking about?"

Hal's voice was hard. "I'm talkin' about how we all come runnin' when we seen the smoke. Then three days later, you come ridin' in."

"From where I was there was no smoke to be seen."

"I doubt that, Chambliss," said Hal, his hand hovering over his pistol butt. "I truly doubt it."

Chambliss felt a surge of anger, but he suppressed it. He understood what was going on in Hal's mind. He had lost a lot of friends in the attack and was unable to punish those responsible. He was angry and was trying to push Chambliss into a fight, using him as a scapegoat.

Chambliss had no desire to kill Hal, and he was terrified of being killed himself before he could go to Jane's aid. He ignored the comment, knowing that by failing to take up Hal's challenge, the man would be further convinced of his cowardice.

As Chambliss stepped into the saddle, Hal said, "Where do you think you're goin'?" When Chambliss ignored him, Hal said, "I'm the foreman of the Diamond J now."

Chambliss reined around and said, "What Diamond J? There is no Diamond J, Hal. The cattle are gone, the horses are gone, the men are dead, and the buildings are burned. You're the foreman of a big piece of dirt."

The words had a noticeable effect on Hal; nonetheless, he persisted. "As long as you ride for this brand, I expect you to do as I say, Chambliss."

"That's fair enough, Hal, but I'm not going to be riding for this brand anymore."

He glanced from Hal to Art and saw distaste in the eyes of both men. He knew what they were thinking.

"Appears Whitey had you figured right," said Hal. "Maybe back where you come from a man drifts when things get tough, but out here . . ."

Chambliss interrupted him. "Back where I come from a man

makes his own decisions and other men keep their mouths shut about it."

Hal's face reddened, and for a moment Chambliss regretted the comment, thinking the man would go for his gun. But Hal said, "Way I remember it, Chambliss, you didn't even own a horse when you come here. That one you're ridin' has a Diamond J brand on it. You come onto this range afoot, and looks like you'll be leavin' it afoot."

"I'm going to need a horse, Hal. I'll buy it. I'll give you the money right now."

"You ain't got the money. That's a fifty-dollar horse."

Chambliss lifted his shirt, removed his money belt, and counted out the money. Then he said, "How much for the saddle and bridle?"

Hal exchanged a look with Art and said, "Another twenty. And that Winchester is Diamond J property too." He spoke the words in an accusatory tone, as if Chambliss had been caught trying to steal the carbine.

"How much?"

"Ten."

Chambliss gave him eighty dollars and rode away.

He needed a packhorse and supplies, but he didn't want to take the extra time to go to Sahuarita to get them. There was a desperation pushing him, and he resented every second he was not on the trail. He decided to take a risk and just start riding, hoping he would pass through a town on the way to Mexico where he could acquire the things he would need.

He had ammunition for his weapons, a canteen full of water, and little food in his saddlebags. That would have to last him until he could get more. He had to get moving. Whitey would probably die, and Hal was in no shape for a long ride. The Diamond J was dead, and it was clear that the other people in the area were leaving it up to the army to chase down the raiders.

Chambliss hoped the army had been successful, but if the outlaws had made it across the border with their stolen livestock and their female captives, the army could not follow. And Chambliss was not willing to wait around to find out what had happened.

Away from the ruins of the Diamond J, away from Hal and Art, he stopped the horse, dismounted, and pulled his moccasins from the saddlebag. Removing his boots, he put on the moccasins and remounted, leaving the boots lying on the ground.

He was no longer a ranch hand.

He rode all that day and into the night. Art had given him rough directions to Skeleton Canyon, but he was following a broad trail of cattle and horse tracks. As long as the tracks were not erased by wind or rain, he would have no need for maps or directions.

Having no cooking implements or even a coffee pot, he made cold camps and rationed out his food and water, eating only what he needed to survive.

The thought of Jane and Josefina in the hands of outlaws was a constant torment to him. He wished he had wings so he could fly and not have to depend on the plodding gait of a horse. He pushed his horse as hard as he dared, but it would do the two women no good if he wore the animal out or rode it to death and placed himself afoot.

As Art had predicted, the outlaws' trail led into a canyon that Chambliss was sure must be Skeleton Canyon. And it was there, on the second evening, that Chambliss encountered the returning troop of cavalry led by an unhappy Captain Roderick. Upon seeing Chambliss, the soldier acted surprised and more than a little suspicious. He said, "What brings you out here, Chambliss?"

"Same thing that brought you."

"Alone?"

"Who else could have come? All the Diamond J men that weren't killed were wounded."

Roderick considered this for a few moments, suspicion on his face, and Chambliss knew what must be in the man's mind.

Chambliss motioned for the captain to follow him out of earshot of his men and said, "Do you remember when Jane told you about the man she was planning to marry?"

"How could I forget?"

"She was talking about me."

Roderick frowned. "Why would . . . ?"

Chambliss interrupted. "She was losing livestock and suspected that some of her own men were in on it. She wanted me to pretend to be one of her riders and find out who it was."

Roderick swore, scrubbing a hand across his whiskery face. "I don't know whether to arrest you or help you, Chambliss. For all I know, you're part of the outlaw bunch and are following them to join them in Mexico."

The thought of being arrested and kept from going after Jane was alarming to Chambliss. He could not allow that to happen. Suddenly he had a thought. He reached under his shirt and fumbled in his money belt, pulling out a small, folded paper. This he handed to Roderick, who unfolded and read it, then slowly nodded, handing it back to Chambliss.

Chambliss picketed his jaded horse, and Roderick invited him to eat. Roderick said, "I never came closer to a court-martial than I did there at the border. If it had only been my career that was at stake, I would have gone after her, Chambliss. I want you to know that. But if I had run into any Federales, it would have created an international incident, possibly even a war between the United States and Mexico. Thousands of people may have died."

He was silent for a while and then he said, "Turning back was the hardest thing I ever did."

Chambliss felt sorry for the man. He had done what he had to do, had done an unselfish thing, and would probably bear the guilt of it for the rest of his life. The two men sat in depressed silence, looking into the flames of the campfire thinking similar thoughts.

After a time Roderick said, "Your horse looks worn out."

"I've been pushing him pretty hard."

"It's against army regulations, but I'll give you a couple of horses and some supplies."

Both men knew the gesture was a necessary one if Chambliss was to have any chance of success. With fresh horses he would not have to remain here tonight and lose that trail time. He could stop and rest a little in the early morning hours.

"Thanks," said Chambliss, still watching the fire. He looked up. "In that case, I guess I'll get back on the trail."

"Wait a minute," said Roderick. He stood and walked to the fire where the Apache scouts were squatted. Clay Lamb was there. Roderick squatted down beside Lamb, and they talked for a few minutes. When Roderick returned, he said to Chambliss, "One of my scouts will go with you if you want him along."

"I'll take any help I can get."

"Least I can do," said Roderick in a low, sorrowful voice.

Roderick told Chambliss the scout went by the name of John

because white men could not pronounce his Apache name. He also said that John, like many Apaches, spoke good Spanish but poor English.

Whatever languages John did or did not speak, he didn't speak at all to Chambliss during the first couple of days on the trail. What little communication passed between them did so through grunts and gestures.

Not long after they crossed into in Mexico, late one afternoon the Apache investigated a side trail. Someone had left the main group and gone up into a small canyon. The Apache was not gone long, and when he came back, he sat on a rock and regarded Chambliss as if in contemplation. Finally he motioned with his head to the little canyon and then looked away.

Chambliss went into the canyon and did not come out of it until the next morning. The Apache was eating breakfast. Chambliss did not look at him but merely turned his horse toward the south and continued on the trail. Later the Apache caught up with him.

The outlaws did not know they were being followed, nor by what kind of man. If they had, they would have worried. For he was not only the kind of man he was, but now he was one who would never stop tracking them no matter how far they went, no matter how long it took. His life now had one purpose, and one alone: To find and kill the men who had murdered Jane Quilter.

The next day, in an arroyo a short distance from the trail, they found Josefina's body. As with Jane, whoever had killed her had lacked even the decency to bury her.

CHAPTER 5

Spring was ending, and the days were growing hot, but these days Chambliss paid little attention to physical discomfort. He only lived to accomplish his purposes, and he was willing to endure anything necessary to that end.

The sun stood high in the sky on the third day into Mexico when the trail they were following crested a hill and descended into a long, green valley where sat a large, tile-roofed, L-shaped hacienda. The stolen Diamond J livestock were grazing placidly in the valley.

There was little activity down below. Quite a number of men were visible, but they were doing nothing. Some of them lounged indolently on the long porch; others came and went through the open front doors of the house.

"Somebody is coming to buy these cattle and horses," said Chambliss. "But they're not here yet."

The Apache nodded.

"Chambliss said, "Either the rustlers got here early or the buyer is late."

The Apache nodded again.

Even from a distance it was easy to distinguish the locals from the outlaws, and whenever one of the locals made an appearance outside the house or one of the other buildings, it was always in the company of one of the rustlers.

These people were being held as prisoners in their own home.

Throughout the remainder of the day, Chambliss and the Apache maintained their positions at the top of the hill, watching. Just before dark, Chambliss drew a rough sketch of the hacienda in the dirt with his finger. He drew a diagonal line through the angle of the L, put his finger on one side of the line, and pointed to the Apache. He put a finger on the other side of the line and pointed to himself.

The Apache nodded.

At dusk Chambliss blacked his face with charcoal and wrapped his head Apache style with a dark scarf he had found with Jane's body. All day he had been resisting an almost overwhelming urge to go down to the hacienda and find Pete Oxley and kill him. The grief and rage within him screamed for action. He hated this enforced inactivity; it gave him too much time to think. And thinking was almost unendurable.

When full darkness came, the Apache silently slipped into the blackness, and Chambliss did the same. Having observed the hacienda throughout most of the day, Chambliss had learned a few things about the situation. One of them was that these men weren't worried. They apparently felt secure in the knowledge that they would not be pursued this far south of the border and did not believe they had any enemies in Mexico.

They had pulled off a successful raid, had gotten cleanly away, and now had taken over this peaceful Hacienda. He believed it to be a safe bet they had had a complete plan from start to finish. That plan had, no doubt, included this remote Mexican ranch and, therefore, also its inhabitants. What Chambliss did not know was what they intended to do next.

Crouched in the concentrated darkness near the main house, he was able to look into the open doorway and see a number of men in the room. He recognized two of them, and Pete Oxley was one of these. The other was a man named Bruce, one of Pete's men who had worked for the Diamond J. Occasionally a man would come out, sometimes more than one, and stroll indolently around the yard.

Chambliss waited.

At one point Pete Oxley and two other men came out and walked in the darkness some distance away from the house. Silently, Chambliss moved closer. Pete was saying, "What do you think we're going to do, Bruce? There's only one way."

"Even the girl?" asked Bruce.

Pete threw his cigarette down and ground it out beneath his boot toe. "Bruce, I don't like it any better than you do, but there ain't any other way."

Bruce said, "The grown-ups I can see, but I hate to think of killin' that purty little Maria gal. What Lencho and Franey did made me want to . . ."

"I guess you're right," interrupted Pete. "And when we're standin' in front of that Mexican firin' squad, we'll all have a warm feelin' in our hearts to think we didn't kill that purty little Maria gal. And when she's pointin' us out to the Federales, we'll blow her a kiss—just before they shoot us."

"He's right, Bruce," said the third man. "We got to see this thing through. Anyhow, once we sell these beeves and horses, I'll take you to a town in Juarez where you can find all the sweet little Marias you want."

Bruce's grin was a gray line in the darkness. "All right, but you two can do it. I'll take care of that sour-faced old sow that threw coffee in my face."

Pete and other man laughed. Pete said, "I don't think Grandma likes you, Bruce."

"She don't like you any better."

Pete made a comment that made the other two men laugh. Bruce started to say something then seemed to suddenly go blank. Pete heard his exhalation of breath and realized that he had fallen to the ground. Immediately thereafter, the other man did likewise. Then, before Pete could react, a dark figure was standing in front of him. Pete tried to speak, but for some reason no sound would come out. There was a wetness on the front of his shirt. He tried to look down at it, and then he knew no more.

Chambliss retrieved his rifle, which was lying on the ground a few feet away, resheathed his knife, put Bruce's hat on his head, and walked toward the house. Through the open front door he could see a dark haired young girl sitting on the floor next to a man in a chair. He was stroking her hair, and she was crying and trying to pull away from him. As Chambliss stepped up onto the porch, a man standing there, away from the open door and barely visible in the pitch darkness, said, "What's the rifle for, Bruce?"

The rifle, as it turned out, was for bashing the man in the head and then, seconds later, levering bullets in and firing them as fast as they would come out of the barrel. The room was filled with the deafening concussions, and the three men inside were caught completely unprepared; only one of them had a chance to pull his gun. He got off one shot before he died.

The girl was screaming. She ran to another part of the house and was silent. Outside, Chambliss heard more shots and knew what was happening: The Apache was doing his part.

Chambliss turned off the kerosene lamps, reloaded his rifle in the darkness, and sat in a chair, facing the door. Presently an owl hooted. He pulled himself to his feet, walked to the door, and replied. The Apache materialized out of the darkness and went to release the people who were being held elsewhere.

Chambliss had already ascertained in what room the family members were being kept. After relighting a lamp, he went there and found the girl standing in front of the door, breathing hard from fear. A bar that secured the door had been recently improvised to keep the family members locked in. Chambliss handed the lamp to the girl and took hold of her arm, gently moving her aside. He set the rifle down, removed the bar, and went back to the main room where he sat in a chair and leaned his head back.

He heard cries and joyful weeping. He heard footsteps as the family members came into the room. He opened his eyes and was aware that lamps were being lighted, but he saw the light as though it were through a cloud. All sound, all perception came to him as across a great distance; indistinct and distorted.

He felt like he was dying, but it no longer mattered. He had done what he had come to do. Nothing mattered anymore. He caught a glimpse in his mind of Jane's face, but only a glimpse; even with his eyes closed, the world was whirling. Someone was next to him speaking words he did not understand. Someone was touching him. He tried to move, to react. He heard the words, *"Mucha sangre."* Much blood. It was a feminine voice. "Jane?" He reached out his hand for her, tried to touch her, tried to grasp her by the hand. He realized he was slipping out of consciousness, and he refused to allow it. He forced himself to concentrate on the words flying around him, though he could not comprehend their meanings. He felt himself being lifted, carried, and placed on a bed. His moccasins and shirt were removed.

In the beginning he did not feel much pain, but later that night it became intense and kept him from sleeping. Finally, in the early morning hours, he slept, and when he woke it was night again. The girl was sitting in a chair just outside the open door and she was looking at him. Seeing that he was awake, she jumped up and called out a string of Spanish words. Soon two women were in the room. The older of the two lifted the bandages, checking the wound. She turned to the girl, calling her Maria. Maria went out and returned only a short time later with the Apache.

The Apache appeared uninjured, and Chambliss tried to think of something to say to him. They had never spoken much, and now, after everything that had happened, they had nothing to say at all.

Finally Chambliss said, "Are they feeding you?"

The Apache nodded.

"Will you be staying?"

"A while. I wait to see if you live." He held up a money belt for Chambliss to see and told him it had been taken from one of the dead outlaws. From his description of the man's death wounds, Chambliss recognized it to be Pete Oxley.

"Keep it," said Chambliss.

———◆———

It was a well-known fact that there was no affection between Apaches and Mexicans, especially those Mexicans within a few days' ride of the border. Because of what he had done for them, the family fed the Apache and tolerated his presence, but he slept somewhere in the hills and came to the house only infrequently and for short periods of time to get food and to see how Chambliss was doing.

On one of these occasions, just two days after they had killed the outlaws, Chambliss said to him, "Pete Oxley and his men were waiting for someone to come to buy the livestock."

"I watch for them," said the Apache. "What we do when they come?"

Chambliss laid his head back. He was too weak and dizzy to deal with these issues, but he knew he had to. "Are there enough men on this place . . ." he asked, "to drive the herd away from here?"

"Maybe. Where?"

Chambliss closed his eyes and considered this question. It would be much easier to answer if he knew from which direction the buyer and his men would be coming. Well, there were four directions on the compass, and the buyers would be coming from only one of them. Three-to-one odds weren't bad. He'd seen worse. He wished he knew more about the buyer and what he intended to do with the cattle and horses. Were they to be sold in Mexico or rebranded and taken back to the States?

He realized now that he was completely dependent on the Apache. He said, "Will these people follow you?"

"If you tell them."

"Bring the men," said Chambliss.

There were few men on the ranch, and Chambliss had met two of them: Maria's father and grandfather. When the Apache returned, he brought with him Maria's father and his segundo, Adolfo, a man who appeared to be in his seventies. Chambliss tried to force his mind to function better. He knew he needed to work out a plan, but his mind was still fuzzy and the situation was complicated. Whether the herd remained here at the ranch or was driven away, the family was in danger. The men who were coming to buy the herd were likely no better than the men who had stolen it. What would they do when they saw that the ranch was not well defended?

Abruptly it came to him that there was really only one way under the circumstances to keep the family safe. He had to let the buyers buy the herd. He had to turn it over to them and let them take it and go.

He shared this observation with the Apache, who sat in silence for a few moments and then gave a slight nod.

Chambliss said, "John, tell them they have to move those cattle and horses somewhere besides here."

The Apache turned to the two men and spoke to them in Spanish. On the face of Maria's father Chambliss saw regret, and he thought he understood why. He had seen very little livestock on this range though there was good graze in abundance. Maria's father had probably hoped to be able to keep some of the rustled livestock now that the rustlers were dead.

Chambliss said, "John, let these men pick out a hundred-and-fifty head of the best breeding stock. A hundred cows, a few good bulls, and fifty horses. And they'll need to hide them somewhere away from here."

The Apache nodded.

The day was hot, and Chambliss was pallid and weak. The Apache had come to tell him riders were coming. A horse was saddled, and Chambliss, with assistance, dragged himself up into the saddle and rode up the hill to meet the approaching men. Behind him, coming from the house, were loud moans and an occasional shriek——the kind made by people in pain.

Chambliss counted nine riders. One of them rode forward, and Chambliss held up his hand. "Don't get too close."

The lead rider was a burly redheaded man. He said, "What's all the noise down there?"

Chambliss said, "Some kind of fever. We've all had it. Some have already died."

The redhead swore. "Where's Oxley?"

"He's sick; he sent me."

"I'm supposed to deal with Oxley."

Chambliss nodded. "Fine with me. Ride down there and deal with him and let me go back to bed."

The redhead looked dubiously at the hacienda and then back at Chambliss. "Who are you anyway?"

"I'm the one Oxley sent. You want that stock or not?"

"How long's this fever last?"

"A week. Some live through it, most don't. The ones who die are screaming at the end. Their skin turns into boils and starts droppin' off the bones. They go blind, and their eyeballs pop like ripe pimples."

The redhead frowned and shuddered. He lifted his hat and ran his hand over his head, an expression of intense disgust on his face as he gazed down at the hacienda. Turning back, he moved his horse farther away from Chambliss and said, "You don't look none too healthy yourself."

"You don't want to get close to me, I'll tell you that."

"The redhead grinned as if enjoying the fact that Chambliss was sick. "Don't worry. I didn't come here to dance." He sobered. "Where's that herd?"

Chambliss' appearance of unwellness was unfeigned, and it was with extreme difficulty that he made the ride to the valley where the herd had been driven. The redhead and his men made a rough count, and he came back and said, "Looks a little shy of what we expected."

"Payin' by the head, ain't you?"

"Yeah."

"Then pay me for what's there and let me get back to bed."

The man produced a pencil and paper and did some calculating, after which he removed some bills from a pouch in his saddlebag and counted. Finished, he started to move his horse forward to hand a stack of bills to Chambliss, then thought better of it and pulled back.

He emptied the pouch into the saddlebag, put the stack he had counted out into the pouch, and tossed the pouch on the ground in front of Chambliss' horse. "Count it if you want, but that's all you're gettin'. Pete's deal was with Slim. I'm just doin' what I was told."

The name Slim cut through Chambliss' consciousness like a knife. Could it be? There were a lot of men called Slim. He said, "When you see Slim, ask him if he'd sell that big roan stallion."

"Lobo?" the redhead shook his head. "Forget it. Slim'd sell just about anything on Antler. He might even sell Sally, but he'd never sell Lobo." Wheeling his horse around, he said, "So long."

Chambliss watched from the hilltop as the riders got the herd on the move. He knew the Apache was somewhere watching too. And he could continue watching. Right now it was going to be all Chambliss could do to make it back to the house.

When he got there the false moans and cries of pain stopped, having served their purpose. Maria came flying through the front door to help him dismount. She made him lean on her as they walked into the house where her mother and grandmother took over. Maria was not allowed to go into the room where Chambliss slept.

Once back in bed, Chambliss spent a few troubled seconds thinking about Slim. He struggled to remember the rancher's last name and then did: Ewart. There was a jumble of questions in his head, but he was too weak and sick to sort them out. He made an attempt, but he fell asleep before he came up with anything that made any sense.

In the main room, Maria's grandmother sat and regarded Maria, who sat alone in somber silence, locked away in her thoughts. After watching her for a time, her grandmother spoke. "You're being foolish, child."

Maria made no attempt to dissemble. She knew her grandmother well enough to know she could not fool the woman.

"Do not do this, child. He will soon be gone, and he will no more think of you when he is away from here than of me."

All conversation in the room ceased. The other members of the family knew of Maria's feelings for Chambliss and had discussed them among themselves. Now Grandmother was discussing them openly.

Maria looked down and picked at the embroidery on her dress.

"Maybe you're wrong," said Maria's mother. "He seems a good man."

"Pssssh," said Grandmother. "He is a man with no heart. A man with no heart is like a horse with bad lungs. He is no good to anyone."

"But he is wounded," argued Maria. He will be different when he is well."

"Wounded in the body and wounded in the soul," said Grandmother. "His body will heal, and you will see; he will still be a man with no heart."

"Perhaps his heart was broken by some woman," said Maria's father. "Broken hearts can heal."

The old woman just shook her head. "I say to you again, Maria, do not love this man. It will bring you only pain."

Maria stood up and left the room.

The next day the Apache came for food, and Chambliss, sitting up in the bed, called him into the room. "Do you know who Slim Ewart is?"

"Man who tell Pete to steal cows and horses."

Chambliss was angry that the Apache had known this and had not told him. He said, "Did Slim tell Pete to kill Jane and Josefina, or did Pete do that on his own?"

"Pete not kill womans. Lencho and Franey, they kill them."

Shocked to his core, Chambliss said, "What are you talking about? Who are Lencho and Franey?" He now remembered hearing Bruce mention those names moments before his death.

"Pete and the others take womans from ranch. Sell them to Lencho Bautista and Jack Franey."

"They sold them?" Chambliss nearly shouted the words. "How do you know this?"

The Apache told Chambliss that two of the outlaws in Pete Oxley's gang had been Mexicans and had talked to some of the workers at the hacienda. One of them in particular had been unhappy with the fact that Oxley and his men had kidnapped the two women. He had been even less pleased with what Bautista and Franey had done to the women and had said that he was going to leave the gang at the earliest opportunity. He was dead now, but the Apache, who spoke far better Spanish than English, had gleaned this information from several of the people employed at the hacienda.

"Where are Bautista and Franey now?"

The Apache shrugged. "Leave before we come. Back to Arizona. Wait for Pete to bring them money."

Chambliss closed his eyes and gritted his teeth against the pain and rage that rose up within him. Presently, with an outward calmness he did not feel, he said, "John, tell me about Bautista and Franey."

"Outlaws. Steal and kill in Arizona, run back to Mexico. Nobody can catch. Too smart. Very bad mans. Kill many peoples."

"Why didn't you tell me this before?"

"You too sick."

CHAPTER 6

Two days later, Chambliss heard shouting. Someone was saying excitedly, "*Rigo—Rigo ha vuelto.*" Rigo has returned.

He heard the sounds of approaching horses, and they stopped in front of the house. There was a great commotion, exclamations of joy, women crying, men's voices being lifted in greeting, the jingling of spurs. There was much excited chatter in Spanish, of which Chambliss understood little. Presently the sound of boots on the stone floor and the jingling of spurs approached his room, accompanied by women's protesting voices.

The door was thrown open and a tall, well-dressed but dust-covered, dark-haired man with piercing dark eyes walked in. This, Chambliss correctly assumed, was Rigo. He was a young man about the same age as Chambliss, and he was handsome and self-assured. "Do you know you are in my bed, gringo?" he said without preamble.

Chambliss said, "No one told me whose room this was."

Rigo dismissed the protesting women and walked over to a chair and sat down. "The two kinds of people I hate most in the world," he said in well-practiced English, "are Apaches and gringos. And you, I am told, are both. I have never heard of such a creature as a gringo Apache. I have only known gringos to be gringos and Apaches to be Apaches."

Chambliss said nothing. He was struck by the resemblance between Rigo and his younger sister Maria. Even in a crowd of people one would have recognized them as siblings.

Rigo said, "Do you not know that it is poor manners when you are a guest in someone's house to refuse to speak when you are spoken to?"

Chambliss began to form a reply, but Rigo continued. "In Mexico we put much greater value on good manners and hospitality than in your country. I hear you have done my family a service, and for that I thank you. And"—he waved a hand toward the bed—"you may continue to use my bed and my room for as long as you need them; that is our way. And when you leave, the women will come in and clean. We place a greater value on cleanliness in Mexico than you do in your country."

There was a pause and Chambliss spoke. "I am very impressed with the cleanliness and manners and hospitality I have seen here in your country."

Rigo made a slight bow with his head. "In case you are wondering why I speak your language so perfectly, it is because I have studied it and lived for three years with an American family in Mexico City."

Chambliss made a guess that the young man had been away at the university and had returned full of opinions and with a very high regard for his opinions.

Tell me now who you are," said Rigo.

"My name is Chambliss."

"I am Rigoberto Gabriel Arredondo Navarrete. I give you my full name, Chambliss. It is the custom in our country. It is more polite."

Chambliss said, "As for the room; I'm feeling much better. It's time for me to move out into your bunkhouse."

Rigo said, "No, I will not hear of it. Despite the fact that you are a gringo and an Apache, you are a guest. You will learn that in Mexico we do not lodge our guests with our hired workers." He rose and said, "If you have any needs, we are at your service," and left the room.

When Rigo was gone, Chambliss lay his head back on the pillow and thought about this latest unexpected event in a long string of unusual events. Until a few minutes ago he had not even known of the existence of Rigoberto Gabriel Arredondo Navarrete, but he was glad Rigo was back. The family needed him, needed his strength. Moreover, there was something likable about the young man.

In the days that followed, Chambliss saw the Apache less frequently than in previous days, owing mainly to the fact that Rigo, with his proficiency in English, was able to act as his interpreter. A few days after Rigo's arrival the Apache showed up at the hacienda, bringing Chambliss the money the redhead had paid for the herd. He set it on the bed and said, "You leave it on the ground. You are strange white man who do not care about money. All white mans care about money."

Chambliss realized that he had not thought about the money at all. He nodded to the Apache, who said, "Soon you better. Where you go?"

Chambliss did not answer immediately, but after a silence, he simply said, "I'm going to find Lencho and Franey." The Apache regarded him impassively, but did not nod. It wasn't his fight, and Chambliss understood that.

He also understood why the Apache had come to see him now, and he said, "You should go now." Had the Apache been a white man, Chambliss would have spoken words of gratitude and friendship. But John was not a white man, and Chambliss had learned that Apaches were not so different from the Indians he had grown up with. And so he looked John in the eye and said, "Keep the horses. Just leave my saddle."

The Apache nodded and left the room.

The next morning when Chambliss was eating breakfast with the family, as he now did, Rigo said, "Your Apache friend has gone, and he stole your horses. But that is the way of the Apache. They are thieves."

"I gave them to him," said Chambliss. "He is no thief."

"All Apaches are thieves. This land was given to my great-grandfather by the king of Spain. Once, there were large herds of cattle and many horses on this ranch. But between the Apaches and the bandidos, our herds have been reduced to almost nothing. It has been the way of things for hundreds of years—the people who live in the northern part of Sonora and those who live in the southern part of Arizona must spend their lives in fear Apaches and bandidos.

There are many bands of bandidos on both sides of the border, and numerous tribes of Apaches.

"Yes," said Chambliss. "I've heard that is true."

"Gringos are thieves too," Rigo added.

Had Chambliss been capable of smiling, he might have smiled at this statement. He knew what was coming.

"Most of the western part of what you call the United States once belonged to Mexico. You stole it from us."

Chambliss leaned back in his chair, stretched out his legs in front of him, and said with seeming irrelevance, "You are descended from

Spaniards."

"Yes, our people came from Spain generations ago. Arredondo and Navarrete are both Spanish names."

"And who was here when your people came from Spain?"

"Aztec and other Indians. They . . ." Rigo stopped himself and grinned. "I know what you mean to tell me, gringo. We stole the land from those people who occupied it before we came."

"And they stole it from someone else," said Chambliss. "It's the story of the human race. Everybody steals their land from someone else and complains when someone comes along later and steals it from them."

Rigo, still grinning somewhat sheepishly, lowered his head. "Yes, I have thought of these things."

"So Spaniards are thieves," said Chambliss, twisting the knife a little. "And what's more, you talk about your good manners, but in my country we would never insult a guest."

"And how have I insulted you?"

"Every time you call me gringo you insult me."

There was triumph in Rigo's smile. "So, you admit that it is a bad thing to be a gringo."

"No, I don't. But you think it is, therefore when you use the word it is an intentional insult. Very bad manners."

Chambliss watched the young Mexican's face as he tried to find a way to turn this argument into a victory, and he was surprised when Rigo humbly said, "You are right, my friend. Thank you for teaching me, a descendant of Spanish royalty, something about good manners. I believe that a well-educated man should always be willing to learn. I am well educated, you know. I spent the last three years studying at the university in Mexico City. It is far superior to your American universities."

<hr>

After he and the Apache had killed Pete Oxley and his men, Chambliss had ceased to think, or care, about the future. But when he learned that Lencho Bautista and Jack Franey were the ones who had killed Jane and Josefina, he understood that the job he had come here to do was only half done. And so he ate the food of his guests and partook of their hospitality with a sterile politeness. He was not ignorant of the fact that Maria was infatuated with him, and he intentionally paid little attention to her, trying to give her no reason to hope.

As his strength returned, he sometimes went riding with Rigo, and the young man showed him places he knew of, special places, beautiful places. On one occasion he took Chambliss to a spot where a stone hut had been built in front of a shallow mine, and said, "This is very old. It was built by the Jesuits. They tried to find gold here. The story is that there was no gold so they left."

Chambliss came to realize that he and Rigo were perfect riding companions. Rigo loved to talk and was seldom quiet. Chambliss had nothing to say and nothing to share. He was as a man who had no past and no future, no stories to tell, no opinions to render, and no friendship to give.

A talker he may be, but Rigo's talk was more than just mindless chatter. The young man was intelligent and articulate. His time at the university in Mexico City had not been spent in vain. He had knowledge and was a gifted storyteller, and the time Chambliss spent with him was a welcome distraction from his grief.

One day Rigo said, "My family is not poor. We still have some money, but it will not last long. My grandfather is old, and my father is not an able man. It is up to me to save my family from poverty.

"Once, my mother and grandmother had many servants who cooked and cleaned and washed clothing. Once this was a great horse ranch. We employed many *vaqueros*. We owned many cattle, too, but our horses were our great pride. They were known throughout all Mexico for their quality. I would have it be that way again.

"My father is a man of great learning. He is a kind man, but he is no fighter. Even before I left for Mexico City, I saw that my father should have armed his men. He should have hired fighting men and purchased rifles and led his men to do battle against the bandidos and the Apache. But he did not. He did not know how to do such things.

"I believe in peace, Chambliss, but peaceful people sometimes have to fight, or that which they have will be taken from them."

Chambliss nodded. He knew these things all too well.

Rigo reined in his horse and turned to face Chambliss. "We Arredondos are proud people. We offer our friendship to anyone who deserves it, but it is not easy to ask for help. I humbly now ask for yours. Not for my sake but for the sake of my family. For the sake of Maria, who loves you—though she is foolish to do so."

Chambliss looked into the young man's eyes but said nothing.

Rigo continued, "You have already done my family a greater service than we can ever repay, and we have not the right to ask more. But I ask it of you anyway. Will you help us?"

"What do you need?"

"There is a band of bandidos who for many years have come often to this part of Sonora. They have stolen from us many horses and cattle. I would rebuild this ranch that my ancestors built. It is my greatest wish. We will assemble men; men who are willing to fight. That is something we can do alone, but I . . . It shames me to say it. I have not acquired skill in battle or in killing."

"You should pray you never have to," said Chambliss.

"If praying would make evil men leave good people in peace, then I would pray all the day long. But I can only pray for the strength and wisdom to conquer our enemies. And I think that perhaps God has sent you here to us for that purpose. So, I ask you now, my friend, will you help us? Will you teach us how to fight the outlaws?"

"There is something I have to do," said Chambliss.

"And so your answer is no?"

There was a long silence, then Chambliss said, "If I go into battle with you and I'm killed, then this thing that I have to do will not get done."

"This thing, this task you must perform is vengeance, is it not?"

When Chambliss said nothing, Rigo continued, "You did not come here to help us. You did not know us then. You did not come for the cattle or for the money that was paid for them; you left that money lying on the ground. You came to kill men, and you have killed them. But there are more men to be killed, and this has become your great need. And so you will place yourself and your need to kill above the needs of your friends."

A sudden wrath rose up in Chambliss. He rounded on Rigo and opened his mouth to speak harsh words, but he could not think of the right ones to say. There was no argument that rang true, no grievance that sounded like anything approaching justice.

His anger drained away and left him with an odd sense of loss and discouragement. And, pragmatic thinker that he was, he realized that if Jane could speak to him from the grave, she would tell him that the needs of the living were more important than any sense of obligation to the dead. He looked away and murmured, "All right, Rigo. I'll help you."

The young Mexican had watched Chambliss' face as he fought this battle within himself and, for once, he said nothing. They rode for a long time in silence until Chambliss said, "Where will you get the men?"

"I have the men. Our hacienda is far from any hacienda or town, but do not think we have no friends. And do not think we are alone in our troubles. For seven years the outlaws have stolen from every ranch and farm in this region. They have killed any who have opposed them. We have tried in the past to hunt them down, but they always go up into those mountains." He pointed. "There are hundreds of miles of canyons and valleys. We have tried to follow, but they have ways of hiding their tracks. We have set traps for them, but whenever we are in one place, waiting for them, they strike at a different place, far from where we are.

We need someone like you to help us, Chambliss; someone who can appear like a ghost out of the night and kill many men; someone who can follow men no matter where they go; someone smarter than the bandidos that we hunt."

Chambliss said, "Gather your men."

"I will leave tonight in the darkness. I will assemble the men in secret at a place . . ."

Chambliss interrupted. "No need for all that. Just gather your men."

"Where?"

"At the hacienda."

"When?"

"As soon as they will come."

"In daylight or at night?"

"Doesn't matter."

CHAPTER 7

It was a jovial group of men who were gathered in the great dining room of the hacienda three days later. Hidden from view on a hilltop, Chambliss had watched as they arrived, one or two at a time or in small groups. All had received friendly greetings from the family, and many abrazos were given.

Maria and her mother and grandmother were well prepared. They had been cooking for two days, and the long wooden table in their dining room was heaped with food. Pozole, birria, empanadas, enchiladas, frijoles, tamales, and more were set before the eager company of men. Lemonade, jamaica, and horchata were prominent among the beverages.

Maria's face shone with perspiration and pleasure as she served the men and endured their good-natured jibes and compliments. Chambliss was not present, nor was his name mentioned at any time during the meal or in the discussion that followed.

When the men were finished eating, Rigo stood up and said, "You all know why you've been invited here. I have acquired a small herd of cattle and horses, and I have no intention of losing them to the bandidos who have stolen so much from us all. We must end this problem now. As all of you know, I have recently spent three years at the university in Mexico City. I returned to find my family's fortunes decimated. We have a new herd of good breeding stock. It is small, but it will grow, and I will not lose it." He slammed his fist on the table.

The assembled men voiced their approval, and there followed a discussion on how this thing was to be accomplished. Several plans were proposed and rejected, and finally one was agreed upon. There were numerous points of disagreement and discussion, but upon one thing the entire assemblage was in agreement, and that was that they should never split into groups. They all understood that when they met these bandits, they must be at full strength.

It was early afternoon when the meeting was declared finished and the visitors departed for their various destinations. One young man stayed behind and spent some time talking with Rigo. "I'm glad you're back, amigo. I have missed you."

"And I have missed you also, Rufino, friend of my youth."

Toward the end of the meal, wine had been served, and Maria came in to refill the two young men's glasses. Rufino said, "Ay, Maria, you have grown up to be a most beautiful woman."

She blushed and left the room.

When she was gone Rufino said, "I should ask that girl to marry me."

"You should, Rufino. You would be a fool not to."

They were no longer laughing. Rufino said, "In truth, I would, my friend, but for the fear that she would turn me down. What have you to say about that? Would Maria accept me or reject me?"

Thinking of Chambliss, Rigo said, "Wait, Rufi. Give her time. Now is not a good time."

"Why not?"

"There is another. He has no interest in her or in any woman, I fear, but she has not understood that yet. He will break her heart and then, when her heart is healing, I will send you word so that you may come and stop her from climbing to the top of the mountain and throwing herself off. And then she may say yes."

"I hope the wait will not be long," said Rufino. "I am not ugly like you, and there are other young women who would find me to be a great prize."

"Ugly? Is it ugly you call me, friend of my childhood? You, whose face can scare fish out of the water? We must assemble all the most beautiful women in Mexico, and you and I will stand before them and tell them to choose between us. We will see which of us garners the largest number."

And so they talked and jested for a while until the wine bottle was empty and Rufino stood to leave. He found his host and hostess, thanked them, and took his leave. After the traditional abrazo, he said to Rigo, "I will wait for Maria, but not for very long."

From his vantage point, Chambliss had counted the men as they arrived and had waited throughout the long hours while they met. Then he had watched and counted as they rode away. One was missing, and now that one also left the hacienda. He rode south as had the others, but when he was well out of sight of the hacienda he turned off the trail, rode up the far side of a small hill, dismounted, made his way to the top, and peered over. For nearly twenty minutes he watched his back trail. No one came. Finally he returned to his horse and followed an eastward trail that led him into the mountains.

Chambliss did not follow. He knew the man would be coming out soon and would easily be able to see if someone had been trailing him. So Chambliss made camp and remained where he was, waiting and watching. It was not until the afternoon of the following day that the man emerged from the mouth of the canyon, rode to the same hill he had climbed the previous day, and from its summit scanned the countryside. Apparently seeing no one, he rode to the main trail and turned south.

When Rigo had told Chambliss of how the land owners' attempts to trap the bandits had consistently failed, and that whenever they had set a trap for them the bandits had shown up at some other place, someplace far away, Chambliss had surmised that there was a traitor among them. And who better to lead him to the outlaws' hideout than that very traitor?

After Rufino came out of the mountains and rode away, Chambliss followed his tracks for miles through the maze of canyons and valleys. There was water in here at places, and grassy valleys. Rufino had made no attempt to hide his trail, and Chambliss made good time. Just before nightfall, he began to smell smoke.

He would need to be careful. The bandits would, no doubt, post lookouts. When it was fully dark, he went on, moving silently in his moccasins. No longer able to follow Rufino's trail because of the darkness, he followed the scent of the campfire smoke, and it was not long before he began to see the reflection of firelight on the sheer side of a mountain. Rather than enter the place that was the bandits' hideout, he decided to find a high point from which he could observe.

In the moonlight he located the most likely looking promontory and climbed up the sloping side, carefully and quietly, stopping frequently to listen.

It took him nearly three hours, but he eventually found himself overlooking a small valley, in the center of which was a large campfire. There were a number of tents and a few people, some moving around, others sitting. Chambliss lay down and slept, alert to any sound or change around him. He woke frequently to look around, listen, and sniff the air.

He saw the sun a good deal earlier than did the people in the valley, and by the time they woke, he had been watching them for some time. With the infinite patience of an Indian, he waited and watched throughout the day, and at midafternoon two more men and one woman arrived. It was nearly dark when another, larger group of men arrived, and with them two women. In all, Chambliss counted eleven men.

Soon a riotous fiesta began. There was guitar music and singing and a good deal of drinking. This went on late into the night. Having learned what he needed to know, Chambliss slipped away and started back.

▶━━━━━━━━●

It was dusk when the eleven men left the little valley and set their horse's hoofs on the trail that would lead them in its circuitous way, canyon by canyon, out of the mountains. Twelve hours from now they intended to return, driving a sizeable herd of prime cattle and horses. The men were confident in themselves and in their leader, a man named Verdugo. Seven years of easy successes had given them this confidence, and now they anticipated another successful raid. After dark they came around a bend in the canyon, and Verdugo reined in and held up his hand. He smelled kerosene. Why would he smell kerosene in this remote canyon?

Suddenly, about two hundred feet in front of him, the night lit up in a blaze of burning brush that filled the canyon from wall to wall. The bandits wheeled their horses around just as the first gunshots from above came raining down upon them. Immediately, two men dropped from their horses, and one horse staggered and fell. The remaining men spurred their mounts viciously, but as they came back around the bend they were met by more burning brush, the light from which illuminated the bandits, exposing them to a withering volley of gunfire from a line of riflemen who were hidden in the rocks. And to make matters worse, here, too, there were men on the

64

rims of the canyon, and they were sending down a hailstorm of lead onto the hapless bandits.

Verdugo screamed useless and incoherent orders as all around him his men fell wounded or dead. Two men were able to drive their horses through the burning brush, thinking they would be safe on the other side, but the attackers had planned for this contingency as well, and the last thing that either of the two men saw with their mortal eyes was a line of rifle barrels spouting flame.

Verdugo threw up his hands and began screaming for the shooters to spare their lives. Rigo gave the order for his men to cease firing. Shouting from the rim of the canyon, he ordered Verdugo and the two other men who were still mounted to lie on their stomachs on the ground. The stretch of canyon from burning brush barrier to burning brush barrier was littered with the bodies of men and horses. A few terrified, riderless horses ran back and forth there.

When Rigo's men were finally able to pass through the smoking brush, they tied the hands of the three bandits, not one of whom was without a wound of some kind, and then tied ropes around their necks, linking one to another so there would be no possibility of any of them breaking free. Nearby was a small box canyon. The prisoners were taken there and put under guard.

In the main canyon Rigo and the other men held a conference. With the exception of Rigo, none of them had met Chambliss or even seen him, though he was nearby and had watched the battle. Now Rigo sent his cry out into the night. "Chambliss, come. We wish to speak with you."

Rufino, standing nearby, said, "Who is Chambliss?"

"He's a friend, Rufi, a gringo. You will meet him."

Chambliss came into the ring of firelight, crossed, and stood next to Rigo, who said, "I present to you all, my friend Chambliss. It was he who discovered the hiding place of the outlaws. It was also he who gave me the suggestion that we change the plan we agreed upon in our last meeting to this plan that we have all taken part in tonight. He also suggested we make sure that everyone accompany us tonight. He said we must all be here together, leaving no one out."

"And why was that?" asked one of the men.

"Because there is a traitor among us."

The statement elicited a few surprised outcries and some of disbelief. Several voices demanded to know who the traitor was.

"I do not know," said Rigo. "But after our meeting at my house on Sunday, my friend Chambliss watched one of you leave the main trail and ride into this canyon. The next day that same man came out. Chambliss followed his trail, and it led him to the camp of the bandidos. And now we understand why none of our former plans worked. The bandidos always knew where we would be and were able to strike somewhere else."

"Why does the gringo not tell us who the traitor is?" asked one of the men.

"He says he did not see him closely enough to identify him. It is our task to find out who it is."

In his short time in Mexico, Chambliss had only begun to learn the language, and he understood very little of this discussion. But though he did not understand the words, he knew what was going on. These men were attempting to determine who had betrayed them.

He could have given them a simple solution to their dilemma by telling them the traitor was the last man to leave the hacienda on the day they had all assembled, but Chambliss was a stranger among these men, and he knew it would be difficult for them to side with him against one of their own. They needed to work it out for themselves.

Several of the men spoke at once, and Rigo raised his hand for silence.

One man said, "I do not believe it. I do not believe what this gringo says. We are friends. We are brothers. He has found the camp of the bandidos, and for that he deserves our gratitude. But now he has planted suspicion in us. He is turning us against each other, for what purpose I do not know. But if we believe what he says, none of us will ever trust each other again. And that is a very bad thing."

Two or three men spoke up in agreement, but Rigo said, "This man is a stranger to you, but he is not a stranger to me. He is a friend. He is as a brother. And I trust him as I trust Rufino, my friend since childhood. Think of it, my friends, does it not make sense? Do you remember how the bandidos always outsmarted us? And how was it that in this vast range of mountains where we have searched many times in vain, seeking the hiding place of the bandidos, Chambliss should find it so easily? How did he do this if not by following someone who came here?"

"Maybe he is one of the bandidos," said Rufino. "Maybe that is why he knew where they were."

"No, he is not one of them," affirmed Rigo. Then he said, "None of us here knows who the traitor is. But the outlaws we have captured know. We will wait here until daylight, and then we will all go and allow them to identify the traitor before they are executed. You have chosen me as your leader, and it is my order that no one should leave this place until this matter is decided. If anyone should try to leave, it will be considered the same as a confession."

Only a few of the men slept that night. The rest of them sat around the fire and drank coffee, speaking in subdued tones. The dead outlaws had been laid together along one wall of the canyon where they would be buried in the morning. Two more of them had been found to be alive, but their wounds received no attention, and they both died during the night.

Chambliss sat alone. He thought about how short a night seems when a man spends it sleeping and how long it can be when he is awake and waiting for it to end. He thought a lot about Jane that night and about Jack Franey and Lencho Bautista, and the world seemed a dark and dirty place.

But, like every other night that had preceded it since the world began, this night ended, and when daylight finally crept into the canyon, Rigo stood up and, without saying a word, looked around at the assembled men. He turned, and the group made the short walk down the canyon to where the three bandits were being held.

During the night the prisoners had been guarded, and the guard had been changed every two hours. Attempts had been made to induce the leader of the bandits to talk but without success. He refused to even reveal his name.

Standing in front of him now, Rigo turned to the assembled group, looking at them one at a time, knowing that one of these men was a traitor and dreading what was to come. He said, "No one leaves until this is over."

Nothing had been done for the wounds the bandits had received in the fight, and all three of them had bled to one degree or another while sitting there during the long night, awaiting their fate. Verdugo's wound was in the arm, and with his hands bound behind his back, he had been unable to do anything for himself. This morning he looked pallid and sick.

Rigo walked over to where Verdugo sat, stood in front of him, and said, "This morning the three of you will die, and it is because you were betrayed. Just as we have been betrayed all these years, now you have been betrayed by the same man. We know he is among us. We know he stands here before you. If you will tell us who he is, I promise we will kill him first, and you will have the pleasure of watching him die—this man who has brought about your deaths and the deaths of all your comrades."

Rufino, who had the previous night stood next to Rigo, was now standing at the back of the group, doing his best to avoid being seen. Verdugo rose unsteadily to his feet, smiled a malicious smile, and said, "Rufi, come and join us. We have shared many joyful times together. Now we must share this unhappy one."

A murmur went through the group, half surprise, half anger. Heads swiveled, looking for Rufino. One of the men directly in front of him spun around and grasped him by the arm.

Rigo stood, frozen, as though turned to stone.

"No," cried Rufino. "You are my friends. How can you believe this *malvado*? It is a conspiracy. This gringo and these men have planned all of it. This gringo is a stranger. He is not to be believed. And Verdugo is a bandido—a murderer and a thief. Will you take his word against mine?"

He moved through the group to stand in front of Rigo. "Rigo, my friend, my brother, you have known me since childhood. Just last Sunday I spoke to you about marrying your sister. Surely you cannot think . . ."

Rigo interrupted him coldly, "So his name is Verdugo."

Rufino flinched as though he had been slapped. His eyes widened, his mouth opened and closed several times, but no words came out. One of the men in the group motioned to another, and they came and stood beside Rufino, each taking an arm. The entire group waited for Rigo to speak.

Verdugo laughed—a low, coarse sound. "Come and stand beside us, Rufi, my friend. Together we will take the journey."

Rigo's eyes sought Chambliss, and in them there was an appeal. Chambliss held his gaze but had nothing to give him. After a few moments, seeing this, Rigo turned back to face Rufino, and Chambliss watched Rigo's face as he had his moment of hell. It seemed that something changed in the young man. His boyish arrogance fell away, and he entered the thorny, exigent realm of men.

Silence was on the group as Rigo stood there looking at Rufino, his eyes boring into the young traitor. Suddenly Rufino began weeping. "I am sorry, my friend. I am very sorry."

Rigo turned away from him. His handsome face was pale. His hand trembled as he pointed. "Stand them over there. All four of them."

Rufino's hands were bound. He was made to stand next to Verdugo. At that moment, Rigo remembered something. "Wait," he said. "I made a promise to you, Verdugo, that the traitor would die first so that you could watch him die."

"No," said Verdugo. "I release you from that promise. Let us die together."

None of the men ever knew if Verdugo had done this as an act of kindness or if he had simply preferred not to see happen to someone else that which was about to happen to him.

CHAPTER 8

There was no jocularity among the group that rode out of the canyon that day into a region whose inhabitants would now be free from the fear that had hung over them for so many years. Rufino's body, slung over his saddle, bore one bullet hole—through the heart—and the men had all taken an oath that, for the sake of his family, they would never tell anyone the truth. Rufino would be remembered as the sole casualty on the side of the land owners, of the battle with the bandits.

Rigo rode at the head of the group, speaking to no one, and, as a gesture of respect, being spoken to by none. When they finally reached the main trail where they would separate, he waited, turned his horse, and nodded to each man in his turn as he passed. Chambliss had lagged behind the group, knowing he was an outsider. Now he stopped his horse next to Rigo's and silently waited.

They did not ride directly to the hacienda. Rigo took a trail that surmounted a high hill that overlooked the valley. There he dismounted and stood gazing across the distance. Chambliss built a fire and made some coffee. When he handed Rigo a steaming cup, the young man said, "You knew it was him, didn't you?"

"I only knew it was the last man to leave your house on the day of the meeting."

"Why did you not say so?"

Chambliss didn't answer. This was something Rigo would have to come to understand on his own.

Rigo said, "I needed your help."

Chambliss did not speak.

"I killed my best friend, Chambliss. I needed help, but you did nothing. You said nothing."

"No one could help you with that. You were the leader. The responsibility was yours alone."

There was a long silence, and then Rigo said, "Did I do the right thing?"

"You did the only thing you could." Chambliss could think of nothing else to say. To kill was hard. To kill for the first time, harder. To kill one's best friend . . .

Rigo picked up a stone and threw it as hard as he could, watching it fly out straight, promising to go far out into the valley, and then seeing it arc downward to land disappointingly short. He picked up another and did the same, and then another, and another, and for a time he seemed lost in this activity. Presently he sat down and said quietly, "My grandmother says you have no heart. If that is true I envy you. Today, I would gladly give you mine. Maria says she is certain you have a heart but that it is broken."

He looked at Chambliss. "Which of those two silly women is right?"

Chambliss gave a faint shake of the head.

Rigo turned away and murmured, "I understand; you do not wish to talk about it. I will never wish to talk about today either. I will keep it inside me and do my best to forget." He turned back to face Chambliss, "Is that possible, amigo? Is it possible to forget?"

"No."

"I have never seen you laugh, my friend, and though you do not wish to talk about yourself, I ask you, for the sake of our friendship, to answer me one question . . . No, I will ask two: Was there a time when you were a man who loved to laugh?"

Chambliss tried to remember the last time he had laughed, and it was Jane he thought of, remembering their joyous times together. Yes, he had laughed. They had both laughed as if the world was a place without sorrow. He answered, "Yes."

"And will you ever laugh again?"

Chambliss understood the question. It did not truly apply to him, so he answered the real question that was being asked. "Yes, Rigo, you will laugh again, and you will dance again, and you will feel joy again."

"Then, if that is true, my friend, so will you. It cannot be true of one and not another."

Chambliss turned away and said nothing. What Rigo had said was logical, but in his heart Chambliss did not believe it.

They rode into the plaza of the hacienda and turned their horses over to Adolfo. Having been apprised of their coming, every member of the family was standing on the porch, waiting for them. Rigo's father walked up to him and put his hands on his son's shoulders. Knowing what they all needed to hear, Rigo said, "The bandidos are dead. All of them."

Unitedly the family gave a cheer of relief and elation. "We shall have a fiesta," said Rigo's father, embracing him.

Rigo's grandmother however, came over to him, took his hand, and said, "What is it? What bad thing happened?"

The cheers and mutual congratulations stopped, and everyone waited. Rigo said, "Rufino is dead."

His mother put her face in her hands. Maria clutched her mother and sobbed.

Later, after a somber meal during which the family spoke of their memories of Rufino, who had many times shared food with them at this very table, Rigo's father took him aside and said, "Did he die bravely, my son?"

Rigo remembered Rufino standing there, desolately looking at the ground, until he had finally gathered the courage to raise his head and meet Rigo's gaze and hold it. And he had held it until . . .

Rigo answered softly, "Yes, Father, bravely."

And after that, never again did Rigo speak of Rufino, the friend of his youth.

On the day Chambliss left, Maria did not come out of her room to say good-bye. Rigo presented Chambliss with a horse, and it was his own favorite—a splendid bay gelding with three white stockings and a white blaze on its face.

Chambliss tried to refuse the gift, but Rigo said, "Remember, my friend, our ways are different from yours. To refuse a gift is an offense."

"Then," said Chambliss, "thank you. Thank you, my friend, for everything."

Rigo embraced him in the traditional manner and said, "Chambliss, you gringo Apache." His voice became thick with emotion. "*Hermano de mi alma,* my brother. *Mi casa es tu casa.* This is your home for as long as you live."

———————▶

Slim Ewart's Antler Ranch was a small spread, and as Chambliss crossed it he wondered how cattle could survive on the sparse graze in evidence here. Nor did the few scrawny cows he saw as he crossed the range enhance his opinion of Antler.

He was not sure what he would do when he met Slim Ewart, but he would meet him regardless, and play the cards as they were dealt. He rode up to the house and dismounted, tying the reins to the hitching rack.

Antler's headquarters were nothing like the Diamond J had been before it was destroyed. The main house was small, and the other buildings were a collection of ramshackle wood and adobe structures. Prosperity had never been a presence here.

He stepped up onto the porch and the door opened. A woman came out—a tall, bony woman with a face that once may have been attractive. This, Chambliss assumed, was Sally. She was holding a pistol in her hand. She did not point it at Chambliss but clearly intended for him to see it. She said, "Go away."

"Ma'am, I just want to talk to Slim."

"Talk?" She laughed scornfully. "I know why you're here, and it isn't to talk."

Chambliss changed the subject. "Did Whitey pull through?"

"Yes. He's gone. You need to go too. There's no way you or anyone else can prove anything against Slim, so just go. He doesn't want to talk to you."

"No, I don't expect he would, considering the circumstances."

She cocked the pistol but did not raise it, "I won't let you kill him. That Captain Roderick came here awhile back with his Apaches. He wanted to see Slim, but I wouldn't let him either. He said you would be coming. He told me what you did down in Mexico."

Chambliss kept his voice low. "Did he tell you why?"

There was a long pause. She seemed to be trying to decide how to answer. At last she said, "Yes." She dropped her eyes, and after a moment he realized that she was crying.

She said through her tears, "I knew Jane. We were friends. She was a lovely person."

She looked at Chambliss. "You did what you had to. I understand that. But isn't it enough?"

Chambliss had not intended to discuss Slim's crimes with his wife, but it was apparent she already knew. He said, "If it was right in Mexico, why not here?"

"Because . . . because . . ." She began to wail. "Because he's all I've got." She uncocked the gun and sat down on the top step of the porch. "I know what Slim did. I'm mortally ashamed of him, but . . . I don't know what I'd do if you killed him," she sobbed.

"I didn't come to kill him."

She looked at him, her expression bleak, wanting to believe but not trusting. She said, "He's already been punished more than you could ever imagine, Mr. Chambliss."

"How so?"

"Slim only wanted some good breeding stock. He's worked so hard to build this ranch, but it's been just one piece of bad luck after another. And after old Joseph died and Jane inherited his ranch, Slim just couldn't take it. He kept talking about the unfairness of the world. He had worked and sacrificed for over twenty years and had nothing to show for it, and she, a young girl, knowing nothing about ranching, had the Diamond J dropped into her lap as a gift. He just couldn't take it, Mr. Chambliss."

Her eyes sought his, as if the earnestness of her gaze could convince him her words were true. "Those men—" she said, "Pete Oxley and the others—took things further than Slim wanted them to. There weren't supposed to be any killings. But they . . ." She began to cry again.

Presently, she wiped her eyes and said, "Slim blames himself for everything. He's in a torment worse than hellfire. He'll never be the same man again. He wouldn't even take the stolen livestock when they brought it back from Mexico, even though he had already paid for them. I know he deserves punishment, Mr. Chambliss, but if you really want him to suffer for what he's done, leave him alive, because, since the day all those Diamond J men were killed, he's never been the same. And since he learned that Jane and Josie were killed, he's been wanting to die himself. You'd be doing him a favor if you killed him."

"I still want to talk to him. I want to see his face."

"What is it to you?" she demanded, suddenly angry. "From what I heard you're just a drifter. "This has nothing to do with you. Why can't you leave us alone?"

Chambliss pulled out the small piece of paper he had shown to Captain Roderick in Skeleton Canyon and handed it to Sally. She unfolded it and read it. Handing it back, she dropped her head, put her hands over her face, and began to sob.

After a while, more composed, she turned to him and said, "Will you give me your word you won't harm him?"

"I give you my word."

She rose and went into the house. Soon Chambliss heard voices; talking at first, and then raised to quarreling. He heard Sally's strident voice say, "He has a right." And then there was silence.

Presently, Sally came back out, leaving the door open. Two minutes passed, then three. Finally, Slim emerged.

Chambliss was shocked by his appearance. Sally had not exaggerated. Slim had suffered. He said nothing; he merely stood there as if it were self-evident that having to face Chambliss was as great a punishment as any Chambliss could have devised.

Chambliss looked at the rancher and waited for him to make eye contact. Finally, Slim raised his eyes, and Chambliss knew he had never seen sorrow like this before. He had once heard a preacher say that Hell was not a place, it was a state of mind. Now he understood what that meant. He thought of many things to say, harsh, cutting things, but he could not say them. He merely looked at Sally and said, "Good day, ma'am. I won't be bothering you again."

He rode away.

It was easy for Chambliss to fill the gaps in the story Sally had told him. Slim had decided to even out some of the unfairness, as he perceived it, in the world, not knowing that the kind of men he was hiring could never be controlled by a man like him. He had devised a simple plan to have some cattle and horses rustled from the Diamond J and taken to Mexico. He would send some men to pay the rustlers for the stolen livestock—and he would only pay a fraction of its real worth—rebrand it, and either bring it back to Antler or sell it elsewhere, probably some of both.

But he had made one serious mistake. He had hired killers and expected them not to kill. Pete Oxley had decided to take away from the Diamond J everything of value. And that had included the two women. Chambliss remembered the money belt the Apache had found on Pete's body, and he wondered how much Lencho Bautista and Jack Franey had paid for Jane and Josefina. The thought sickened him, and a flush of rage coursed through him. Again, he promised himself that he would find Bautista and Franey. He would find them, and when he did, he would not be as merciful as he had been with Slim Ewart. He would make sure they never harmed another human being.

He rode over to the Diamond J, remembering Jane as she had been when he had last seen her alive. He remembered how he had held her in his arms and kissed her. He remembered the things she had said to him, and he wished he had known she was in danger. He wished he had remained with her and protected her. More than that, he wished she had stayed in Wisconsin and married him and never come here.

He wished many things that would never be.

Unbidden, a few lines of a poem he had heard years before came into his head:

Our lives are ruled by God's decree
And sorrow comes to you and me
And reaching for eternity
We wish for things that cannot be.

He tried to remember the rest of the poem but couldn't.

The Diamond J was abandoned now, and the elements had begun to reclaim that piece of ground. Weeds and grasses and brush and volunteer Palo Verde trees were already taking over. The long row of wooden markers was a tragic reminder of what had turned this place from a bustling ranch to a lonely, desolate graveyard. Jane's few remaining riders had long since dispersed and gone to work on other ranches or to parts unknown. Adjacent ranches had moved onto the range that had formerly been the Diamond J and were using the land.

Someday, Chambliss promised himself, he would go back to Mexico, to the place where he had buried Jane's body. He had chosen a place that would not be disturbed by man or by the elements; a place he would be able to easily locate again. He would go back and visit when this was all over.

But for now, he had things to do.

Captain Roderick had sent the news of Jane's death back to her family. Now, Chambliss sent them the money he had been paid for the cattle. Long months of unrewarded searching followed. Months of riding from town to town fruitlessly questioning everyone he met. He went to New Mexico, then back across Arizona to California, even down into Sonora in his hunt for Jack Franey and Lencho Bautista.

In the Apache-plagued, Arizona town of Tubac, he learned that the two outlaws had had a falling out and gone separate ways, but as to their whereabouts, he was given no clue. Finally, in the tiny, austere community of Arivaca, eleven miles north of the Mexico border, he encountered the outlaw Lencho Bautista.

He went there intentionally to talk to Hal Dean. He had heard that Lencho frequented the area. He also had learned that Hal was working on a small ranch nearby. The fact that Hal had a low opinion of him made no difference to Chambliss. After all that had occurred, he had weightier matters on his mind, and if Hal had any information regarding the whereabouts of the men Chambliss sought, Chambliss would put up with the cowboy's scorn in order to get it.

It was midafternoon on a hot and breezeless day. He stopped at the ranch headquarters a few miles out of town, dust-covered from the trail, sweaty from the heat, and jaded from long months of riding. He was informed that Hal and another rider had gone into town for supplies. He rode on in to Arivaca and found Hal in front of the mercantile loading the supplies into a spring wagon. Hal turned an unfriendly gaze on Chambliss and then made a point of sending a disdainful glance at his moccasins.

Ignoring this, Chambliss nodded and said, "Hal."

Hal looked at him, saying nothing.

Chambliss said, "Seen Whitey?"

"Why?"

"No particular reason."

"Then it don't matter if I've seen him."

Chambliss' lips formed a faint, ironic smile. So this was how it was going to be. He looked at Hal and said, "I don't care what you think of me, but if Jane mattered at all to you, at least give me what help you can. I'm trying to find the men who killed her."

Skepticism on his face, Hal considered this for a long moment and said, "What do you figure on doin' if you find them, challenge them to a footrace?"

"I'll decide what to do when the time comes." It was a lie. Chambliss had made that decision in the canyon where he had buried Jane's body, but he had no intention of discussing it with Hal.

Hal said, "Do you even know who they are?"

This was another subject Chambliss did not wish to discuss, but there was no way Hal could help him unless he did. He simply said, "Right now I'm looking for a Mexican outlaw named Lencho Bautista."

Hal gave a derisive laugh. "Lencho could kill you in his sleep and not even interrupt his snorin'."

A stocky cowboy had come out of the store and was standing next to Hal, listening to the conversation. Now he volunteered, "Lencho likes to hang around these parts. It's close to the border, and there's not much law to speak of. Sometimes he comes here to Arivaca."

Chambliss felt a faint stirring of excitement, but before he could ask another question, Hal interrupted. Shooting a dark look at the stocky cowboy, he said, "Yeah, but he ain't here now."

"You know that for a fact?" asked Chambliss.

"Yeah," said Hal, "He rode back to Mexico a week ago."

"Do you know what he looks like?"

"Never seen him, and if you're smart, you won't either. Greenhorn like you wouldn't stand a chance against Bautista."

The stocky cowboy next to Hal laughed and uttered an epithet, spitting tobacco juice on the ground to put the exclamation point on this last statement.

"Thanks for the advice," said Chambliss sardonically. He started to ask another question, but Hal turned away and walked back into the store, followed by his friend.

Chambliss rode down the narrow, dusty street to what appeared to be the only saloon in Arivaca. Carrying his Winchester as he always did, he walked inside. It was a shabby little saloon in a shabby little town.

It was not a large room, and aside from the bar itself and a few tables and chairs, it sported little in the way of furnishings. The mirror behind the bar had been shot; the bullet holes in the bare boards it had once covered could be clearly seen, and a jagged fragment of it still hung from a nail higher than a man's head. The air in the room was stale and hot and smoky.

Four Mexicans were playing cards and drinking at a table at the far end of the room. They looked up and noticed Chambliss as he, likewise, briefly surveyed them. They did not appear to see anything of interest in him, nor did he in them, and they all turned their attention away.

The saloonkeeper had been dozing on a stool, his head on his chest, his face shiny with sweat. He looked up and raised his eyebrows questioningly as if speaking would take too much energy.

"Beer," said Chambliss.

"We're out. Freight wagons got hit by Apaches. We got whiskey."

Chambliss nodded. The saloonkeeper poured, and Chambliss took a sip and said, "I'm looking for a Mexican named Lencho Bautista. I hear he comes here sometimes. I'd like to know what he looks like."

The saloonkeeper's face underwent a subtle change, but he said, "Never heard of him."

"I heard he comes here sometimes."

"Lot of men come here sometimes. You might have noticed I don't have a register where you sign your name when you walk in."

Disappointed, Chambliss took another sip of whiskey. The saloonkeeper had not moved, and his face held no expression, but his eyes flicked almost imperceptibly to one side, and Chambliss recognized this as a signal. In an action the saloonkeeper would later describe as being faster than any cat could move, Chambliss whirled to find a Mexican behind him with a pistol in one hand and a long, slender-bladed knife in the other. He was within striking range, clearly intending to use the knife but holding the pistol in case he was discovered before he could sink the blade. Now facing Chambliss, he brought the pistol up.

Using his momentum as he spun around, Chambliss knocked the gun aside with the barrel of the Winchester just as the Mexican pulled the trigger. The Mexican's knife hand flashed forward, but Chambliss twisted his body so the sharp steel merely cut a shallow groove in the flesh of his side. As he did so he jerked the Winchester back to center, and with the tip of the barrel touching the Mexican's chest, he fired.

Immediately he levered in another cartridge and raised the Winchester to cover the men at the table. One of them started to rush forward, crying out, "Lencho!" Another was raising his gun when Chambliss fired again.

Chambliss stopped Lencho's concerned friend with a command. "Get back to the table." The man obeyed. There were two outlaws left standing, and one on the floor moaning. Chambliss ordered the two who were standing to set all the guns on the table and back away. Now, recognizing he owed a debt to the saloonkeeper, he shot a glance at the man and barked, "You could have warned me."

The saloonkeeper was no fool. He recognized the gift he was being given. "You come in here, you take your chances like everybody else. I'll warn no man."

Chambliss looked around for something to destroy as a way of underscoring his point, but aside from the bottles of liquor on the shelf behind the bar, which represented the saloonkeeper's livelihood, he saw nothing. The mirror had already been shot and was gone; the room's single window held no intact panes of glass. Even the two lamp brackets on the wall hung empty.

Finally, his gaze rested on the single adornment in this bleak room; a painting of a reclining, thinly clad woman. He raised his rifle and fired, puncturing a hole in her navel. Afterward, he gathered up the outlaws' guns and backed out of the saloon, and when he was out of view of Lencho's friends, he gave the saloonkeeper a brief nod.

He stuffed the guns in his saddlebags, and as he was untying his horse, Hal Dean and the stocky puncher pulled up in the spring wagon.

Hal said, "Shootin' in there?"

Chambliss nodded.

"Loud noise scare you away?"

Keeping his eye on the door of the saloon, Chambliss stepped into the saddle and said, "You knew Lencho was there. That's why you told me he'd left town. You let me go in there figuring he'd kill me."

Hal sat looking at him, stone-faced, unspeaking. Chambliss reined his horse around and rode away.

CHAPTER 9

It was spring and the desert was in bloom. The life-giving moisture imparted by the recent rains had not yet been sucked from the soil by the brutal heat of the unforgiving summer sun.

George Durfee looked around in awe. Why had he never noticed how beautiful the desert was? He had always thought of it as a dead place, a place of snakes and lizards and rocks and cacti and little else. He had seen it as a thing to be feared, a malevolent entity, certainly not a place filled with green plants and wildflowers, humming insects and abundant life.

It was that time of day when the world is at its best—just past sunrise. The sun was bright but not glaring or hot. The pleasant light showed off the radiant colors of the desert. Man and beast felt revitalized by their night's sleep. The air was clean and invigorating, and George breathed in deeply and filled his lungs. He regretted never having taken time to appreciate the beauty he now saw around him.

He had spent the last thirty-two months in self-enforced slavery, working his claim from dawn to dark, seven days a week, wresting from the clutching grasp of the rock the precious metal which he had exchanged for the money he now carried with him.

During those months he had lived like a miser, never gambling or indulging in any form of entertainment that cost money. And, though he had frequented the Frisco Lady, one of the many saloons in the town, he had done so only for companionship, seldom taking a drink, reluctant to spend any of the fruits of his labors on liquor.

His home had been a tent, purchased at a song from a miner who was giving up and moving on. Durfee had shared it with scorpions, tarantulas, and the occasional visiting rattlesnake. His meals he had prepared himself, cooking them on a campfire in front of the tent.

For thirty-two months he had been a man with a purpose, and that purpose was to gouge out of the earth as much ore as he possibly could. Now, with the money he carried in his saddlebags, he could go back and start a business and still have money left to buy a house large enough for a family.

Cynthia was as excited as he was. It showed in her letters, especially the last one, written after she had received his letter informing her that he would soon be coming home. She was already planning the wedding.

He noticed a group of riders off to his right, three of them, perhaps four hundred yards away, riding toward him. He quickly took stock of the situation, wishing now that he had listened to Martin Chambliss, who had advised him not to travel alone.

For the past half hour he had been riding down the center of a wide, flat valley, staying away from the hills on either side as a precaution against ambush. He turned and angled toward the open mouth of a canyon on the opposite side of the valley. If he could reach it he could climb up the side and hold off his pursuers with the rifle he carried in a saddle scabbard.

He spurred his horse, and the animal lunged forward. His pack mule struggled to keep up. Glancing back, he was puzzled by the fact that the riders were not closing the gap. It was almost as though they were intentionally maintaining their distance, never lagging behind, never coming closer.

He wasted no time wondering about this. His main goal was to reach the canyon and get up into the rocks. From there he could hold them off all day. He spurred his mount hard, whipping it with the reins.

Approaching the canyon, he glanced back over his shoulder to check the distance between his pursuers and himself. No change. Why were they hanging back? A few seconds later he knew. From the mouth of the canyon emerged three more riders, coming straight at him. There was no way to escape. He could only hope they intended to rob him and would not kill him if he did not resist.

The bullet knocked him out of the saddle, and he landed in a clump of cacti. He lay on his back and looked up at the sky. It was beautiful.

Martin Chambliss topped the rise overlooking the town of Pick-Em-

Up and sat still for a moment, resting his horse. He looked down on the town below, its haphazard sprawl making it appear as though its buildings and streets had fallen from the sky and lay where they had landed. Some of them rested on the sloping hills, and others on relatively level ground. It was anything but pretty.

It had begun with a single establishment, the First Chance Saloon, and the rest had grown up around that core into a collection of establishments, around the perimeter of which was a sort of mining camp. The town, if such it could be called, possessed all the lack of permanence of a mining camp. Its buildings were mostly canvas tents, though there were a few hastily built, unpainted, rough wooden structures. It was a town that could be torn down and hauled away in a day, leaving nothing but holes in the ground and trash heaps, and the ugliest, most unappealing graveyard Chambliss had ever seen.

Pick-Em-Up was a raw and lawless place, and with only a few exceptions, its businesses were of the type that catered to the basest appetites of men. It had one definite street, which was lined on either side by rows of these businesses facing each other like soldiers. It was a narrow street, and the dust on its surface was fine and powdery and easily stirred, and when it rained, that dust was turned to a thick, ankle-deep soup.

For Chambliss the town had one attraction and one alone: there was a reasonable hope that Jack Franey would show up here sooner or later. And Chambliss had been waiting for that to happen for over two years now.

After killing Lencho Bautista, having no clue as to where to even begin looking for Franey, Chambliss decided to go to a place where there was a strong likelihood the outlaw would turn up, and wait for him there. He had settled on Pick-Em-Up; it was the kind of lawless town that would appeal to an outlaw, it was near the area where Franey and Bautista had formerly operated, and it was just a short ride away from the Mexican border.

Knowing little about mining, Chambliss had chosen a spot for his claim based on advice from other miners and, trusting more in luck than any geologic knowledge, had marked his boundaries, filed his claim, and begun working it. His mine was not a great one, he had discovered no bonanza, but it had so far paid him well for his labors, and he had saved a fair sum of money, part of which he had invested in a small herd of cattle.

No one he had talked to thought Pick-Em-Up had much of a future. It was generally agreed that the town was a temporary one. Chambliss too believed this to be true, and yet he had no desire to go anywhere else. He was a man with no roots, no ties, no plans. He was here for one reason and one reason only: to wait for Jack Franey to turn up and kill him when he did.

He spurred down the slope and rode into town, passing Shaw's store. A few men had brought their families to Pick-Em-Up—a bad idea in Chambliss' opinion—and Ralph Shaw was one of them. Shaw owned a freighting business and the store—a lucrative combination. He and his family lived in the back of the store. They were cramped quarters, and Shaw could afford to build a house, but, being a frugal man, he was waiting to see if the town would survive. He had no desire to waste money on a house that he would have to abandon in a year or two. To make such an unsure investment was a thing completely against his nature. However, despite his tight-fisted shrewdness, Ralph Shaw had the reputation of being a fair man who, though he liked to make a healthy profit, would not do so dishonestly.

As Chambliss passed Shaw's store, Ralph waved him down. "Martin, could I have a word with you?"

Chambliss dismounted and tied the horse at the hitching post.

"Martin, would you go find Ricky for me? He's been gone for two days, and his mother is worried. It's those new friends of his; they're a bad influence on him. He's a good boy, but he's just too young to understand the ways of the world, and I'm afraid those young men he's running around with might corrupt him."

"I'll do what I can, Ralph."

"And, Martin, when you do find him, maybe you could have a talk with him. I think he would listen to you. His mother and I have tried, but he's at that age . . . you know."

Chambliss nodded but refrained from voicing his opinion, which was that at nineteen years of age, Ricky Shaw was well aware of what he was doing and why. When it came to their only son and youngest child, the Shaws were completely blind. Ricky was aware of this and took advantage of it constantly, as Chambliss suspected he had been doing since infancy.

He rode away, wishing Ralph Shaw didn't have so much faith in him. He was not sure why he did. He didn't know the Shaws very well, and he didn't like Ricky at all. Ralph Shaw had the idea that Ricky looked up to Chambliss. It was a belief Chambliss did not share. But he had promised he would try to find the young man and talk some sense into him, and, though he knew it would do no good, he would keep his word.

He noticed a huddle of men in front of one of Pick-Em-Up's saloons and rode over to see what it was about. Looking over the heads of the men from atop his horse, he saw a body stretched out on the ground in front of the saloon. The man had obviously been dead for several days, and his body and face were bloated beyond recognition, but Chambliss could not fail to recognize the blond hair and the clothing, and he felt the sudden wave of shock that accompanies the first realization of the death of someone close.

Several men spotted Chambliss at once. One of them spoke, his voice hard with anger. "Chambliss, look here. It's George Durfee."

Chambliss dismounted and handed his reins to the nearest man. The others moved aside to let him through, all watching his face. He stood over the body and felt his pain begin to turn to anger. The bloody hole in George Durfee's chest told how he had died. He turned away and took a deep breath, fighting the rage he had carried with him constantly since Jane's death. Finally, he asked, "Who found him?"

Curly Archer, short, wiry, and bald, standing at Chambliss' elbow, said, "I did," and needing no more prompting, he began telling the story.

"I was checkin' out an old claim and smelled somethin' bad. I looked down one of the test holes, and there he was. Sorry, Chambliss, I know he was a friend of yours."

Chambliss looked at Curley and nodded.

"There's somethin' else," said Curly. "You can see he was shot in the chest and bled all over his clothes, but there was no blood where he was a lyin'. I looked all around, and there wasn't a spot of blood anywhere. Somebody must've killed him and throwed him in that hole. After I saw he'd been shot I come to town and got Haws and Jackson to help me get him out."

"Find anything on him?" asked Chambliss without much hope.

"Nope. Pockets were emptied. Turned inside out like you see 'em. No sign of his horse or pack mule neither."

Now that the initial shock was passing, Chambliss began thinking of all the ramifications of the tragedy. George Durfee was not married. He had no children, but he came from a large family and was engaged to be married to a woman who was anxiously awaiting his return. He had a mother, too—aged and infirm—who was counting on him to provide for her for the rest of her life.

Bitterly, Chambliss wondered if murderers ever thought about these things. He wondered how he would notify Durfee's loved ones of the tragedy. How would he tell them their lives had been irreparably shattered? He had no address. He knew only that Durfee's mother's last name was also Durfee. The fiancée's name was Cynthia—Chambliss did not know her last name—and the family lived near Richmond, Virginia. Beyond this he had no information.

The men around him were murmuring. Like Chambliss, they were angry. They were also afraid. He heard one of them say, "This makes three. All of them shot and their bodies moved somewheres else. This kind of thing ain't been happenin' around here since Lencho got put in the ground."

Another man added, "And all of them that was killed was carryin' money. Somebody had to know about it."

Somebody else said, "That's right. There's lots of comin' and goin' on the trail in either direction, and people that ain't carryin' money or haulin' somethin' valuable never get killed."

Curly Archer, still at Chambliss' elbow, said softly, "We ought to get him buried, Chambliss. Me and Jackson can do that if you want."

Chambliss shook his head. "No. Just find me a shovel, will you? And send somebody to get Bledsoe and Westmoreland."

"Sure," said Curly. "I'll borrow one of Ralph Shaw's wagons. Man ought to go to his grave in somethin' with wheels."

Chambliss stepped away and took a deep breath, trying to clear his nostrils. He said, "Curly, never mind about sending someone for Bledsoe and Westmoreland. I'll do that. You just get me a shovel and maybe get him wrapped in a blanket before you haul him up there. We'll do the rest." Curly nodded and took off at a brisk walk.

Chambliss reached for the reins of his horse with a brief nod to the man who had held them. But instead of mounting, he started up the street on foot. Right now he preferred to walk.

Tory Shaw was working in the storeroom when Martin Chambliss rode into town. She saw her father hail Chambliss, and she went out and stood just around the corner and listened to their conversation. When Chambliss had gone, Tory came back and stood in the front doorway of the store and followed him with her eyes. She was a tall, blonde-haired girl with a slender figure and large, deep-blue eyes. Ralph Shaw, aware of his daughter's beauty, strictly forbade her to go out unescorted under any circumstance. He walked past her into the store and her mother, Myra, met him there and motioned him to follow her to the back of the building where the family's quarters were. "Ralph, why do you even speak to a man like Chambliss?"

"Because I'm worried about Ricky."

"I know that, but what makes you think Chambliss can do anything?"

Ralph Shaw hesitated, searching for the reason. After a moment, he said, "Because he's respected."

At this Myra Shaw scoffed. "Respected. Oh yes, Ralph, respected and admired—as a killer. Let's invite him for dinner, and while we're at it, let's make sure Ricky spends a lot of time around him."

Ralph bristled and said, "Don't be ridiculous, Myra. He killed an outlaw, and good riddance. That doesn't make him a dangerous killer. But, frankly, I don't care what he's done or who he's killed. If he can help Ricky, that's all I care about."

Tears appeared in Mrs. Shaw's eyes. She dropped her head; her shoulders slumped. "I wish we had never come to this awful place. There aren't any boys Ricky's age except for those delinquents he runs around with."

Tory's voice came from behind Myra. "Yes, there are, Mother."

"Well, where are they, then?"

"They're working, like Ricky should be doing. And they're not boys, they're men. At Ricky's age they're supposed to be called men."

There is a particular facial expression; a sort of closing up of the features, that people exhibit when struggling to disbelieve something that is self-evident—it takes a good deal of effort to block out logic. Mrs. Shaw's face took on that look, and Tory, recognizing it for what it was, said, "Mother, I love Ricky too. You know I do. It's just that . . ." She could find nothing more to say.

Tory went back up front and heard a murmur of voices coming from up the street. She stepped out the front door to investigate. A few men were standing around in a semicircle, looking at something on the ground. Martin Chambliss was among them. "Maybe he's killed another man," she thought.

While she watched, Chambliss turned around, and even at this distance she could tell there was something different about him. His back seemed bent as though a great weariness had suddenly come upon him. As she watched, he squared his shoulders and turned and walked up the street, leading his horse.

When Chambliss approached the Frisco Lady, one of many saloons that lined both sides of Pick-Em-Up's single street, several men who were sitting on barrels and upturned crates casually stood up and walked inside. Too preoccupied to wonder at this, he pushed through the batwings and started across the room.

A massive, square-jawed man sitting at a table by the door hailed him. "Evenin' Martin."

"Evenin', Tiny," responded Chambliss distractedly. There was little place in his mind for pleasantries at the moment.

The big man slammed a huge fist down on the table, disrupting the unnatural silence in the room, a silence Chambliss had just begun to notice.

"What did you say to me?" demanded Tiny Webster.

Chambliss looked at him and frowned. "I wished you a good evening."

"No, you didn't. That's not what you said." Webster stood up, overturning his chair.

Chambliss, disinclined to repeat himself and completely baffled, made a quick survey of the room as he attempted to appraise the situation. Webster walked toward him, and Chambliss noted a certain hesitancy in his demeanor. Webster said without emphasis, "No man talks to me that way, Chambliss."

"All right, Tiny, have it your way. I am sincerely sorry for having wished you a good evening."

Webster looked irresolutely at something beyond Chambliss and, seeming to draw assurance from that source, moved closer to Chambliss and, without warning, swung a massive right fist. Chambliss was quick enough to block the blow, and then he swung his own right and delivered a blow to Webster's square jaw, but with no significant effect. Webster swung again, and again Chambliss blocked the punch. Chambliss was mystified. Webster was not this slow. Now Webster backed up a couple of steps. He was toying with Chambliss. But why?

Chambliss kept his guard up, waiting for the big man to move in. But Webster did not. Chambliss became aware of the shouts of the men around him. Some were urging him to try harder while others literally screamed at Webster to move in and fight.

Chambliss looked at the man, vainly trying to figure out what was happening. Webster was grinning now; there was no malice in his expression. Excitement showed in his eyes, and Chambliss understood why: Webster loved fighting. He was in his element.

Chambliss dropped his hands to his side. "What's this all about?"

Tiny Webster's good-natured grin widened. "Nothing personal, Martin, just a little fun."

"I'm not having much fun, Tiny," said Chambliss, an edge of irritation in his voice.

Webster chided, "That's no kind of an attitude for a sportin' man."

Chambliss looked around again at the eager faces—some worried, others jubilant—and then he understood. He crossed his arms on his chest and said, "Go ahead and have your fun, Tiny, but I'm not going to join you."

The character of Webster's grin changed, and he moved in and threw a quick, right-hand jab, which stopped about an inch from Chambliss' nose. Chambliss was unable to restrain himself from blinking, but otherwise he didn't move. Webster aimed the next punch at Chambliss' midsection, again stopping within an inch of connecting. Then he sent two lightning-fast jabs that stopped short of Chambliss' jaw. Still Chambliss didn't move.

Disappointment pulled down Webster's features. "Ah, Martin, I expected more from you." He dropped his hands and turned back to his table. At this gesture, the crowd erupted in shouts, those who had bet on Chambliss arguing that they should not have to pay up because the fight had not ended with a winner or a loser, and those who had bet on Webster arguing that clearly Chambliss had lost by forfeit. Chambliss watched as the bickering became more animated. Violence threatened to erupt in several quarters. But Tiny Webster stood, raised his big arms, and bellowed, "Quiet. Quiet!"

All sound in the room ceased.

"What just happened here," said Tiny, "was not a proper fight, and I'll not be acceptin' any money for my part in it, so I wouldn't expect anyone else to either. I have the greatest of respect for Mr. Chambliss, but it appears his sportin' blood is a little weak today. No matter. There'll be other opportunities, and I've no doubt we'll convince the gentleman at a future time to participate. And I'm sure if he puts his heart into it he'll be a worthy opponent." With a nod to Chambliss, he sat down.

This speech was met with some laughter and some grumbling, but everyone seemed to accept Webster's statement as the final word. Chambliss now remembered the unpleasant task that had brought him here.

His two friends Rome Bledsoe and Frank Westmoreland were at their usual table against the wall near the bar—the same table at which they and Chambliss and George Durfee had often sat talking and playing no-stakes poker. At this moment quite a number of men stood around the table, and to each in his turn, Rome Bledsoe was refunding bet money and speaking reassuring phrases. As he did so, he shot an occasional worried glance in Chambliss' direction. Chambliss waited until each man had gotten his money and the group had dispersed. He went over to the table, sat down, and turned a hard glare on Rome Bledsoe.

That Bledsoe was uncomfortable was obvious, and the fact that Chambliss was saying nothing seemed to make him more so. Finally he blurted, "Sorry, Martin, it was just a way to make some money. I was going to give you half."

"Make money?" Chambliss said incredulously. "You have to win to make money. Is there something wrong with you, Rome? Webster is an animal. He outweighs me by forty pounds. He's already fought seven men in this town and never lost once."

"Now, don't get angry," said Bledsoe. I know he's big and he's strong, but you're smarter than he is, and quicker. A big man like that . . ."

Chambliss' voice was rising. He pointed to Tiny Webster. "You've seen him fight. Did he look slow to you? Do you think that just because a man is big he can't be fast?"

Bledsoe put his hands out in a placatory gesture. "Now, calm down, Martin. Everything is fine. Next time . . ."

"What?" Chambliss nearly shouted. "Next time? Are you joking?"

"You're an easy-going man, Martin, but if he gets you mad, you'll fight him. And you'll win. I know it."

"I've never been that mad."

Bledsoe shook his head. "I've known men like you: Slow to anger, but when they did get mad—when there was really a reason—they'd rip apart anyone who got in their way. I told Webster to do something to insult you, to make you very angry. He said he'd try, but . . . he's just too good-natured."

Chambliss looked at Bledsoe and shook his head in disgust. He looked over at Westmoreland, who had watched the exchange with obvious amusement. "Did you know about this, Frank?"

"Not until just before you came down the street. I knew something was afoot, but nobody was telling me anything."

"We didn't trust you not to tell Martin," said Bledsoe.

Chambliss looked down at the table for a moment, and then he looked up, his features grave. "I came to tell you both something. George is dead. Murdered and robbed."

Their shocked expressions heightened Chambliss' own sense of sorrow. Westmoreland looked away at nothing in particular. Bledsoe reached for a drink, his constant companion and daily comforter. After a while, Westmoreland and Bledsoe wanted to know more, and Chambliss told them everything he knew, which amounted to very little.

The three men went up the hill together to bury their friend, and afterward they went back down to the Frisco Lady, where their table was waiting empty. They sat in silence for a time, but as the evening wore on they talked more, mostly about George Durfee and of his fiancée and his mother, whom they would need to notify.

"Sooner or later they'll write," said Westmoreland. "There'll be a return address, and we can let them know."

"By the time that happens," said Chambliss, "I hope we can also tell them George's killers are as dead as he is."

───────•

Later that night, when Chambliss brought Ricky Shaw home, the young man was so drunk he was unable to stand.

CHAPTER 10

The next morning Chambliss arose early, put on his moccasins, and walked to town. Occasionally someone commented on his choice of footgear, but Chambliss didn't care. He had always worn moccasins and did not feel comfortable wearing anything else. The exception to this was the work boots he wore when he worked his claim.

When he got to town, he went directly to Shaw's store to buy some supplies. He liked this time of day when most of the people on the streets were working men beginning their labors. The saloons and dance halls had not yet opened, there were no singing drunks in the street, there was no fighting, no shooting, no raucous laughter to be heard anywhere. The gamblers and drunks and night-working men and women were asleep. It was the day people's time now, and their minds were on their business.

When Chambliss arrived at Shaw's store, he found it crowded. Myra and Tory Shaw were busy selling everything imaginable, from canned goods to pick axes. Ralph Shaw tried to carry as wide a variety of goods as he possibly could, thereby decreasing the opportunity for competition. His system seemed to work. His competitors were few and small, and none of them could boast counter help that came anywhere close to being as attractive as Tory.

It was no secret in Pick-Em-Up that a significant portion of the patrons in Shaw's Mercantile took their custom there in order to have a chance to gaze at the proprietor's daughter. In fact, it was jokingly—and not altogether inaccurately—said, that in Pick-Em-Up, if a man needed salt and pepper and flour, it meant three trips to Shaw's.

Chambliss awaited his turn, wondering idly if it would be Tory or her mother who attended him. He observed Tory as she helped some of the other men in the store. She was businesslike but friendly, sometimes joking and exchanging small pleasantries. With him, however, when his turn finally came, she was cool almost to the point of being severe, asking only questions that pertained to his purchases and offering no comments. Her mother had always treated him in the same way, and he wondered why it was so. To his knowledge he had never done anything to offend them. In fact, he had a good relationship with Ralph Shaw, who seemed to see him as a potential savior for his errant son.

Chambliss continued to wonder about Tory's coolness toward him as he watched her fill his order—some food items, a new shirt, and two shovel handles. She totaled up his bill and put his smaller purchases into the flour sack he had brought. He paid and thanked her and left.

His claim was about a mile and a half north of town, and it didn't take him long to get there on foot. Having grown up with Indians, Chambliss liked to walk, and he liked to run, and he often took a day off from his labors and went exploring. Sometimes—especially when the weather was cool—he would choose a direction or a particular trail and go for a run, and these runs could last a few hours or most of the day. He took care when he ran to avoid being seen, if possible, remembering the occasions when people, seeing him, had become alarmed, thinking he was running from Apaches or some other danger.

He had worn out several pairs of moccasins that way, but he had found a half-breed Apache woman outside Tombstone who did excellent leatherwork and would make moccasins to his specifications. He had even taught her the Ojibwe way of waterproofing them.

Chambliss had spent much of his life around livestock, but he had never raised cattle for a living. He made no pretensions to being a true cattleman, nor did he aspire to be the owner of a big ranch like the one Jane's grandfather had built. But miners liked to eat meat, and his small herd provided him with a steady income. He saw the cattle business as a way to make a meager living but a poor way to try to get rich. The simple truth was, the demand for beef in Pick-Em-Up was limited by the size of the town; moreover, there were a number of large cattle ranches in the area, some of which were competitors in the Pick-Em-Up market.

Chambliss' claim represented another source of income, but it was an income that fluctuated. He sometimes encountered pockets of silver, but there were long stretches in between when the pickings were slim. What the mine did represent was the possibility of sudden wealth. This was not an unrealistic hope. More than a few men had walked away from Pick-Em-Up with wealth jingling in their saddlebags. George Durfee had been one of them.

When Chambliss arrived at his camp, he lighted a kerosene lamp and went inside the mine, finding everything as he had left it. There was a new section that would need timbering, and he was almost out of timbers. He would need to remember to purchase some from Ralph Shaw next time he was in town.

Like most of the miners in the area, Chambliss kept a canvas tent near his claim. This would not have been adequate shelter in an area where winters were cold and snowy, but here in this desert a warm bedroll and a tent were more than enough protection from the coldest winter night, and in the brutal heat of the Arizona summer, he slept inside the mine where it was cooler.

In fact, rarely did Chambliss sleep in the tent at all, except when it rained. Outside the tent his acute senses were better able to detect the approach of an enemy. Sounds and smells were messages borne on the air; and those messages could be muffled and distorted by the canvas of a tent. He preferred to lie out in the open and gaze up at the stars and wonder about what was out there as humans have done since there have been humans on the earth.

He kept most of his foodstuffs in metal tins inside the mine. There was a spring nearby, which served as his water supply except in the late summer months when it dried up and he had to buy water from one of the men who made a living carting it in barrels from the nearby San Pedro River.

After packing his supplies into his saddlebags, he tidied up his campsite. When he picked up the two shovel handles he had bought at Shaw's, he felt a sharp edge protruding slightly from one of them. Not wanting to get splinters in his hand when he used it, he made a closer inspection of the rough spot to see if it could be rubbed off with sandstone. Visible only upon close inspection, there was a long section of the grain that seemed to be elevated. He laid it over his thigh, pressed down on the ends, and saw that there was a six-inch-long split along the grain of the wood. Any significant leverage on the handle would break it completely in two.

He set the handles just inside the mine entrance, making a mental note to take the defective one back to Shaw's next time he went to town, then he mounted up and rode out.

Using Curly's directions he soon arrived at the test hole where George Durfee's body had been so unfeelingly thrown. During the ride he had tried to avoid thinking of George by concentrating on the beauty of the desert around him, oblivious to the irony in this. Now, as he looked down into the hole, its bottom strewn with jagged rocks and debris, his anger returned, and he remembered the solemn, three-man funeral ceremony of the night before.

He and Westmoreland had taken turns digging the grave. Bledsoe, already too drunk to effectively participate in that activity, had watched, cursing whoever was responsible for Durfee's death. Curly Archibald had thoughtfully provided some ropes, and when the hole was deep enough, Chambliss and Westmoreland lowered the body into it. They each spoke a few words about their friend—Bledsoe waxing maudlin—then they refilled the hole.

Chambliss dismounted, taking care not to disturb any tracks, and walked around the test pit in ever-widening circles, searching for any prints not belonging to Curly or his friends. He knew that if the man or men who had dumped Durfee's body in the pit had then ridden to town, their prints were already obliterated by all the traffic on the main trail, but if they had gone elsewhere, he should be able to find their trail.

He found several sets of horse tracks going northwest. Shortly thereafter he found where the same horses had ridden in from the east. He was certain that if he followed these, they would lead him to the spot where Durfee was killed. Right now, however, his main priority was to find out where these riders had gone after dumping their victim's body.

His desire to locate the killers was based not only on the fact that they had killed a friend of his, but also on the fact that there had recently been several other similar killings. It was a familiar pattern in mining camps. Some men, too lazy and worthless to work for their own living, stole from others the fruits of months and years of honest toil, taking from these diligent workers even their very lives in order to avoid discovery. Chambliss could think of no more despicable kind of person. Moreover, he knew that unless something was done quickly, there would be more deaths.

The tracks led straight to the Dragoon Mountains, a wild and incredibly rugged area of high, barren peaks and deep, steep-sided canyons. These mountains had been previously used for years by the Apache chief Cochise and his band of Chiricauha Apaches, as a place to hide from the white soldiers who hunted them.

Chambliss observed that the outlaws had initially made no effort to hide their trail, but as he penetrated deeper into the mountains, the trail became increasingly difficult to follow.

It grew late, and as the light faded, he was forced to dismount and follow on foot, leading his horse, in order to be able to bend down to see the tracks. It was in this way that he discovered a set of hoofprints leading off at a tangent from the main group of tracks. Ground tying his horse, he followed these tracks to a hidden spot where a man had waited, watching the back trail. And it appeared he had waited there over night and well into the following day before returning to the trail his companions had taken. Knowing this, Chambliss was certain it would be foolhardy to follow the trail as he had been doing. The nearer he got to the outlaws' hideout, the more closely would the trail be watched.

The terrain here reminded him of the area where Verdugo's bandidos had had their hideout down in Sonora. But Verdugo's band had become complacent, and their complacency had led to carelessness. These outlaws were very much the opposite. It would require different tactics to apprehend them.

It was now fully dark, and there was no more he could do at this time. He went back to his horse and rode back the way he had come. It was past ten o'clock when he hit the main road. His horse was weary, and so was he. He debated in his mind whether to ride straight to his camp or to stop first at the Frisco Lady to inform Westmoreland and Bledsoe of his lack of progress in locating George Durfee's killer. He was still trying to be angry with Rome Bledsoe but was finding it difficult. This was usually the case in dealing with Bledsoe. He was one of those men for whom people always seemed to make excuses.

Westmoreland was an entirely different story. He was a shrewd businessman, and though he owned a saloon, he never drank to excess. He was a man who could be trusted, someone to count on, whereas Rome Bledsoe was likeable enough, but no one would ever turn to him in a time of trouble.

There was, Chambliss considered, no more varied and unusual assortment of human beings to be found anywhere than in a mining camp. Most of the men were just faces in the crowd, but there were a few exceptional characters that stood out. Tiny Webster was one of these. Tiny had been born in Pennsylvania and christened Osman Webster. By the time he was two years old, both his parents had died and he was taken in and raised by two puritanical maiden aunts. He was an obedient boy, but despite all their best efforts, his aunts could not stop the boy from getting into fights. Nevertheless, they managed to instill in him their religious zeal, and now in his adulthood, Tiny was still a church-going man.

By far the most religious man in Pick-Em-Up, it was said that Tiny never missed a day of reading his Bible. No one had ever heard him say a swearword or use coarse language. He refused to break the Sabbath and would not drink liquor or do work of any kind on Sunday.

There was no church in Pick-Em-Up, so Tiny rode to Tombstone every Sunday morning to attend church there. He was a light drinker, and, like George Durfee, he frequented only one saloon—the Frisco Lady—and that, primarily for reasons of companionship and the hope of an occasional fight.

Despite his size and his bluster when in the company of men, Webster was shy around women. In fact, the mere mention of matters involving the opposite sex would cause him to blush, and he would find a reason to excuse himself. No one had ever heard him make a comment that so much as implied disrespect to the feminine gender.

He was incredibly tenderhearted and could never refuse a loan to a miner who came to him with a sad story. He was polite to a fault and, had it not been for his brute strength and his love of fighting, he probably would not have survived amid this rough and savage crowd.

The night was in full swing when Chambliss reined in at the Frisco Lady. The town was alive with the raucous sounds of coarse men enjoying their coarse pleasures, a shrill female voice frequently sailing above the other sounds. He went in and ordered a beer and carried it to the table where Westmoreland and Bledsoe sat. Briefly he told them about his day, and they both nodded grimly. They had hoped for more. He noticed Tiny Webster walking toward the table, an odd expression on his face. Tiny looked uncomfortable. Chambliss turned to face him but did not stand up.

Tiny stopped in front of Chambliss and said hesitantly, "Your mother was . . . a harlot . . . and your father left . . ." Here, there was a long pause as the big man searched for the right words ". . . before breakfast."

Bledsoe moaned and dropped his head, resting it on the table. Westmoreland almost choked on his beer. Chambliss sat looking at Tiny for a moment, and Tiny stared back apprehensively. The barroom had fallen silent as men waited.

Finally Chambliss spoke. "That pretty much sums it up, Tiny. Can I buy you a drink?"

An expression that mingled embarrassment and relief spread over Webster's features. "No, thank you, but it's a kind offer." He held out his hand, and Chambliss shook it, and a rush of noise rose up from the throats of the men in the room, some laughing, others complaining.

Bledsoe looked glumly down the table, still shaking his head. When Webster had gone back to his own table and the noise level had returned to its normal pitch, Chambliss leaned his chair back on two legs. "It's hard to say for sure, but I think I've just been called a bastard."

Westmoreland, no longer able to stifle his mirth, began silently laughing as Chambliss had seen him do at rare times. Tears rolled from the man's eyes, his shoulders shook, and his bent head moved up and down. After a while, when he had regained control, he wiped his eyes and said, "If all insults were given as politely as that one, there would be peace in this sorry old world."

Early the next morning when Chambliss was cooking his breakfast, Curley Archer rode up on a mule and said he was making the rounds of all the claims in the area to invite the miners to a meeting at the Eureka Saloon at about midmorning.

"What's it about?" queried Chambliss.

"It's about somebody murderin' people and robbin' 'em. Clyde Roth thinks it's time we organized a vigilance committee to do somethin' about the problem."

"We already have a vigilance committee."

"Roth thinks they ain't done much, and I agree."

Chambliss couldn't disagree with that, but he also understood the reasons. The vigilance committee was composed of miners who had claims to work and didn't have days and weeks to spend on the investigative work that would be required to solve a problem of this nature. They had, on a number of occasions, apprehended criminals whose identities were known and whose guilt was obvious and had dispensed justice in standard vigilante style. They had even erected a small shed for a jail, though it was rarely used.

Because there were no laws in Pick-Em-Up, the vigilantes were only concerned with major offenses, and when a major offender was taken by the committee, punishment was usually dispensed immediately.

Chambliss invited Curley to step down and eat, but Curley said, "I'll have some coffee, but I got to do some ridin'."

While they sipped coffee, Chambliss said, "Some people are saying that what we really need to do is to start acting like a town and elect a marshal."

"Well, you can bring it up at the meeting, but you'll probably be the one they'll pick, so don't mention it unless you're willin'. As for me, I wouldn't take the job if it come with a bucket of gold nuggets and a wife. I was workin' up at Canyon Diablo when the railroad got stalled 'cause the bridge they ordered was shorter than the canyon was wide. That place was every bit as wild as Pick-Em-Up. It was roarin' twenty-four hours a day. Got so bad some folks decided we needed a marshal. Well, we got one, and he was swore in at three o'clock in the afternoon and we buried him at eight o'clock that night. After that, we had five more marshals and five more burials. The longest any of 'em lasted was a month. And none of 'em died from indigestion, if you know what I'm sayin'."

Chambliss offered no comment. He had no desire to be a lawman. Mostly he just wanted to be left in peace to work his claim and wait for Jack Franey to show up. But he knew that when good men do nothing, bad men prosper, so he said, "I'll be at the meeting."

"Thanks for the coffee," said Curley, climbing into the saddle. "See you there."

CHAPTER 11

The meeting had to be held out in the street because of the size of the crowd. Most of the male population of the area around Pick-Em-Up was there, and it was an unruly group. There were more than a few women present too; in fact, it appeared to Chambliss that there were too many of them. These were not what in other places would have been called decent women; there were very few of that kind in Pick-Em-Up, Myra Shaw and her daughter Tory being prominent among them. These were the women who worked in the saloons and dance halls and other such establishments, and Chambliss had the idea they were out here for a purpose. He suspected that purpose would become apparent later, but for now they stayed on the fringes, speaking only to each other.

Looking around him, Chambliss sensed fear in the group. No one felt safe anymore. These men all knew it was in the nature of mining camps to have saloons and gambling and women and violence. There would always be killings in a wild and lawless place like Pick-Em-Up, but they were usually spontaneous things, more often than not the end point of an argument over a woman, or a partnership breaking up and a disagreement over how to split the claim. Liquor played a role in most of them.

These recent killings, however, were different. They were methodical and cold-blooded, and robbery was the motive. It was part of a system, and the miners knew that any one of them could be next.

In the beginning, the meeting was pretty much what Chambliss had expected: a lot of men voicing strong feelings and conflicting opinions about what should be done. Everyone seemed to be angry that no one had yet done anything, but few were willing to take on any of the responsibility themselves.

Clyde Roth, the man who had called the meeting, was the owner of the Eureka Saloon. He was, in Chambliss' assessment, one of those people who liked to be the center of attention. Acting somewhat self-important, he called the meeting to order, and soon a lively discussion began. Feelings ran high. There was a great deal of shouting, a couple of fights erupted and had to be quelled, and one man shot another in the leg.

The vigilance committee was profanely criticized for failing to do its job, and after a number of insults were exchanged, its members resigned in disgust. Roth asked for volunteers for a new vigilance committee, and from the crowd someone called out, "We need a town marshal." A portion of the crowd voiced agreement with this opinion, but a much louder group began shouting its dissent. This group, Chambliss observed, included all the women present, and every owner of any kind of establishment in Pick-Em-Up as well as every bartender, doorman, swamper, spieler, or employee of any kind, be he ever so lowly.

Chambliss now understood what was happening. This meeting represented the dispute between those who wanted real law and those who wanted this to remain a wide-open town. Though it was a small place, Pick-Em-Up boasted a remarkable number of saloons and dance halls and dives that in more civilized places were relegated to the "bad side of town." Here, for the most part, they were the town. They were temporary, makeshift affairs, most of them just large tents, but their owners were the wealthiest people in the community.

Liquor and gambling and women were the real bonanza here, and it was no secret that men from nearby towns like Charleston, Fairbank, Contention City, Watervale, Tombstone, and others came to Pick-Em-Up to frequent its establishments, liking the fact that there were no laws and no peacekeepers strutting around with stars pinned to their vests.

The disagreement between the two factions quickly turned into a quarrel, and Chambliss, not caring either way, walked over to Shaw's store. He was drawn there and tried to convince himself that he didn't know why. As he thought about it, it seemed silly, even a little presumptuous. After all, he didn't know the Shaws all that well. He liked Ralph, though he sometimes dreaded being around the man because he was always expecting Chambliss to perform some sort of miracle on his son, but Tory and her mother both seemed to hold him in contempt.

When he got to Shaw's, he remembered the cracked shovel handle and wished he had thought to bring it. There was nothing else he needed to buy, no excuse to go in, but after a moment's hesitation he stepped through the door.

Tory Shaw was sitting in a chair behind the counter, reading a book. She looked up and spoke in the same flat tone she always used with him. "Good morning, Mr. Chambliss, what can I do for you?"

Chambliss was caught unprepared. He had assumed there would be other customers in the store and he would have time to look around and decide on something to purchase, but evidently everyone was at the meeting. Caught flat-footed, he said the first thing that came into his mind.

"Uh, I'd like to buy a shovel handle please."

Her eyebrows raised slightly, and as Chambliss pulled a handle from the barrel where they were kept, she said, "You must be a very hardworking man."

He laughed uneasily, "Don't know about that, ma'am. I just do a lot of digging."

Myra Shaw was stocking shelves. She turned now, looked at him squarely, and said, "Holes to bury people in, I suppose."

Chambliss felt the disapproval in her demeanor and assumed she was referring to the burial of George Durfee. He didn't understand. Surely she did not disapprove of him burying his friend. This left him with nothing to say.

Now, he thought, would be a good time to say something pleasant or amusing, something to dispel some of the coldness between him and the two Shaw women, but he could think of nothing, and the moment quickly became awkward. "How much is it, miss?" he asked Tory.

"For one shovel handle, you pay just half what you paid when you bought two," she replied.

But for the complete lack of expression on her face, the statement could have been a joke. Nor was there any censure in her voice, and Chambliss was unable to categorize the comment. Myra Shaw was looking at them intently, making him all the more uncomfortable. He paid Tory, thanked her, and left, feeling a complete fool.

After Chambliss left the store, Tory mentally reviewed the incident. She knew her mother to be a good woman, but in Myra's treatment of Chambliss, she reminded Tory of one of those outspoken, razor-tongued women they both disliked.

Many of the men who came into the store were coarse, foul smelling, poorly groomed, and often ungentlemanly. Dealing with them was part of the job. She and her mother helped them make their purchases, took their money, and most times thanked them. Chambliss may be a killer, but at least he was a gentleman. Except for the fact that he usually wore moccasins, he was always well groomed and displayed every sign of good breeding. It seemed unfair to treat him so badly.

Tory knew that Chambliss must think she disliked him, but in reality he intrigued her. It went against her nature to be rude to anyone, but she tried to maintain a neutral attitude with him out of respect to her mother, who would be displeased if she thought there was any friendship between the two. Tory was trying in every way she could to be a dutiful daughter as a way of mitigating some of the pain her parents were having to endure because of her younger brother's recent behavior.

The quip about the price of shovel handles had been an attempt at humor, Tory's way of trying to show Chambliss that she did not dislike him, but it had fallen flat because she had not followed it up with a smile. She was sorry now that she had said it.

That night Chambliss heard distant gunshots off to the east. He lay awake for a while, wondering what they meant, listening for more. None came. Later, he was awakened when the wind came up and it began to rain. He picked up his bedroll and went into his tent. He knew the tracks he had been planning to follow tomorrow—the tracks he was certain would lead him to the men who had killed George Durfee—would be obliterated.

"Sorry, George," he murmured aloud. "Seems like I just keep letting you down."

He lay awake for a long time, listening to the sounds of the wind and the rain slapping the canvas of the tent. It was pleasant, but it made him feel very much alone.

He rode out the next morning to check on his cattle. While crossing a low hill, something caught his eye about a hundred yards away. He rode over to investigate. It was a dead steer. It had his brand on it, and it had been shot. Nearby, he found another, also shot to death.

Chambliss knew that in the cattle business one had to accept a certain amount of losses. Indians would sometimes steal and butcher a steer when they had the need, white settlers who had a hankering for fresh beef would sometimes do the same. And there were rustlers, coyotes, screwworm, and any number of other ways that cattle could die or disappear. But this was the first time he had ever known of someone killing beef animals just for the fun of it and leaving them to rot.

He searched the area around each kill for clues, but the rain had washed out any tracks that had been left. He wondered if whoever had done this—and he had a pretty good idea who it was—had known the rain would wash away their tracks, or if they even cared.

He rode into town, a deep anger settling on him, and stopped at Shaw's store. Inside, Tory was speaking to a customer. Chambliss interrupted her. "Is Ricky here?"

Before she could speak, Ralph Shaw walked into the front carrying a crate. Chambliss turned away from Tory and said, "Ralph, I'd like to have a word with Ricky."

"Certainly, Martin. He's in the back. I believe he's still asleep. I'll wake him."

"No need. Just take me to him."

Myra Shaw came in from the back. She protested, indignation in her voice. "Mr. Chambliss, you can't just walk in here and demand . . ."

Chambliss swung around and interrupted her, his voice polite but hard. "Mrs. Shaw, I have my reasons for wanting to see your son, and they're between him and me."

She looked as though she had been slapped. She reddened and glared at him, and then, aware that everyone in the room was watching, she turned her attention back to her customer.

Ralph led Chambliss to a small stock room where Ricky was sleeping on a mattress on the floor. Except for his boots, he was fully clothed. The room smelled of liquor and alcoholic breath. Chambliss nudged Ricky roughly with his boot until the young man finally awoke, acting by turns confused, then surprised, then apprehensive. He sat up, scratching his head with one hand and his chest with the other.

"Where were you last night, Ricky?" Demanded Chambliss.

"Out with some friends."

"Where?"

"Around."

"Around town?"

"Yes."

"Tell me where you were in town so I can go talk to people who saw you."

"Well, we were only in town for a little while. We bought some whiskey and went off by ourselves to drink it."

"You and who else?"

"Nobody you'd know."

"Where'd you go?"

"Over by the river. We just sat around and had a few drinks and talked." Now fully awake, Ricky started to act indignant. "Look here, Chambliss, I ain't done nothin' wrong. You got no business comin' in here and askin' me a lot of questions."

"See any cattle last night, Ricky?"

Ricky dropped his eyes, and Chambliss could tell he was getting ready to lie.

"Don't recall noticin' any." He raised his eyes and asked innocently, "Why?"

"Somebody killed some of my steers last night." Ricky's eyes flickered, and Chambliss was sure he already knew about the dead steers. He said, "This is cattle country, Ricky. You may not know it, but around here, rustlers and cow killers get hanged." He turned to leave the room, and over his shoulder, he said, "You'd better straighten up, Ricky. You're not smart enough to be an outlaw."

Myra Shaw had come in and had observed this exchange from the doorway, and Chambliss read shame and grief on her face. They seemed to be settling there, etching their permanent lines in her visage. He felt sorry for her. He nodded to her as he walked past, and she flashed him a cold look.

Leaving his horse tied at Shaw's, Chambliss walked over to the Eureka and found its owner, Clyde Roth, in the back room, conferring gravely with several other members of the new vigilance committee. "Mornin', gents," said Chambliss. They all turned to look at him.

"Mornin', Chambliss," said Clyde Roth. "What can I do for you?"

"There's a matter I need to bring to the attention of the committee."

Glances were exchanged.

"Go ahead. What's one more matter?" said Roth.

"Last night somebody killed two of my steers."

"Any idea who it was?"

"I think it was Ricky Shaw and his friends, but I have no proof."

"What do you expect us to do about it if you have no proof?" demanded Chick Massey, one of the men at the table.

Chambliss was not in a good mood this morning, and he had never held Massey in high regard. "I don't expect you to do anything about it. I'm just informing you of the situation so that when I do something about it myself, you'll know why."

"Gentlemen," said Roth placatingly. "We're all on the same side here." Looking at Chambliss, he explained, "Last night three miners were beaten and robbed here in town. One of them is in pretty bad shape. We suspect it was Ricky Shaw and his friends."

"And do you have any proof?" asked Chambliss.

Roth gave a wry smile and shook his head. "Some, but not enough."

"Good luck," said Chambliss, and left.

He walked back over to Shaw's store and saw Ralph Shaw working out back, stacking timbers onto a pile. When Ralph saw him coming, he stopped what he was doing and stood, watching Chambliss approach, his expression grave, almost defensive.

"Mornin', Ralph."

"Mornin'."

It was clear to Chambliss that Ralph thought he wanted to talk about Ricky, but Chambliss said, "I need to buy some timbers."

Ralph watched his face for a moment, then looked away. He said in a subdued tone, "Got some good, straight ones here, from the Huachucas."

"They look fine. I'll take ten."

Ralph nodded. "I'll deliver them for you. Help me load them up, and we can do it right now."

They loaded the timbers, and Ralph hitched the team to the wagon. He drove while Chambliss rode along side. During the short ride they spoke of nothing weightier than the weather and the price of silver. They unloaded the timbers, and afterward, Ralph said, "I forgot to ask if you needed caps or wedges?"

Chambliss shook his head. "Still have plenty. How much do I owe you, Ralph?"

Ralph had trouble meeting his gaze. "Nothing, Martin."

"Why nothing, Ralph?"

Ralph flushed and looked at the ground. "I just . . . those cows you lost. I thought maybe I would pay you off in goods whenever you need them until . . . well, until the debt's paid off."

Chambliss felt a wave of sympathy for the man. Softy he asked, "Did you kill my steers, Ralph?"

A small, ironic smile twitched at the corners of Ralph's mouth. He faintly shook his head.

"Then it's not your debt."

Ralph looked up and said earnestly, "Ricky's not a bad boy, he's just . . ." He was silent for a moment, then he shrugged.

"Chambliss started to say something, "Ralph . . ." Ralph looked at him, and Chambliss saw in his eyes that the man already knew everything he might possibly say. He changed his mind and said, "How much do I owe you for the timbers?"

Ralph took his money and drove back to town.

That night it rained again, harder than the night before, and the wind blew. It didn't bother Chambliss; he was comfortable inside his tent, and the more rain the better as far as he was concerned. It meant more grass for his cattle during the hot, dry summer months to come.

The rain, however, was not the reason he didn't sleep well that night. He couldn't stop thinking. He thought about the Shaws—about Ricky, who would probably never amount to anything even if he didn't wind up at the end of a rope; about Ralph and Myra and how they must have made excuses for Ricky's behavior all his life. They would never figure things out, he knew—at least not until it was too late. And for Ricky, it probably already was.

His thoughts turned to Tory Shaw, and he wondered why she disliked him. He didn't know why it should matter to him at all. Perhaps it was because decent women were so scarce in this town. It was just that he was lonely, he told himself, and she was pretty.

Anyway, who cared about a woman who would judge a man without even knowing him?

Presently these thoughts went out of his mind, and he lay listening to the rain strike the canvas of the tent. And, as he did every night before going to sleep, he thought of Jane. She had been dead for over two years now. Her face came less vividly into his mind these days, and he was not certain he could recall her voice. The grief was not as sharp either, as it once had been, and when it came, instead of the terrible desperation of a hopeless future that it had formerly brought, and the agony of remembering all the beautiful times they had shared, it merely left him feeling hollow and incredibly sad.

He tried to never allow himself to think of the awful sight in the canyon where Jane's body had been left unburied by her murderer. He tried to keep that acid memory from entering his conscious mind. But sometimes it did, and at those times his insides twisted in pain and rage, and he thought of Lencho Bautista and Jack Franey, and reminded himself that Franey was still alive.

Not long after he had killed Lencho Bautista, Chambliss had given up looking for Franey. The outlaw seemed to have disappeared from the earth, and Chambliss had been weary of searching. In truth, he was weary of everything.

There were just a few people in Pick-Em-Up that Chambliss trusted, and he had asked those few to keep their eyes and ears open and to let him know immediately if Franey showed up in town. And so he waited, and while he waited he worked and lived a life that had very little meaning to him.

CHAPTER 12

Big Bill Cross sat on the hard seat of a freight wagon several miles east of Pick-Em-Up, feeling every bump and jolt in his tired, stiff low back. He huddled inside his slicker, grateful for its protection against the rain and the wind tonight. The kid beside him on the seat had dozed off, his body moving and swaying automatically with the movements of the wagon. The kid was fifteen and big for his age. This was his first freight run. He had turned out to be a willing helper and pretty good company. It was his first time away from home, and Cross had enjoyed regaling him with stories of his experiences and adventures in thirty-odd years as a teamster.

Right now Cross was tired. He was glad this run was almost over. Yesterday, just after noon, they had broken a wheel and lost over four hours repairing it. If not for that, they would already be in Pick-Em-Up. And they would have gotten there before the rain started.

A gunshot shattered the night and his thoughts. Cross heard the thud of the slug hitting the kid. He heard the involuntary grunt as the kid was thrown off the seat into the darkness. He reached for his rifle, but there was another shot. He didn't feel the bullet. He didn't even hear the sound.

The sound of gunshots rolled up from the southeast, and Chambliss thought of his dead cows. It only took him a few seconds to roll out of his bedroll and pull on his moccasins, a minute to run down the hill to where his horse was picketed, and two or three more to get back up the hill, leading the horse by the long picket rope. The rain had stopped, but as he was saddling up, it started to sprinkle again. He ran to the tent and grabbed his slicker. By the time he was in the saddle and spurring down the hill, a hard rain was coming down and the wind was beginning to blow.

As he rode, he analyzed the situation. Whoever had fired the shots had done so in the rain. Would Ricky Shaw and his rowdy friends enjoy killing cows so much that they would be willing to get cold and wet doing it? He doubted it.

He pushed the horse as fast as he dared in the darkness over the rugged, muddy terrain. There was a well-used trail that led down to the main road. It had been made by animals—mostly his own cattle—but Chambliss used it often too. His horse knew every dip and rise and curve in it. When he hit the trail he urged the animal faster and gave it its head. The wind was blowing harder now and the slanting rain slapped him in the face.

He came around a bend in the trail and collided with another rider. The man's horse was thrown off balance, and he had to leap out of the saddle to avoid being thrown.

Chambliss reined in and swung his horse around just as the rider fired his pistol. Chambliss' horse flinched and shied, shot through the ear. The unhorsed rider fired again, and Chambliss felt the disturbance in the air as the bullet flew past his cheek. He had his pistol out now and fired at the spot where he had seen the muzzle flash, but he couldn't tell if he had hit the man or not.

He heard the sounds of other riders just before he saw them. There were several of them, their rifle barrels preceding them, slim outlines in the darkness. He moved off the trail into the brush, hoping they hadn't seen him. The rifle shots that followed him told him they had. He heard their urgent shouts, heard their horses tearing through the brush behind him. He also heard another sound: the clinking of glass striking glass.

Chambliss was grateful for this swift, sure-footed horse Rigo had given him, and soon he believed he had lost the riders. He didn't want to lose them by too far, however, just enough so they would give up the chase and turn back. Then he would follow them. He knew that these could very possibly be the men who had killed George Durfee, and he hoped they would lead him to their hideout. He pulled up beneath a mesquite tree, his ears alert to every sound. He still had his pistol in his hand and took advantage of the opportunity to eject the spent brass and reload.

He didn't have to wait long. Soon he heard the sounds of a single horse—and more clinking. He saw the dim figure of horse and rider as they crested a small hill in front of him. The outlaw stopped not more than twenty feet away, and Chambliss knew the man was listening, hoping to locate his position.

For a long, suspenseful moment, nothing happened. Then a jagged, long-flickering lightning flash lit up the darkness for several seconds and Chambliss could see the rider clearly. The man was looking away, but just before darkness returned, he swung his head and saw Chambliss. He raised his gun and Chambliss shot him.

Another rider nearby called out in Spanish, "*Lo mataste?*"

Chambliss spurred out into the open again. These were smart men, and more determined than he had expected. He would have to ride hard and outdistance them. There would be no more tricks. The rain and the wind were dying down now—not a good thing. He needed them to cover the noise he and his horse were making as they crashed through the brush.

He topped a small rise and spurred down the incline, not wanting to make a silhouette on the horizon. At the bottom of the slope there was a narrow wash. The horse easily jumped it, but when his hoofs hit the other side, the wet earth of the low bank crumbled and the horse went backward.

Chambliss kicked his feet free of the stirrups and narrowly missed being crushed by the animal as they fell noisily into the shallow wash. The moon was shining through a clearing in the clouds. A rider crested the rise, clearly visible in the bright moonlight. Chambliss had dropped his pistol in the fall and had no time to reach for his rifle in the saddle scabbard. The rider was leveling his rifle even as Chambliss dove to the side around a bend in the wash. From there he scrambled up the sloping bank into the brush, hunched over like an ape, using his hands as much as his feet. He heard his horse running down the wash and hoped the animal would go back to camp.

He went over a rise and found a deeper arroyo. Behind him he heard shouts as the message was relayed to the other riders that their quarry was now on foot. In the interest of speed and silence, he ripped off his slicker, balled it up, and shoved it under a bush.

He followed the arroyo for about a hundred feet, then left its shelter, going into the brush again, trying to make as little noise as possible. The clouds had once again passed in front of the moon and brought back the darkness—his only ally now.

He lay flat on his belly in thick brush as a rider passed close by. When the rider was far enough away, Chambliss began moving again.

After about twenty minutes of alternately hiding and moving, he found a deep wash of which one side had been undercut by floods. A recent flash flood had left a tangle of debris in the undercut. Chambliss wormed his way behind this debris and lay there, knowing that if they guessed at this hiding place there would be no more escape.

Two times men rode past him, but neither time did they notice him. Finally, after a seemingly interminable wait, all was silent. Even the rain had stopped. Chambliss was convinced the searchers had given up, but he waited another half hour, just to be safe, and then crawled out of his hiding place and slipped up the side of the wash into the brush. Keeping low, he made his way south to the main road, alert to every sound or movement. The bright moon shone down, no longer shrouded by clouds, and illuminated the landscape almost as if it were daylight.

Not long after striking the main road, he heard sounds behind him. He slipped out of sight into the shadows and waited. Soon he recognized the creaking, jangling sounds of a freight wagon and its plodding team. When the wagon was abreast of him, he saw that there was a saddled horse tied to the back. He stepped out of the shadows. The driver grabbed the rifle that was resting on his lap, but Chambliss held his hands out away from his sides. "It's all right."

The man did not move the rifle. "You alone?"

"I'm alone. Could use a ride into town."

"Chambliss?"

"Yes."

"No horse, no gun, not even a hat," observed the driver, but he asked no questions. "Climb up," he said.

As Chambliss climbed up onto the wagon seat, he heard the sounds of an approaching rider. Still wary, he asked the driver, "Anybody you know?"

"Friend of mine. We ride together."

They waited as the newcomer rode up. The man held his rifle at the ready and eyed Chambliss suspiciously.

"Where you been?" demanded the driver.

"Horse picked up a stone. Had to stop and pry it out."

"Well, stay with me. I'm spooky tonight."

Addressing Chambliss, the new man said, "Who are you?"

"He's all right, Owen," said the wagon driver. "It's Chambliss."

"Hear any shots tonight, Chambliss?" asked Owen.

Chambliss said that he had.

"Come back here. I want to show you something."

The driver reined in the team. Chambliss got down and went to the back of the wagon. Owen dismounted, dropped the tailgate, and raised the tarp. The load had been readjusted to make room for the two bodies, an older man and a young boy who looked to be sixteen or seventeen."

"We rode up onto 'em a couple of miles back. The man was still on the seat, dead. The kid was on the ground. Whoever did it was long gone. The tarp was pulled back and some of the freight was gone."

What were they hauling?" asked Chambliss.

"Liquor."

"Liquor?"

"Mostly whiskey, a few kegs of beer in the front."

"Any of it missing?"

"Looked like four or five cases gone."

Chambliss remembered the sounds of clinking glass he had heard earlier and was sickened. "You mean they killed two men just to steal some whiskey?"

"Maybe they didn't know what they was freightin'," offered Owen.

Chambliss shook his head in disgust. "Seems to me you'd find out what you were stealing before you killed somebody for it."

"Some men will kill for just about any reason. Some'll kill just because they like it."

Some rainwater that had pooled on the tarp rolled off onto the faces of the two bodies, and Chambliss heard a sound. Owen was about to replace the tarp, but Chambliss said, "Wait."

Using the hub of the wheel as a step, he climbed up and gently shook both of the bodies. The boy gave a soft moan.

Myra Shaw couldn't sleep. Ricky had taken off again, had sneaked away like he always did. "You'd think a person would get used to it," she thought, but it was worse now since those drunks had been beaten and robbed and Chambliss' cows had been killed. She told herself that Ricky had had nothing to do with those things—he was wild, but underneath it all he had a good heart. But doubts kept creeping in. She worried that things would keep happening. She worried that people would come and blame Ricky for them—like Chambliss had. And what if something really bad happened and they blamed Ricky and the vigilance committee came and took him out and lynched him? She didn't think her heart could stand any more of this pain and worry.

She was standing in the front doorway of the store in the darkness as she had been for almost two hours. She had gotten up to watch the rain and listen to the wind. Those things always soothed her. There was a rustling sound behind her, and Tory was by her side, putting her arm around her mother's shoulders.

"Tory," chided Myra, "why aren't you in bed? You should be asleep."

"The rain was nice, wasn't it, Mother? And the wind was so soothing. The sounds helped me to sleep, but when they stopped, I woke up. Isn't that odd?"

"No, dear, I do that sometimes too."

The store was situated at one end of town, away from the saloons, the dives, and the dance halls. The sounds of their nightly revelry could be faintly heard, and gunshots were a common thing. At first those sounds had bothered Tory—especially the gunshots, but she had grown accustomed to them, and she thought now that she may even miss them if they were suddenly gone. Mostly she didn't notice them at all anymore.

"I wonder where Ricky is," said Myra.

Tory hugged her more tightly, not knowing what else to do.

After a while the rain started again—lightly this time and without wind. Myra, who had not yet been to bed, said she was going to try to get some sleep, but Tory was no longer tired, and she was enjoying the sound of the rain and the delicious smell of the wet desert earth.

She moved a chair over in front of the door, just inside in the darkness, where she wouldn't be seen in her nightdress and wrapper, and sat, thinking. Like her parents, she worried about Ricky. She had tried to counsel him, but Ricky never listened to counsel. She thought of her father's desperate hope that Martin Chambliss could have some beneficial influence on Ricky, and she knew it was a false hope. Why couldn't he see that? she wondered. And why did her mother hate Chambliss so? Was it because he represented what she feared Ricky would become?

The Mexican outlaw Lencho Bautista had been feared all around this area, and so the story of his killing had been of great interest to many people, especially the miners and freighters who had been his favorite prey. After Lencho's death, his men had permanently departed Arivaca, leaving the saloonkeeper free to recount the story of the outlaw's death whenever and to whomever he chose. And this he did often, adding such embellishments as he saw fit. Nor was the grim nature of the story in any way detracted from by the humorous element of the shooting of the woman in the painting, and the saloonkeeper always ended his recitation by proudly pointing to her perforated navel. The painting now hung prominently behind the bar, and for it he had been offered—and had turned down—significant sums of money.

And so, Chambliss' reputation had grown disproportionately large in this small part of the world. Tory knew that her mother had heard the story more than once and from more than one source and was repulsed by every aspect of it. It had been Ricky who had told her and Tory about the shooting of the woman's navel, and he had laughed at their blushing embarrassment.

"That was an indecent thing," Myra had said to Tory afterward. And many times since then Tory had thought about it and suspected that her mother disliked Chambliss more for that indecency than for the killing of a man.

She dozed and was awakened by the sounds of a freight wagon coming into town. This was not an unusual occurrence, but as the wagon passed, the bright moon illuminated the profile of the man sitting on the seat next to the driver. It looked like Martin Chambliss. This seemed strange to Tory, particularly since Chambliss was hatless and without a slicker. He would be, no doubt, soaked by the rain.

When the big wagon stopped in front of Doc Stender's place, part of the mystery was resolved. This had something to do with death. Death and Martin Chambliss seemed to be often connected, thought Tory.

Doc Stender wasn't really a doctor, but he was the closest thing to it in Pick-Em-Up. Before the war, he had studied medicine at some eastern college for a year. After the war, for reasons known only to him, he had gone west rather than continuing his education. Of the roughly twenty intervening years, nothing was known by anyone in Pick-Em-Up.

Like most others, Stender had come to this area with the idea of striking it rich, but the rich veins of ore had eluded him as they did so many. Not long after his arrival in town he had, as favors to friends, successfully doctored a sick mule, a couple of horses, and a dog that had been shot by a drunken miner. In the land of the blind, as they say, the one-eyed man rules, and Stender soon found that he could make a better living doctoring men and animals than he had been able to do as a miner. Moreover, being past fifty years of age, he was happy to leave the brutal labor of mining to younger men.

No one in the camp seemed to care about Stender's truncated medical education, though he had never made a secret of it, and when he built an office for himself—half tent, half frame construction—his prestige expanded.

He was a gruff man, but not an unkind one, and patients received the same respect and attention from him regardless of their ability to pay, or, for that matter, their species. If two patients were brought to Doc Stender at the same time and one of them was a mule and the other a man, Stender ministered first to the patient whose needs were of greater urgency.

Nor was dentistry excluded from the good doctor's list of available services, though, alas, anesthesia was.

Death was a frequent visitor to Pick-Em-Up, violent death being far and away the most common variety, and in addition to being the closest thing to a doctor in town, Stender was the closest thing Pick-Em-Up had to an undertaker. And though most of the time the dead were merely wrapped in a blanket and buried, sometimes Doc Stender's back room was used to store the cadaver during that brief interval between death and burial, it being considered unseemly to lie around on the street, dead.

So when Martin Chambliss knocked on Stender's door in the middle of the night and presented him with one dead body and one that was barely alive, Stender was not particularly moved. Like a true professional, he checked the dead body to make sure it was truly dead, and the live one to ascertain what should be, or could be, done for it, and then Stender and Chambliss carefully carried the boy inside while the other two men took the body of the older man into the back room and covered it with a blanket. Stender examined the unconscious boy's wound, looked at Chambliss, and asked, "You know him?"

"No."

Stender drew Chambliss to the other side of the room and said in a low voice, "He won't make it."

Chambliss nodded. Together they removed the boy's wet clothing, and after Stender had dressed the wound and placed a warm compress on his stomach, they wrapped him in a dry blanket. The other two men watched. One of them spoke apologetically. "We'd handled him easier if we'd knowed he was alive."

"I checked both of 'em," said the other man. "He looked awful dead to me, layin' there in the mud."

Stender said gruffly, "Wouldn't have made any difference, no matter what you did."

After the two men had gone, Chambliss remained and stood gazing at the unconscious boy. Stender watched him for a moment, and Chambliss, in response to the obvious but unasked question, said, "Just thought I'd stick around for a while."

"Friend of yours?"

"You already asked me that."

"Hmm," said Stender, his eyes narrowing, "You the one that shot him?"

Chambliss shook his head. "Road agents."

They could do little more for the boy than try to keep him warm. This seemed to do some good, and after a while Chambliss saw the boy's eyes open.

Stender spoke a few soothing words to him. Tears formed and ran out the corners of the clear young eyes. The boy tried to form words with his mouth but failed. Finally, a barely audible sound escaped—a single word. Stender could not understand what the boy was trying to say, or perhaps he could not bear to acknowledge to himself what the word was.

Chambliss understood and said, "I'll be right back."

———

Tory Shaw watched with interest as Chambliss and Stender and the other two men carried the bodies into Stender's place. Soon afterward she saw two of the men leave. After a while Chambliss came out the front door. He seemed in a hurry. He walked purposefully up the street to one of the dance halls and without hesitation went in. A short time later he emerged with a woman, and they walked hurriedly down to Stender's place.

Tory felt like someone who was peeping in windows or reading someone else's diary, and she felt ashamed. She was not the type of person who would normally do such things, but she was intrigued by what might be occurring within the flimsy walls of Doc Stender's place and tried to convince herself that this had nothing to do with the fact that Martin Chambliss was involved.

The wind was still blowing, and it was lightly raining again when Chambliss and the dance-hall girl both emerged from Stender's front door. Tory watched as Chambliss reached into his pocket and withdrew some money, thrusting it at the girl and wheeling angrily away. The girl hurled some words at him and turned, stomping up the street.

Chambliss stopped on Stender's threshold and stood as if in deep thought for half a minute or more. Then he turned and looked in Tory's direction and started walking that way. She was astonished by this and a little fearful. What could it mean?

Halfway to the store he stopped, stood unmoving for a moment, and turned back toward Stender's place. But after a few paces, he stopped again, turned, and resolutely strode toward her. Upon reaching the open door, he raised his hand to knock, hesitated momentarily, and then knocked lightly on the frame and said softly, "Hello? . . . Ralph? . . . Mrs. Shaw? . . ."

Tory was glad she was wearing her wrapper. She pulled it tightly around her and said with more confidence in her voice than she felt, "Yes, Mr. Chambliss?"

Momentarily he seemed surprised. Of course he had not expected her to be just inside, hidden by the darkness. He said, "Miss Shaw?"

"Yes?"

"Sorry. Hope I didn't wake you. I'm here to ask a favor of you."

"What would that be, Mr. Chambliss?"

"I know it's late and this must seem strange, but I need you to come with me to Doc Stender's"

"What on earth for?"

"Miss Shaw, there isn't much time. It would be a lot easier if I could show you when we get there."

She hesitated, weighing the urgency in his voice against the impropriety of the circumstances and the unusualness of his request. He waited, trying to divine her thoughts, wishing he could see her face. And then he said in a soft, pleading voice, "Please, Miss Shaw."

"I'll get dressed."

"Please hurry."

When they got to Stender's place, Chambliss opened the door without knocking and took her over to the bed where the dying boy lay. His cheeks were smooth and unwhiskered, his hair damp and matted with mud. Without being told, she understood that he was going to die.

Chambliss spoke to her softly. "He was asking for his mother."

Stender brought her a chair, and she sat by the bed and caressed the boy's forehead. She found his hand and held it and leaned over and whispered something in his ear. Immediately his chest heaved with a convulsive sob and tears rolled out from beneath his closed eyelids. She kissed him on the cheek and held his hand to her lips. He tried to speak, but nothing intelligible came out. She whispered, "I love you, my sweet boy."

When it was over she sat there for a long time, holding his hand and softly weeping.

Chambliss turned away. He felt the need to leave the room. "Be right back," he murmured to Stender.

When Chambliss had gone, Tory looked at Stender, who gave her a sad smile. He said, "You did well. It was good of you to come."

She dried her eyes with a handkerchief. "I'm glad I did."

"You weren't the first woman he brought here tonight."

"I know. What happened?"

"Chambliss told her he would pay her. That was why she came. She didn't . . ." Stender looked over at the boy, and his voice dropped in pitch. "She just sat there, and after a while she asked how long I thought it would be before he died. Chambliss was furious."

"I saw."

She stroked the boy's forehead and wondered what his name was. A swell of emotion caused her to put her hand over her mouth to stifle a small sob. Why he had been killed? What possible reason could there be? Could Chambliss claim self-defense? The thought was absurd. What chance had this boy had against a gunman like Martin Chambliss?

Stender, seeing her agitation, felt the need to say something comforting, but he couldn't think of the right thing. All he said was, "You did very well, Miss Shaw." Then he added, "It was good of Martin to bring you."

She looked at him, and he didn't understand the anger in her eyes. "He must have felt guilty," she said.

Perplexed, Stender said nothing, and it wasn't until after she had gone that it came to him that she thought Chambliss had shot the boy.

Chambliss returned with a steaming pot of coffee, and Stender thought he seemed disappointed when he learned that Tory had left. Stender went to a cupboard and got a bottle of whiskey and added some of it to the coffee. They sipped in somber silence for a while, and finally Stender said, "It's a hard world we live in, Martin. Sometimes I wonder why people keep on struggling."

After a thoughtful interval, Chambliss said, "I guess it's because people have the hope of happier times."

Stender turned inquisitive eyes on Chambliss, and seeing this, Chambliss said, "These miners come here and break their backs and their hearts pounding away at the rock, expecting the next shovelful, or one tomorrow, or next week, to be full of riches. Every one of them expects he'll ride away from here with his pockets full of money and go find a woman to marry and a mansion to put her in and live happily forever and never die."

"Aren't you doing the same thing?" asked Stender.

"Me? No. I know I'll never hit any mother lode. I can work hard at my claim and make wages. I can sell a few cattle and get by. That's about it."

"What about the woman and the mansion and the happy life?"

There was a long pause while Chambliss remembered the Martin Chambliss of a few years before, the one with dreams and plans. That young man had looked at the world very differently than he did now. He avoided answering by saying, "You're older and wiser than I am. You tell me."

Stender's heavy mouth twitched in irony. "Well, as you can see, I don't have them either. Difference between me and most of the men

124

in this camp is that I don't hope for them. I know I'll never have them. Makes me wonder sometimes why I go on living."

"Why, Doc, I suppose a man can get off the train anytime he wants to. If you haven't done that by now, there must be a reason."

For a long moment Stender regarded Chambliss gravely and finally said, "You're right." He found his pipe and took some time packing and lighting it, then he said, "It's because I don't want to see myself as a coward, Martin. I figure there've been billions of people who've lived in this world—billions that still are. Most of them have put up with whatever the world handed them, cried their million tears, shaken their fist at the Almighty, and stuck it out until their time came. I'd hate to think I'm weaker than all of them."

He uncorked the whiskey bottle and took a long pull, then passed it to Chambliss. Presently, he spoke again. "But it's more than that, Martin. I'm not as cynical as you might think. I think a man has got to believe there's a purpose to all this working and struggling and hurting and crying and bleeding and dying. There has to be a reason, otherwise . . ." he paused, and his voice became low, "I guess I just couldn't stand to think it's all for nothing and we die and that's the end of it."

"Well, Doc, it seems to me that if you wanted to be fair you'd need to mention all the laughing and dancing and loving and just plain living that goes on too."

Stender looked at him, surprised. "Why, Martin, you're less of a cynic yourself than I had imagined, especially in view of the fact that I haven't known you to do much laughing or dancing or loving—or even smiling."

"I suppose that's more my fault than anyone else's. What's your excuse?"

"Excuse? Oh, I've got excuses by the kegful, but there really is no justification for not living life to the fullest. Giving up is a choice, and it's a cussed poor one at best." Stender drew deeply on the whiskey bottle and turned to gaze at the dead boy. Gravely, he said, "Go to bed, Martin. You're a young man, and you'll have work to do tomorrow. I'm not young, and I want to get drunk . . . And I want to do it alone."

Chambliss stood up and said, "I'll come in the morning and help you with the burials."

By the time Chambliss arrived back at his claim, dawn was not far away. It seemed like a long time had passed since he had ridden away in haste. He looked for his horse, but it had not returned, and he was sorry about that. He hated to lose that fine animal.

He had a hard time getting to sleep, and when he woke it was full daylight. He felt groggy and morose. The boy's death had left him feeling deeply depressed, and Tory Shaw's leaving Stender's without waiting for him to come back had made him more aware of the bleak and lonely nature of his life, though he didn't quite understand why. He thought of Jane and couldn't remember her face, and his sadness deepened.

CHAPTER 13

There being no bank in Pick-Em-Up, Chambliss kept his money in a tin box, which he buried inside his mine. At one point the mine made a right-angle bend, and the spot where he kept his money hidden was just beyond this point. He lighted a lantern and went in, uncovered the box, and took out enough to buy a hat, a pistol, a rifle, and a horse and saddle to replace those he had lost the night before. He reburied the box and headed back out of the mine. As he came around the turn it struck him that the tunnel was darker than it should be. Ordinarily, more light came in through the entrance.

In an instant he realized what was wrong. The opening to the mine was completely choked with men. He held up his lantern and approached them, and there, at the front of the group, he saw Tiny Webster. Webster—the shy, bible-reading, mountain of a fighter.

Webster stepped forward and began speaking as though he were reciting well-rehearsed lines, which, in fact, he was. "Chambliss, your sister . . ."

Chambliss interrupted angrily. "Get out of here, Tiny. All you men, get out of my mine. Now!" He looked around. "Bledsoe, where are you? I know you're here. Get these men out of here."

Rome Bledsoe crouched lower behind the men in front of him so Chambliss couldn't see him. There was an excitement among the men; he could sense it. Excited whispers were passed back and forth. The recent killings and robberies had raised the emotional pitch of the camp, and the men needed a release.

Chambliss was not in the mood for any of this. Moreover, he knew that Bledsoe was wrong. No matter how angry he got, he would never be able to beat Tiny Webster in a straight-up fistfight.

A man in front of the crowd, one of Bledsoe's friends, came forward. "Chambliss, we ain't leavin' and neither are you, until you fight Webster."

Chambliss' mind raced furiously as he tried to come up with a

C.M. CURTIS

plan. This problem was not going to go away until these men got what they wanted. No doubt some of them were betting on him, but that was because of the long odds Bledsoe was giving. Mostly the miners just wanted to see him and Webster fight. It didn't matter much who won. He glanced quickly around, searching for an idea. And it came. The men watching him saw the activity of his mind reflected on his face, and when he smiled, a tremor of excitement coursed loudly through the crowd. He blew out the lantern and hung it on a timber. "All right," he said. "Let's go outside."

While the group of men cheered and clamored, Webster removed his shirt—revealing massive muscles—and assumed a boxer's stance.

"Not with fists," Chambliss said.

"What?" said Webster incredulously. The crowd voiced its disapproval.

"I said not with fists."

"I only fight with fists."

"Well, you challenged me," said Chambliss.

"So?"

"You're a bible-reading man, Tiny. The bible says, "If thou challengest another to fight, let the choice of weapons be his, lest thou be smitten with a pestilence."

Webster didn't like this at all, but the last thing he wanted was to be smitten with pestilence. "Where in the bible?" he demanded. "What book?"

Chambliss, who hadn't been to church in years, tried to remember the name of a book in the bible, any book. After only a second of hesitation he said, "The book of Elijah."

Webster seemed to accept this. "No guns or knives, Martin. I don't want to kill you."

"No guns or knives," agreed Chambliss.

"What, then?"

"Shovel handles."

"Shovel handles?"

At first the crowd didn't seem to know what to make of this suggestion, but after a moment, though there were dissenting voices, the majority registered their approval. A shovel-handle fight was something they had never seen before. There was novelty as well as excitement in this.

Chambliss had grown up more Indian than white man, and

128

anyone who knew Indians knew they loved competitions. He and his friends had competed in every conceivable way and fought in every way they knew how, always testing to see who would come out the winner. The grown men of the tribe would teach the younger men and the boys all their techniques of fighting, and these were very different from the white man's ways of fighting. Chambliss and his friends had fought many times with sticks, delivering and receiving some punishing blows.

Chambliss walked over to where he had left the two shovel handles he had purchased at Shaw's store days ago. He picked up one of these and casually slid his hand up and down its length, feeling the sharp edge of the split. This one he handed to Tiny Webster, keeping the intact handle for himself.

Webster grasped the handle in different ways, testing different positions, feeling its balance and weight. With a nod that he was ready, he took a defensive stance, and the two men began circling. Ever the aggressor, Webster swung the handle sideways, and a solid crack resounded in the clear desert air as Chambliss parried. Chambliss backed up a little as Webster bore down on him, swinging his handle around to the other side. Chambliss again parried, but this time the force of the swing was so great his shovel handle was thrust back and slammed hard against his rib cage, partially knocking the breath out of him. Webster's cracked handle seemed to be taking the punishment pretty well. This was obviously going to be harder than Chambliss had thought.

Webster feinted a swing to the left but let go with his left hand and swung the handle overhand at Chambliss' head. Chambliss barely had time to dodge, taking a glancing blow on his arm. Now he took advantage of Webster's position, thrusting his handle forward like a spear into Webster's belly. Webster grunted and stepped back, fighting for breath. The men around them were screaming wildly, venting their pent-up frustration.

Chambliss thrust again at Webster's chest, but Webster, with amazing speed, grabbed the handle with his left hand. Now Chambliss, fearing he would be unable to pull the handle from Webster's grip, grasped it with both hands, stepped back, and jerked it free.

Webster was still struggling for air. Taking advantage of this, Chambliss moved in and thrust hard again, this time striking Webster in the midabdomen. Webster tightened his muscles before the impact, and the blow had no appreciable effect. Webster came on fast now, swinging first from one side and then the other, forcing Chambliss back. He swung hard at Chambliss' head, and Chambliss ducked and swung low, delivering a stunning blow to Webster's left arm, temporarily paralyzing it. Chambliss thrust again at Webster's abdomen, but the big man shifted sideways, and the shovel handle slid along his sweaty skin.

Holding the handle in his right hand, Webster swung and struck Chambliss again in the rib cage, this time harder than the first. Both men were struggling for breath now, oblivious to the frenzied shouting going on all around them. Webster's left arm was beginning to work again, and he grasped the shovel handle with two hands, swinging it overhand with all his strength. It came down toward Chambliss' head, but Chambliss raised his handle aloft, holding it with both hands held wide apart. Webster's handle hit it square in the center, and there was a loud crack as the defective handle split in two, leaving the big man holding a piece no more than two feet long.

Chambliss swung his handle sideways. Webster lifted his stub to parry the blow, but it was not long enough, and Chambliss' handle knocked it back, striking Webster a wicked blow on the side of the head.

Webster went down. His left ear began bleeding before he hit the ground. He got up again, but not quickly, and stood unsteadily on his feet, holding his short club protectively in front of him. Chambliss took advantage of this moment of weakness and charged, holding the handle with both hands, hitting Webster across the chest, throwing all the weight of his body into the blow. Tiny Webster was knocked off his feet onto his back and lay there moving his head back and forth, dazed.

Chambliss dropped his shovel handle and took Webster by the hand and pulled him to his feet. "Come on over to the Frisco Lady, Tiny. I'll buy you a drink. He shouldered his way through the screaming, cavorting crowd of men.

At the Frisco Lady, Tiny downed two beers like they were water. He reached up to touch his swollen ear and suddenly froze, an odd look coming over his face. He said, "Wait a minute, Chambliss, there is no book of Elijah in the Bible."

Tory Shaw was attending a solitary customer, wondering why there were so few of them this morning. She couldn't stop thinking of the events of the previous night. Doc Stender had come in early and told her she was mistaken in believing Chambliss had killed the boy.

"How do you know?" she had demanded.

"He told me."

"You have no more proof·than that?"

"Miss Shaw, Martin Chambliss' word is good enough for me."

Now Tory pondered the way he had said it—as a definite affirmation of loyalty. She remembered her father saying something similar about Chambliss, and in the same way. For some reason, men respected Martin Chambliss.

The sound of running hoofs approached, and a man rode a horse up to the door of the store, poked his head in, and breathlessly and loudly proclaimed, "Chambliss licked Tiny Webster."

"What?" said Tory's customer incredulously.

"You heard right. Chambliss licked Webster."

"Chambliss licked Tiny Webster in a fistfight? I don't believe it."

The breathless messenger laughed gleefully, scarcely able to contain his excitement. "No, not a fistfight. It was wonderful. It was the best thing I ever saw."

"Not a fistfight?" How did they fight, then?"

"With shovel handles," the messenger fairly screamed the words, and then he was off, galloping down the street, crying, "Chambliss licked Tiny Webster!" at the top of his voice. Tory's lone customer left the store on the run and followed him, shouting questions.

Tory was left alone. "Shovel handles," she said aloud. And she smiled.

Early that afternoon a wagon pulled into town with three people sitting on its high seat. One of them was an older woman. Her faced looked haggard and gray. A young man sat on one side of her, his arm around her, and on the other side sat an older man with a lawman's star pinned to the front of his shirt.

The three looked around them uncomprehendingly. Though it

was a time of day when everyone should be working, the town was alive. The streets were full, and the boisterous sounds of drunken men could be heard all over town. Some of these men could be seen wandering from one saloon to the other, others had been at it long enough to be headed in the direction of their tent or a flophouse. And from where the three newcomers sat on their wagon seat, they could see two fistfights going on. The man with the star on his shirt said aloud, "What is this, the fourth of July?"

He handed the reins to the younger man and climbed down. It took him a while to locate someone who was sober enough to answer questions coherently and provide the marshal with the information he sought, and then he climbed back up onto the wagon seat and drove a short distance down the street.

Finding a spot that was not directly in front of a saloon, he left the wagon, telling his two companions wait for him. As he entered the Frisco Lady, he murmured to himself, "Bad day to come to Pick-Em-Up."

He stepped over to the bar and told the barkeep he was there to see Mr. Westmoreland. The barkeep went in the back and returned with Westmoreland. The pair shook hands, and the lawman said, "Name's Ashworth. I'm the marshal of Watervale. I'm looking for a man named Chambliss and was told you could probably direct me to him."

Westmoreland was a good friend first and a good citizen second, so he asked, "Why are you looking for him?"

I want to talk to him about a murder. John Day, a storekeeper in Watervale, was shot this morning. A man wearing a bandanna over his face walked in and robbed the store. John gave him the money, but the man killed him anyway. There were two other people in the store. Mrs. Day was one of them. Somebody who saw the killer ride away recognized Chambliss' horse—and his hat too.

"It wasn't Chambliss," said Westmoreland.

"How do you know?" asked the marshal.

"I was with him this morning."

"At what time?"

"What time did the shooting take place?"

"About seven forty-five. What time were you with him?" repeated the lawman.

"Around eight, and no one can get to Pick-Em-Up from

Watervale in fifteen minutes; I don't care how fast their horse is."

But Ashworth was unconvinced. "Not that I don't trust you, Mr. Westmoreland," he said, "but did anybody else see Chambliss besides you at eight o'clock this morning?"

Westmoreland smiled. "I'd say there were fifty men, maybe more." He offered Ashworth a drink and told him about the fight between Martin Chambliss and Tiny Webster.

When he had finished his drink, Ashworth said, "Well, looks like I made the trip for nothin'."

Westmoreland escorted him outside, where they encountered Chambliss, who was just tying up a horse at the hitching rail. It had taken him several hours to locate a horse and saddle that he cared to purchase, and then he had spent considerable time haggling over price with its owner. Westmoreland greeted him and introduced him to Marshal Ashworth, briefly explaining the purpose of Ashworth's visit.

Chambliss was interested. "You say they recognized my horse?"

"That's right," said the marshal. "White blaze on the forehead, three white stockings." Then he said, "Mr. Chambliss, according to Mr. Westmoreland, you've got an alibi and a town full of witnesses. I've got an old woman in that wagon over there who lost her husband this morning and just made the ride over here to see if she could identify the man who killed him. Would you mind stepping over there and letting her look at your face?"

Chambliss agreed.

Mrs. Day was sitting on the wagon seat, her head lowered, her shoulders slumped in grief and fatigue. A younger man who was introduced as her son-in-law was sitting beside her, his arm held protectively around her.

"Mrs. Day," the marshal said. "I brought someone for you to look at."

She looked up and dabbed at her eyes with a handkerchief. Her physical and emotional exhaustion were clearly printed on her face.

Ashworth pointed to Chambliss. "Take a good look at this man, Mrs. Day." Chambliss looked up at her and said sincerely, "I'm sorry to hear about your husband, ma'am."

Her eyes met his and subjected them to a sharp, brief scrutiny, and she said, "This isn't Chambliss."

Ashworth said, "This is Chambliss, ma'am."

"Then it wasn't Chambliss who killed John."

"I don't believe it was, Ma'am," responded Ashworth. "But I want you to be sure to your own satisfaction. You said the man was wearing a bandana on his face."

"Yes, he was, but the eyes are different, and he had a red beard. It was almost covered, but when he turned sideways you could see it behind the bandana. He wore a different hat, too."

"Describe the hat," said Chambliss. She described the hat, and Chambliss recognized the description of his own hat, lost the previous night.

Ashworth thanked Chambliss and Westmoreland and started to climb up onto the wagon. "Guess we'll be on our way."

Chambliss said, "Marshal, Mrs. Day looks tired, don't you think it would be a good idea to let her rest some before you head back?"

Marshall Ashworth turned to her and said, "Mrs. Day, how do you feel about that?"

"Mr. Chambliss is right, Warren. I could use a rest."

Ashworth looked at Chambliss. "Is there a place?"

Chambliss and Westmoreland exchanged a glance, each trying to decide in his mind which of the town's meager accommodations would provide the most comfort to the bereaved woman. After a moment they agreed that the Shaw's place was the best choice. "You'd better be the one to speak to Mrs. Shaw," said Chambliss. "She doesn't like me."

"Why not?"

"No idea."

Chambliss and Westmoreland walked down to Shaw's store while Ashworth turned the team and wagon around. The store was busier than usual for this time of day, but then the whole town was busier than usual. Tory and Myra Shaw were both attending customers.

Westmoreland approached Mrs. Shaw and explained the situation. "Why, certainly," she said. "She can stay as long as she needs to."

"I'm so sorry to hear about your husband," Myra told the older woman when her two traveling companions escorted her inside the store. "We want you to feel free to stay here as long as you need to. If there is anything at all we can do, just tell us."

"Thank you. You're very kind."

Mrs. Day was introduced to Tory, who went with her to the back, where the family had its living quarters. Tory took her to her own room and helped her lie down. It was a small room but pleasant and immaculately clean. Mrs. Day looked around and exclaimed, "Oh, my, I didn't expect to find any place this nice in Pick-Em-Up."

Tory helped her remove her shoes and lie down and then went to the kitchen, started a fire in the stove, and put the teakettle on. Afterward she went to the front to help her mother with customers. When the kettle whistled, she went back and made the tea and took it into the bedroom, trying to make as little noise as possible in case the woman was asleep.

But Mrs. Day could not sleep, and Tory found her softly weeping. Tory set the tea on a tray beside the bed, sat down in a chair next to it, and held the older woman's hand. "I'm so sorry about your husband, Mrs. Day."

Mrs. Day dabbed at her eyes with a handkerchief. "We were married for fifty-two years. I woke up this morning, just like always. I fed him breakfast, just like always—just like I've done every morning, rain or shine, for fifty-two years. And now I'll never do it again." A great sob swelled up from within her. "So many things . . . never again." Tory put her arms around the grieving woman, knowing there was nothing else she could do, and for the second time in less than twenty-four hours she had reason to wonder why there had to be men who liked to kill.

Presently Mrs. Day's sobs subsided, and she spoke apologetically. "I'm sorry. I should never have come here. It's just that I was so angry, and I hoped to find the man who killed my husband. I wanted to see him swing at the end of a rope. Isn't that awful?"

"Under the circumstances," Tory assured her, "just about anyone would feel that way." And she added, "So I take it you have some clues as to who it was."

"There were some people who recognized the horse. They said it belonged to a man named Chambliss. We came looking for Mr. Chambliss."

Tory's heart froze. Last night she had been willing to believe anything of Chambliss. Now she was surprised to discover she didn't want it to be so. She wanted the witnesses to be wrong. She had a brief insight into the minds and hearts of her parents and realized how they felt when they learned of things Ricky had done. She understood their need to deny them.

But then her logic took over and she was forced to admit to

herself that it couldn't possibly be mistaken identity. There could be no other horse like Chambliss' horse in the region. Its distinctive markings made it quite unique. She asked. "So, did you find Mr. Chambliss?"

"Yes, we did." Suddenly Mrs. Day glanced sharply at Tory, her clear eyes subjecting the young woman to a hard scrutiny. After a moment she said, "Dear girl, please forgive me. I had no idea. If I had known, I would have made myself clear from the beginning. Yes, we did find Mr. Chambliss, and he is not the man who killed my husband."

For some reason, Tory felt she did not have to disguise her relief from this woman. She said, "Are you sure?"

"Oh yes, absolutely sure. It's the eyes; I read people's eyes. I always have. The man who shot my husband has the devil's own eyes. Mr. Chambliss has kind eyes. No, my dear, have no fear. Your Mr. Chambliss is no murderer."

Tory blushed. "Oh no, Mrs. Day. He's not my—We're not in any way connected."

Mrs. Day spoke soothingly, "That's all right, dear, you just be patient. Men usually need more time than women."

CHAPTER 14

While Tory was having her conversation with Mrs. Day, Martin Chambliss was at the Frisco Lady conferring with Marshal Ashworth and several members of Pick-Em-Up's vigilance committee. After Ashworth told him the direction the red-bearded man had taken after killing John Day, Chambliss said, "I have a rough idea where the hideout is. It's over in the Dragoons.

Ashworth said dryly, "That's a rough idea, all right. You got it pinpointed to within about fifty square miles. Years ago I prospected that area for some time. It's a rugged pile of rocks. There's a lot of places in there to hide. Cochise and his band did it for years."

Chambliss said, "These outlaws are doing just what Cochise did. They're not just hiding out for a couple of days, they're living in there. That means they have to have water. And there can't be many places in those dry mountains where there's water."

"No," agreed Ashworth. "I only know of two."

"Would either place make a good hideout for outlaws?" asked Clyde Roth, the head of the vigilance committee.

"One of them would. It's an old mining claim. Even had a little cabin as I recall. The roof had caved in, but the walls were still pretty good. You'd have to evict the snakes and the scorpions and put a new roof on it, but it could be fixed up."

"What's the name of this place?" one of the other men asked.

"Don't know that it has one," answered Ashworth, "except the one I gave it. Dry Heaves Canyon. I ate something that didn't agree with me while I was there."

"Can you tell us how to get there?" asked Clyde Roth.

"Nope, I couldn't tell you how to get there; I'd have to show you. I'm pretty sure I could find it again, though I was lost the first time I found it." He paused for a moment and said, "If I took you there, when would you want to leave?"

"Soon as possible," said Roth. Then he pointed out, "We'll be going out of your jurisdiction."

"I won't be going as a marshal. John Day was my friend."

"I'd like to go along too," said Chambliss.

"Why?" asked Roth. "You're not on the vigilance committee."

Chambliss wasn't sure how to answer this question. It was more than the desire to recover his horse that motivated him, but he wasn't sure he understood it completely himself, so he said, "They shot at me last night and stole my horse."

Roth nodded. It was agreed that Chambliss and seven members of the vigilance committee would accompany Ashworth into the mountains in search of the outlaws' hideout. It was also agreed that it would be best for Mrs. Day to spend the night in Pick-Em-Up and that someone would take her home the next morning. Ashworth went over to Shaw's to give her this message in person and to explain why he would not be present at her husband's burial. He told her that he felt a greater need to find his friend's killers and hopefully bring them to justice than to attend the funeral.

Mrs. Day agreed. "He's gone on," she said. "You go and find his killer. That's what he would want you to do and what I want you to do. And be careful, Warren. Don't take any chances. Your wife needs you, and getting yourself killed won't bring John back."

It was a riotous time in Pick-Em-Up that night. The contagious spirit of celebration that had started after Chambliss fought Tiny Webster had spread, and it seemed to Chambliss that every man within twenty miles had come to get drunk. Pick-Em-Up's single street was thronged so thickly that Chambliss had to shoulder his way through just to cross to the Frisco Lady. When he was almost across he heard a voice behind him. It said, "Chambliss, Chick Massey's workin' for Franey. He's going to draw you into a fistfight and kill you."

Chambliss turned, but whoever it was had melted into the crowd and the darkness. He went on into the saloon, and someone he barely knew came over and said, "Don't fight him, Chambliss. Ain't worth it."

Apparently the word had gotten around.

Chambliss went to the usual table, where he found Westmoreland and Bledsoe to be in a somber mood. Bledsoe said, "I had nothing to do with it, Martin. I would never . . ."

"I know. This is something different."

Tiny Webster came to the table and sat down uninvited. He said, "Martin, make sure to get in the first punch and never let him get close to you. He's not as tall as you, but he outweighs you. He's big-boned, and his arms are just as long as yours are. He's built like an ape. He's not like me, Martin. I fight to fight. He fights to do harm. Both his thumbnails are long and filed sharp. He blinded a man he fought last month. Almost killed him—and then bragged about it."

A man Chambliss did not know came up to stand behind Webster. Looking at Chambliss, he said, "Chick Massey wants to see you over at the High Grade."

"Don't go, Martin," said Westmoreland.

Chambliss said, "Tell Massey if he wants to see me, I'm right here—unless he's afraid to come."

The man sneered. "He ain't afraid of you."

"He can prove it by comin' over here. Go tell him that."

After the man left, Bledsoe said, "He won't come, Martin. He wants to fight you on his terrain."

"He'll come. He has to or be seen as a coward. And when he comes in, he'll say something about me being afraid to go over and meet him."

Chambliss was right. A short time later Massey swaggered through the door with a sneer on his face. Men began moving to the periphery of the room, making space for the fight. Other men pushed their way in, crowding at the door, and it sickened Chambliss. It made him feel like a circus attraction.

Massey stood in the center of the barroom and said, "I guess you were afraid to come over to my side of town, Chambliss."

Chambliss knew Massey would want to talk; bullies always did. He would want to boast and tell Chambliss what he was going to do to him—putting on a show for the crowd.

Chambliss stood up and walked over to him and said, "Massey, I've got just one question for you."

"Wha—" began Massey.

There was a blur of hands as two wicked blows—one to the throat, and one to the base of the breastbone—took away Massey's ability to breathe. He gasped and started to bend forward, but Chambliss stepped past him, hooking an elbow around his throat and rolling him over his hip. Viciously, he thrust out the hip and pivoted and felt something crack in Massey's spine.

He dropped Massey to the floor, rose up, and slammed his bent knees down onto the man's rib cage. He did this twice, and each time he felt ribs break.

There was a break in the ring of men, and four men rushed forward, one of them pulling a gun. Westmoreland had given his floormen explicit instructions, and they rushed this group en masse, swinging sawed-off pool cues. Soon all four of the interlopers were on the floor.

"Drag 'em out," ordered Westmoreland, holding a shotgun.

When they had dragged the men out and left them in the street, the floormen came back in, and Westmoreland said, "Massey too."

Two floormen took hold of Massey's legs. "Wait," ordered Chambliss. Massey was breathing again, and his eyes appeared to be focusing. Chambliss bent down and said, "Chick, don't hang around these parts. Next time I see you, I'll kill you."

The posse left the following morning at first light. Nine riders and two pack mules with supplies for three days. From the doorway of her father's mercantile, Tory watched the men ride past. Chambliss glanced at her briefly, resigned now to the fact that for her own obscure reasons she would never like him. He gave a quick nod and then looked away, missing the smile she started to send him.

Later that day, the low, rounded, brushy mountains around Pick-Em-Up gave way to a dramatically different kind of terrain, and the men found themselves in a land of abrupt changes: from horizontal to up and down, and from shallow, wide valleys to narrow, deep, vertical canyons.

Ashworth, the only member of the group who had ever spent time in these mountains, was in the lead. He followed no trail, and at times Chambliss worried that the man might not know where he was taking them. The fact that Ashworth on three different occasions during the day sought a high point in order to gain a clearer view of the terrain did nothing to assuage these fears. Therefore, it was a great relief to everyone in the party when at dusk the marshal led them into the small box canyon where there was a narrow stream formed by water that seemed to ooze rather than flow out of the rock at the base of a towering mountain.

Roth looked around and asked, "How did you know they wouldn't be here, Ashworth? Seems to me this would be a fine outlaw hideout, right here."

"It would," Ashworth responded dryly, "until June, when the spring dries up."

The horses and the pack mule were greedily sucking water from the several pools along the little stream. The animals were unburdened of saddle or pack and hobbled so they could feed without straying. The men found places to sit or lie down and rest. They munched on jerky and dried fruit and enjoyed the quiet and the relaxation after long hours in the saddle.

Presently, Clyde Roth called a conference. "We need to decide how we're going to do this. First off, Marshal Ashworth, how far are we from the place you believe may be the outlaws camp?"

Ashworth scrunched up his face as if in deep concentration. "We're probably about a mile from them as the crow flies."

Roth seemed surprised. "That close? Isn't that a little risky?"

Ashworth chuckled. "It might be if they were crows, but bein' they're just men with horses, it would take them a couple of hours to get from there to here."

The members of the group seemed to relax a little at this. Chambliss spoke. "Marshal, why don't you tell us about the layout of the spot where you think the outlaws are and show us where the cabin is situated and how the trail comes in to the canyon."

"Trails," corrected Ashworth. "There's three of them. That's one of the things that makes that canyon so perfect for outlaws. There's a front door and two back ones." He took a stick and drew outlines on the ground, detailing as best he could from memory the trail that led from the where they were to the canyon where he believed the outlaws were hiding. He described the canyon in as much detail as his memory permitted, not omitting the other two trails.

When he had finished, Chambliss said, "We ought to leave here at midnight. We'll get there around two in the morning, when they'll be sleeping the soundest. We'll have to divide up and cover all three trails so no one slips past us, then we'll move in and surround the cabin."

"When we've got them rounded up, how do we play it?" asked

one of the men.

"What do you mean?" asked Chambliss.

"Well, I don't know how we'll hang anybody. I haven't seen a tree in these mountains that's taller than me. I say we just shoot 'em and leave 'em for the coyotes."

As head of the vigilance committee, Roth was the leader of the group, and he stepped in to assert his authority. "We won't shoot anybody unless we have to. And we won't hang anybody out here. One of the rules of the vigilance committee is that we hang no one until all the members of the committee are present. The idea is to round them up and take them back to Pick-Em-Up. They'll get a trial there with all the committee members attending, and if they're found guilty, they'll hang. Is that understood?" He swiveled his gaze from face to face until each man had either nodded or murmured assent. "All right," he finally said. "Check your weapons. We leave at midnight—and no fires."

"No smoking either," added Chambliss.

That night in Pick-Em-Up, Ricky Shaw and two of his friends were celebrating Ricky's twentieth birthday. Mrs. Shaw had wanted to have a small family celebration at home and had baked a cake for the occasion, but Ricky had scoffed at such feminine sentimentality and gone out to drink with his friends at one of the saloons.

Ricky sat at one of the tables with a bottle in front of him. His two friends sat opposite, eyeing him with displeasure. Ricky was already moderately drunk. He held the whiskey bottle jealously by its neck. "Buy your own whiskey," he told the other two, "like I bought mine."

Across the table from him, Reed Cole, who was about a year younger than Ricky, said, "That's fine for you to say, Shaw. Your old man's rich. Me, I ain't even got a job."

Ricky Shaw smiled the smile of a man who knows something he's not telling. "This money didn't come from my old man. I don't ask him for anything anymore."

The third member of the trio, the youngest of the three, a small, fair-skinned, blue-eyed eighteen-year-old named Reuben, said, "Forget it, Reed. Don't beg."

Ricky laughed and took a long pull on the bottle and said, "Come on, let's go."

"And do what?" demanded Reed sulkily.

"What we always do. Raise hell."

They followed him outside and down the street, weaving their way through the masses of men that filled the street. Hours from now the throng would thin out, and in the early morning hours the town would finally sleep, only to wake a short time later to a new day, which would begin and end the cycle of working, carousing, and sleeping that was the lifestyle of this place.

They took their horses a short distance behind the town and tied them to a mesquite. Ricky then led his two companions into the darkness of a trash-strewn strip where there was a gap between two saloons, and there he sat down on overturned crate. "I'll show you how to get some money," he said. "Sit down."

They did as they were told, and when one of them started to ask something, Ricky quickly shushed him. "Just wait."

It didn't take long. In fact, less than ten minutes had elapsed when a man in soiled work clothes appeared in the opening between the two buildings, framed there by the light from the street. He staggered through the narrow passageway, probably headed for his tent. He never made it. The blow Ricky Shaw dealt him to the side of the jaw knocked him off balance, and he went down. He grunted as he hit the ground. He said, "Hey, what's—?"

Ricky was there, kicking him in the chest and the face. The man rolled onto his back, dazed, his labored breathing the only sound he made as Ricky hurriedly went through his pockets. Reed Cole rushed over to help subdue the dazed miner while Reuben hung back. When Ricky found the money, he exclaimed in a loud whisper, "We did good tonight."

"How much?" asked Reed in an excited whisper.

"We'll count it later. Let's go."

The miner had started thrashing, and Reed was having difficulty holding him down. When Reed let go, the man grasped Ricky by the sleeve and flailed with his other hand, striking Ricky on the side of the face. There was little power behind the blow, but it infuriated Ricky, and with his free fist, he began pummeling the drunk. The man released his grip, and Ricky leaned back and stood up. But as Ricky tried to walk away, the drunk man grasped the cuff of his trousers and started to yell. "Help me! They've robbed me!" Ricky's booted foot struck him hard in the face, but the miner clung stubbornly to the other leg. Ricky kicked him in the head, and the miner released his grip.

"Let's get out of here," Reed Cole said urgently.

"Yes," hissed Reuben, clearly not liking any of this. They started to leave, and the miner began to yell again.

"Shut up," said Ricky, his voice husky with anger. He reached down and pulled a knife out of a sheath in his boot. He bent down and grasped the miner by the hair and thrust the knife into his throat, giving a grunt of satisfied rage. Quickly, he stood up and turned around, still holding the bloody knife. "Let's go."

As Ricky ran off into the darkness, Reed Cole came along beside him, and there was excitement in his voice. "Guess you shut him up."

"Where's Reuben?" Ricky asked. They stopped and turned around. Reuben was standing a few feet away from the dead miner, staring in shock. Ricky ran back and said urgently, "Do you want to get hung?"

"You killed him. He's dead."

"Shut up. You're part of this; do you want to get hung?"

The reply was hesitant, almost inaudible. "No."

"Then come on," commanded Ricky, urgency and anger in his voice. He pulled roughly on Reuben's arm, and Reuben followed. They ran to their horses, where Ricky washed the blood off his knife and his hands with water from a canteen. Reed was excited and couldn't stop talking about what Ricky had done. Reuben vomited.

CHAPTER 15

It took the party longer than anticipated to reach the canyon where Marshal Ashworth thought the outlaws would be, but a half hour more or less to a sleeping man is insignificant, and the men figured the outlaws would be just as sound asleep at two thirty as they had been at two. From where they sat at the opening to the little valley, the trail dropped, leaving them on higher ground than the cabin. The moon was not full, but it was bright enough for them to see the cabin and the rocky, trash-strewn area around it. A faint smell of wood smoke still lingered in the canyon, though last night's cook fire had probably died hours ago. Beyond the cabin was a horse corral, which held some horses. "They're here," said Roth excitedly.

A hasty conference was held, and it was decided that they would leave their horses and go the rest of the way on foot, keeping in the shadows and being as quiet as they could. Chambliss could feel the tension in the group. The men spoke in hushed, short phrases. They all knew what kind of men occupied the cabin below.

Chambliss took a long minute to scan the high points around the cabin to see if he could see any sign of a lookout. Then, telling the others to wait for him; he slipped away and spent over an hour scouting the area. When he returned he said to Roth, "All right."

In a raised whisper, Roth said, "All right, men, keep your weapons ready. Don't take any chances. Anybody so much as acts hostile, shoot 'em. If we go back with any bodies hanging over a saddle, I don't want it to be one of ours."

The men started off, moving in pairs, each pair going in a different direction so as to surround the cabin as Roth had instructed but trying not to get too far separated from the other groups. Marshal Ashworth and Chambliss went together, taking the left flank. Ashworth whispered to Chambliss, "I'd like to sneak around to the back of the cabin. It never used to have a back door. I'd like to make sure someone didn't cut one out."

"How about windows?" asked Chambliss.

"Couple of small ones up high, not big enough for a man to wiggle through."

When they were still about three hundred yards from the cabin, Chambliss picked up the smell of decaying flesh. "Smell that?" he asked quietly.

A few seconds later Ashworth whispered, "Now I do."

"I think I'll check it out," said Chambliss.

"Okay, I'll meet you at the head of that little wash to the west of the house."

Chambliss suspected the source of the smell was in the wash, so he entered it and let its crooked course lead him. He came around a bend and froze as the skulking shapes of several coyotes slipped away into the night. The stench was almost overpowering here. Its source was out in the open, and he recognized it immediately. He saw the white blaze on its forehead; he saw the two white stockings on the front legs. The carcass was bloated, and the legs stuck out at an unnatural angle from the body. It had been partially eaten by scavengers, but he had no difficulty recognizing his horse.

He moved closer and struck a match. Clearly visible was the bloody froth that had dried around the mouth and nose. He saw the raw gashes on the flank of the exposed side of the animal, showing where it had been cruelly roweled with spurs. This splendid horse Rigo had given him as a token of friendship had been ridden to death.

The heat of rage washed through him, and he strode past the animal and broke into a trot. When he reached the head of the wash, he stopped to wait for Ashworth, his anger stirring up memories of Jane and Josefina and of George Durfee, making his breath come out hard. When Ashworth arrived, he said, "Find anything?"

Chambliss forced control into his voice, "My horse."

Ashworth swore softly.

As they approached the cabin, Chambliss saw that it was made of stones that appeared to have been mortared together with mud. The roof was flat, made of poles overlaid with brush. The plank door hung on leather hinges.

While Ashworth waited near the cabin, Chambliss scouted the immediate area. He returned and whispered, "No one here."

A lantern protruded from a stick that had been driven into a gap between two stones in the wall beside the door. Chambliss took a match from his pocket, went around the corner of the cabin, and lighted the lantern. He came back and whispered to Ashworth, "Hold it up above my head when I go in."

He jerked the door open and stepped inside. There were two bunks in the single room, each with a man in it. One of the men had a red beard. Chambliss crossed the room in two strides, to where the startled red-bearded man was reaching for a pistol in a holster hung at the head of the bunk. With his gun barrel, Chambliss struck the man's wrist a solid blow, knocking it away from his gun. A quick sideways glance at the man in the other bunk told Chambliss he had not yet reacted. He took hold of the red beard, and with all the strength of rage, jerked the man completely out of bed, dragging him halfway across the room. Then he thrust his gun barrel into the outlaw's throat.

Behind him, Ashworth crossed the room quickly, holding the lantern high, his pistol trained on the inert form in the other bunk. He pulled the blanket away and revealed the man's dark-skinned, shirtless chest, the right side of it covered with bloody bandages.

Two by two the rest of the men arrived, crowding the doorway. Ashworth ordered, "Check all around. Don't go putting your guns away just yet."

Presently, they all returned with nothing significant to report except for Roth, who said, "I don't see your horse in the corral, Chambliss."

"You won't," growled Chambliss, turning a hostile glance on the outlaw on the floor. The red-bearded man returned it with equal hostility.

Roth ordered two of the men to tie the outlaw up. While this was being done, Ashworth approached the outlaw and bent down to look at his face. "Well, I'll be. This is Jack Franey."

"Are you sure?" asked Roth.

"Oh, I'm sure. Franey's not the kind of man you forget."

The realization that this man was Jack Franey hit Chambliss like the kick of a mule. Already angry, he felt an upwelling of rage such as he had never before experienced. This was the man who had killed Jane, the outlaw Chambliss had sought for over two years. Franey had taken from him two things of incredible beauty, and not so he himself could enjoy their beauty but to destroy them. The picture of

Jane's body as he had found it in that canyon in Sonora came into his mind, and the grief and rage returned.

"Franey." The name came out of Chambliss' throat as a feral growl. He shouldered Ashworth out of the way, reached down, and grasped Franey by the front of the shirt and stood him up as though the outlaw had no weight. He roared and thrust Franey against the cabin wall and pulled back his balled fist.

Roth was there, and so was Ashworth, catching hold of Chambliss' arms and restraining him. "No, Martin," said Ashworth. "Not this way."

When Franey had been tied up and Chambliss had gotten control of himself, Roth asked the outlaw, "Where's the rest of the gang?"

Franey glared at him, not speaking.

"What happened to him?" demanded Roth of Franey, indicating the dead Mexican in the bunk.

"Shot," replied Franey.

"Who shot him?"

Franey inclined his head toward Chambliss, "He did."

Chambliss remembered his narrow escape from the outlaws several nights before. This must have been the man he'd shot.

"How long has he been dead?" asked Roth.

"He was alive when I checked him last night."

Roth shuddered. "Don't think I'd enjoy sleepin' with a dead man."

Pointing to two men, Ashworth told them to round up the horses in the corral and get hackamores on them, and he sent three other men for the posse members' own horses. Chambliss stepped outside, trying to get a rein on his emotions, and a minute later Ashworth and Roth joined him. "What do you think?" asked Ashworth, directing his question at both of them.

"I think we need to get out of here quick," said Roth.

"Why's that?"

Roth looked at Chambliss and said, "You saw it too, didn't you."

"Yes," growled Chambliss, in no mood to be civil.

"What?" said Ashworth.

Chambliss got another lantern from the cabin and lighted it, leading the way. About a hundred feet back of the cabin was an area at the base of the canyon wall, seventy-five or eighty feet long, where the sheer rock wall sloped outward, creating an overhang. There were quite a number of makeshift shelters, each with some sort of bedding inside. The entire area was littered with bedrolls, dead campfires, some trash, and the personal possessions of the men who slept there. Among them, Chambliss found his saddle.

Roth said, "There's more of them than we thought."

"And," added Ashworth, "they could be comin' back at any time. It's pretty clear that Franey is their boss, else why would he be sleepin' in the cabin while everyone else sleeps out here?"

"Thing I don't understand," said Roth, "is why he's here alone. Where's the rest of the gang?"

"Been thinkin' on that myself," said Ashworth. "I figure it this way: Everybody in Pick-Em-Up seems to know that Chambliss is gunnin' for Franey. Everybody knows he is the one that killed Lencho. And he shot that feller inside in the bunk. Franey's got plenty of reason to want Chambliss out of the way. So when he and his pals found Chambliss' horse and hat the night he had his run-in with them, he decided to frame him up for a murder. Franey rode the horse into Watervale wearin' the hat and went in and robbed John Day. I'd been wonderin' why he killed John when there was no reason to. John had already given him the money."

"So," supplied Roth, "he killed an innocent man so another innocent man would hang."

"That's it. And then he killed the horse getting away."

"He had to kill the horse anyway," murmured Chambliss. "It was too recognizable. It would draw attention to anyone riding it."

"How about the rest of the gang?" asked Roth. "Why aren't they here?"

"Don't know," said Ashworth. "And it makes me nervous."

"Me too."

Holding the lantern, Chambliss walked slowly around the area, looking at items scattered on the ground, some stacked against the rear wall of the cabin, some under the overhanging rock. There were empty tin cans, crates full of whiskey bottles, canned foods, and other booty—the spoils of thievery.

Roth walked over to him. "I agree with Marshal Ashworth, Chambliss. We've got the leader, and we know he was the one who killed John Day. We came out here expecting to find four or five men, but now we know there's more than that. We don't have enough men to fight that many desperados. At least now we know where they've been hidin' out. We'll ride back to town, gather up a bigger posse, and come back."

"They won't be here," said Chambliss.

Roth did not reply. The men who had been sent for the horses came, and they all began checking their cinches and stowing their rifles. Chambliss asked a man to saddle one of the horses in the corral with his own recovered saddle and went back into the cabin. Ashworth and Roth followed him.

Jack Franey was still seated on the floor. Chambliss looked down at him and thought of Jane. She had been a remarkable person inside and out, beautiful in every way that a woman could be beautiful, and this man had destroyed that beauty. Chambliss felt his insides begin to churn again, and he tried to check his anger. He needed control. He said, "Where's the money?"

The outlaw merely glared at him.

"All right," growled Chambliss. "We'll have it that way." He went outside and came back with a rope.

He slipped the loop over Franey's head and tightened it, then dragged the outlaw outside by the neck. With his hands tied behind him, Franey could only push with his feet in an effort to take some of the tension off his neck. Chambliss threw the loose end of the rope over a thick roof pole that jutted out from the cabin wall, took out the tension, and said, "Ready to talk, Franey?"

Franey, sitting on the ground, merely glared at him. Chambliss hauled on the rope, pulling the outlaw upright. Men started gathering around now.

Roth came up to Chambliss and said, "What's going on, Chambliss? I thought we were going to take him back to Pick-Em-Up alive."

"We will," growled Chambliss, "if he tells me what I want to know. If he doesn't, we'll leave his carcass hanging here for the buzzards to eat."

Franey's face was turning blue, and his legs were starting to tremble. Chambliss eased the tension on the rope and loosened the loop, "Where's the money?" he demanded.

"It's all been spent," Franey gasped.

"Spent? How?"

"What does it matter? It's all gone."

"You're a liar." Chambliss stood back and tightened the rope again.

Roth said, "Maybe he's tellin' the truth, Chambliss. Anyhow, he won't be able to tell us anything after he's dead."

Chambliss said, "He's lying. There's got to be a lot of money stashed around here somewhere. He released the tension on the rope again. This time Franey dropped to his knees, choking and gasping. Chambliss bent down to get close to the outlaw's ear. "Franey, I believe you've got a big pot stashed, and you'll either tell me where it is or you won't live out the night. I'll stretch you out with your friend in there."

Franey rasped, "What's the difference, Chambliss? You'll hang me anyway once you get me to Pick-Em-Up."

Chambliss said, "I'll be honest with you, Franey. I plan to do everything I can to see you hang, even if you tell me where the money is. And I wouldn't give a bent horseshoe nail for your chances of seein' next week. But I'm going to hang you right now unless you talk. This is the last time I'm going to lean on this rope, so you decide."

With that, he pulled the rope tight, lifting the outlaw onto his feet again. He hauled back a little more, and Franey was pulled onto his tiptoes.

Chambliss said, "I don't guess you can nod your head now, Jack, so if you want to signal me that you're going to take me to the money, you'll have to lift one of your legs."

The hatred in Franey's eyes had turned to genuine fear. His feet began to tremble, then his legs. He opened his mouth, but no sound came out. His eyes were red and bulging, his lips blue.

Looking worried, Roth said, "Chambliss . . ." but Marshal Ashworth touched him on the sleeve, made eye contact with him, and shook his head.

Finally, when it seemed to Chambliss that he had to either give in to the outlaw's stubbornness or carry out his threat, Franey lifted one leg, bending it slightly back at the knee. Chambliss felt the outlaw's weight settle onto the rope, and he released it.

Franey slumped to the ground and lay there, gasping. Standing over him, Chambliss said, "Now, I want some answers. First, who has been telling you when a miner with money is leaving Pick-Em-Up?"

"Franey did not reply immediately, but when Chambliss straightened and started to take the slack out of the rope, Franey croaked, "Chick Massey."

"We'll need to add him to our hangin' list," commented Roth dryly.

"Who killed George Durfee?" said Chambliss.

"Who?"

"Blond-headed, tall man. His horse is in your corral."

"Don't know who you're talking about."

Chambliss was sure Franey was lying, but he had no way of proving it, so he let it go. He started to speak again, and couldn't continue. He had been holding back, dreading this part for fear he would lose control in some way or other. He took a few deep breaths and said, "Do you remember Jane Quilter?"

"Never heard of her."

Chambliss knew he was on the verge of doing something drastic. He had a nearly overwhelming need to kill this man. He found that his hand was on his pistol and forced himself to pull it away. "Yes, you do, Franey. You killed her—and you . . ." He stopped, unable to say more. The image of Jane's body was before him, and he pulled back his fist and struck Franey a vicious blow in the face.

Franey was knocked completely unconscious. Chambliss swung around and walked a distance away, breathing heavily. Ashworth came over and put his hand on Chambliss' shoulder. "I didn't know. I heard about the two girls couple of years back, but I didn't know that you . . ."

"It's all right," interrupted Chambliss. "Let's get on with it."

Ashworth went back to Franey. Someone had poured water on the outlaw's face, and he was conscious again. Ashworth said, "Time for you to show us where the money is, Franey."

Franey led them to a spot several hundred yards from the cabin where there was a rock that weighed at least two hundred pounds. Franey told them the money was buried beneath it.

The rock was rolled away, and using a shovel he had found behind the cabin, Chambliss began digging. The dirt was loose. About two feet down he struck something soft. It turned out to be a canvas sack wrapped in oilcloth, and it contained a large amount of money, some in scrip and some in gold and silver.

When they had opened the sack and gotten a rough idea of the value of its contents, Roth said, "We'll need to decide where this money goes."

Chambliss said, "The vigilance committee can try to find its rightful owners, but I'd like to see George Durfee's and Mrs. Day's money taken out first."

"That's fair," said Roth. "Now we'd better slope, Chambliss. I'm nervous."

"Me too," admitted Ashworth.

Chambliss looked at Franey and struggled with the emotions he was feeling. He had a savage need to take this man in his hands and maim him. He wanted to tear the outlaw's body to pieces. But at the same time he felt a deep sense of revulsion at the thought of it and was ashamed.

Vaguely he wondered which of them was more unhappy at this moment, himself or Franey, and he made the decision then that he would not attend the hanging.

CHAPTER 16

It was early afternoon when the posse arrived in Pick-Em-Up, a tired and dusty group of men. The recovered horses were taken to a feed lot where they would be boarded until the vigilance committee had ruled as to their disposition, or until some rightful owner came forth with proof of ownership. Chambliss pointed out George Durfee's horse and pack mule, and he asked Roth to sell them and add the money to Durfee's pile.

"I don't know how much money George had with him when he was killed," he told Roth, "but Westmoreland does. Will you take his word for it?"

Roth said he would.

Marshal Ashworth approached the two. "I know you're figurin' on hangin' Franey. I guess you know there are some people in Watervale who were hopin' to do the same thing."

"Hard to hang a man twice," said Roth.

"Keep a close eye on him," admonished Ashworth. "And if you were to decide you couldn't find enough evidence to hang him on . . ."

"Not much chance of that," interrupted Roth.

"I know, but on the off chance, we won't have any problem doin' it. John Day was pretty well liked."

Roth said, "I'll meet with the rest of the group this afternoon. The plan is to have a quick trial and hang Franey and Massey today. Why don't you and your witnesses come up here, and we'll try Franey for John Day's murder at the same time if you think it'll make some of your people feel better about things."

Ashworth thought it over for a moment and nodded his head. "All right."

Just then Orville Manning, one of the members of the vigilance committee who had not gone with the posse on their long ride, came walking up briskly, his expression grave. He said, "I need to talk to you, Roth." He looked at Ashworth and added, "This concerns you, too, Marshal.

"Last night a miner named Harvey Vanover was robbed and killed. Stabbed in the throat."

"Vanover?" exclaimed Roth. "I know him. Comes into my place all the time."

"Used to. It was out behind your place they killed him."

"Do you know who did it?"

"Well, you know Harv had a lot of friends, and three of us—Dick Parks and Hugh Mason and me—followed the three that done it and caught up with two of them over in Watervale."

"Where are they now?" asked Roth.

"Well, that's the problem." He looked at Ashworth. "Marshal, your deputy helped us apprehend the two, but he's got them in jail and won't let us bring 'em back here. And he won't say why."

"Who are they?"

"Nobody I ever heard of. One of them says his name is Reuben Greer, the other goes by Reed Cole. The one that got away was Ricky Shaw, Ralph Shaw's boy."

Roth turned to Ashworth and said, "Well, Marshal, I guess there's another favor you can do for us. Go home and tell your deputy to turn those two prisoners over to us."

Ashworth left for Watervale immediately, accompanied by several members of the Pick-Em-Up vigilance committee, all grimly determined to bring back the two men incarcerated in the jail in Watervale.

When they got there, they found Dick Parks leaning back against the hitching rail outside the marshal's office, arms folded on his chest and a scowl on his face. Howie Studer, Ashworth's deputy, was sitting in the doorway with a shotgun balanced across his knees.

Watervale was a busy town, but it was not the pit of iniquity that Pick-Em-Up was, and Ashworth was glad to be back. He missed his wife and wished he could go straight home, but he had this business to take care of.

He dismounted and tied his horse to the hitching rail. Dick Parks strode over to him, a stubborn determination on his face. "We want those two men, Marshal, I want you to know that. We want 'em."

Without speaking, Ashworth stepped past him. Howie Studer stood up and pulled his chair aside. They had been friends for a long time, and Ashworth tried to read Studer's face now and couldn't. "What's goin' on, Howie?"

Studer shot a warning look at Parks and the others, pulled Ashworth into the office, and closed and locked the door. He turned to Ashworth, his face grave. "We got two boys locked up. One of 'em is in the back cell and the other is in the shed out back. They ain't talked to each other since we caught 'em, but they both tell the same story."

"What's that?" asked Ashworth.

"They was with this Ricky Shaw kid. They robbed a drunk, and then Shaw stabbed him in the throat. Then they ran away cause they figured they'd all get hung for it. After that, they panicked and rode out of town. I seen 'em ride in this morning. They went over to Frank's saloon. Must've thought nobody was followin' 'em by then, but these three fellers come into town, trackin' 'em. They came here first, and we all went to the saloon to question the three boys.

The Shaw kid was the smartest one. Must've seen us comin' and slipped out the back. He rode off. Those Pick-Em-Up fellers tried to follow him but lost him. Meanwhile, I made the arrest and brought the other two boys over here to the jail."

Ashworth's face was quizzical. He reached his hand up under his hat and scratched his head. "So why didn't you just let them take the both of 'em back to Pick-Em-Up?"

A look came into Studer's eyes, one that might not be described as anything but compassion, and Ashworth mistakenly thought he'd gone soft on these two boys.

"Come with me," Studer said.

Ashworth followed him into the back room. There in a cell sat a young man—nice looking, blond haired, and blue eyed, and he had the frightened, depressed look about him that Ashworth had seen many times on young men who were not accustomed to being in trouble.

"Doesn't look much like a killer," Ashworth thought, but then, you never could tell.

Studer ignored the young man and used his keys to open the back door, which led outside to a stone shed. The young man locked inside stood up and turned to face them as they opened the door, a look of apprehension on his face. For the briefest instant nothing happened, then Ashworth recognized the face. He stopped as if he had run into a wall. His breath caught in his throat. Howie Studer turned away.

"Hello, Father," said the young man in the cell.

For a moment, Ashworth stood transfixed. Then he turned and walked back to the jail, passing the back cell on his way to the office without glancing at the young man inside. Studer followed, locking doors behind him.

Ashworth sat in the chair behind the desk, leaned his head back, and closed his eyes. "Pour us a drink, Howie."

Studer opened one of the desk drawers and withdrew a bottle and two glasses. He filled both glasses. Each of the men took one and downed it.

"Tell me everything," demanded Ashworth.

"Well, it was like I told you, only I didn't tell you it was Lyle. Evidently he's been goin' by the name of Reed Cole. I didn't recognize him until he told me who he was; he looks different. Well, you saw."

Ashworth nodded, but his expression was distant. He was thinking of his wife, remembering. They had been childless for so many years, and then . . .

She had called it a miracle. "We're like Sarah and Abraham in the bible," she said.

And how they had doted on him—as only a middle-aged couple with an only child can. Nevertheless, they had tried to raise him right. They had tried not to spoil him, but . . .

What had they done wrong? They had asked themselves that question ten thousand times, as Ashworth asked himself now and had no answer. "Maybe nothing," he thought. "Maybe it wasn't us. Maybe it was just him—a bad seed." Who could know?

It had been over two years now since Lyle had left; just slipped away in the night. No note, no nothing. He had taken his horse, a few of his things, and all the money he could find in the house and sneaked away. He had never written to them or sent word that he was well or even alive. And how many times had Warren Ashworth awakened in the night to find his wife beside him, crying softly. And how many times had they prayed for Lyle's safety and for his return.

And now he was back. And no pain he had ever inflicted on them could compare with the pain Ashworth felt right now.

Studer broke the silence. "Listen, I've been thinkin' all day, sittin' out there in that chair. Those men outside are pretty riled. They say that miner had a lot of friends, and somebody has to hang for killin' him. You know as well as I do that if they had caught all three of them kids before I got there, they would have took 'em back to Pick-Em-Up and hung 'em all. I've been talkin' to the feller outside, and he pretty much knows that Shaw was the one who done the killin', but they can't hang Shaw 'cause they didn't catch him. Way I figure it, all it's gonna take to satisfy them is that they hang somebody who was involved.

We can tell 'em they can have one of the two and that's all they get. They won't like it, but I think they'll accept it. What do you say, Warren? Do you want me to try?"

For a long moment Ashworth looked away at nothing. Finally, he nodded.

Studer went outside, and a short time later Ashworth heard raised voices. He didn't bother listening to the words of the argument. His mind was on other things.

After a while things were quiet, and Studer came back in. He gave Ashworth a nod.

Ashworth lifted himself wearily out of the chair, and the two men went into the back, not bothering to lock the door behind them. Neither of them looked at the young, blond man in the back cell as Studer unlocked the back door and went out, but the young man stood up and approached the bars. "Marshal, I heard your deputy talking outside. You're going to give him to them ain't you? You're going to give Reed to them and not me. Why? Is it because I'm younger? Marshal, listen to me. The two of us are partners. Whatever he did, I did. We killed Chambliss' cows. We stole whiskey from the back room of the First Chance. We robbed that drunk miner. We raised lots of hell, and we did it together, and that's because we always stick together.

"Shaw wasn't like that; he deserted us. But me and Reed, we stick together and whatever he's got coming to him, I've got coming to me. Marshal, please let me go with him. We'll tell those men out front what happened. We'll tell them the truth, and then whatever they do they can do to both of us. Even if they hang us it's got to be both of us. Do you understand how I feel, Marshal? I don't want to spend the rest of my life knowin' my friend got hung and I didn't."

Howie Studer had come back in. He opened his mouth to speak, and Ashworth knew he intended to set this young man straight, to tell him that he, not his friend, was going to hang and hang alone. Ashworth spoke sharply. "Howie, shut up."

Studer clamped his mouth shut, turned away, and went across to unlock the shed door. Ashworth went in first and said, "Close the door behind us, Howie."

Ashworth stood in front of his son, the heaviness in his heart actually making it hard for him to breathe. Lyle had been standing by the door, and there was excitement in his eyes. "Is it true, Father? I heard Reuben talking to you. Is it true they're just going to take one of us?"

"Yes." Ashworth's voice was low, almost inaudible.

Enormous relief spread over Lyle's features, and his eyes filled with tears. He leaned his head forward and said, "I thought I was dead."

The pain in Ashworth's chest spread and threatened to suffocate him. He thought he would have to sit down, but he steadied himself. He said, "That boy in there says you two are pardners."

Lyle wiped his eyes. "Yeah, why?"

"Does he know I'm your father?"

"No."

"He says you raised a lot of hell together."

Lyle dropped his gaze. "Well, some."

"How long you been friends?"

"Year and a half or so, why?"

"Because he's going to hang, Lyle, that's why."

Lyle saw what his father was getting at now, and his face assumed a grave expression, "Yeah, I know. It's too bad. He's been . . . a good friend."

There was no feeling behind the words, and Ashworth knew it. Lyle felt no more sorrow now than he had felt when he had robbed his parents and slipped away in the middle of the night, leaving them to grieve.

Ashworth could no longer bear the shame. He turned away and walked slowly across to the jail, leaving Studer to lock the door.

Back at his desk, he poured himself another drink and then poured one for Studer when he came in. For a long time neither man spoke, and when they finally did it was in the low tones of depressed men. Very little needed to be said, and after it was said, Ashworth rose wearily and picked up his hat. Halfway to the front door he stopped, turned, and said, "Howie, give me your word you will never tell a soul who that boy is out there in the shed—especially not my wife."

Howie Studer's voice choked in his throat as he said, "I'll die first, Warren."

Satisfied, Ashworth turned and walked slowly outside. He neither looked at nor spoke to any of the men from Pick-Em-Up who were waiting there. He untied his horse, climbed into the saddle, and rode away. He didn't go home. He went the opposite direction, out into the desert, far from town, far from people, where he dismounted, dropped to his knees, leaned forward, and released his emotions in huge, choking sobs.

Hours later, when he finally went home, he kissed his wife and held her tightly for a long time. He tried to act cheerful, but she could tell something was wrong. She didn't ask him what it was, knowing he would tell her if he wished. She had long ago learned that a man in his line of work sometimes saw and did things that he wished he hadn't had to and that sometimes he didn't want to talk about them.

The following morning when she went down to the emporium to make some purchases and to gossip, she heard the story about the young man who had been taken back to Pick-Em-Up to be hanged— removed from the shed behind the jail house and taken away after dark, according to the marshal's instructions. Someone said his name was Cole Reed, and someone else thought it was Reed Cole. Maybe that was what her husband had been upset about, she thought. Oh, well, he would get over it. He always did.

At no time during the rest of his life did Warren Ashworth ever talk about the incident to anyone. And, except for that one brief episode in the desert and one other—much later—he did not allow himself to shed any tears for his son. He was a strong man, and he mastered his emotions well.

But one day, many years later when they were quite old and Watervale and Pick-Em-Up and most of the other mining and milling towns in Cochise County were mere memories, Ashworth and his wife were sitting in church, listening to a sermon about Abraham and Sarah and Isaac. The preacher read Genesis 22:12, which told of the angel that had stopped Abraham from sacrificing Isaac, his only son.

Suddenly the dam inside Warren Ashworth burst, and the old man began sobbing, unable to control himself despite the fact that there were people all around. He got up and hurried out of the church, holding a hand over his mouth, his concerned wife following closely behind. He walked to a tree and leaned against it, unable to stem the torrent of emotions. His wife stood beside him with her arm around him. It was long before he spoke, and in a broken voice he said something she thought she understood but never would: "Oh, Lord," he sobbed, "where was my angel?"

CHAPTER 17

On the evening of the day the captive outlaw Jack Franey was brought into Pick-Em-Up, the vigilance committee held their meeting, and it was agreed that hasty action was indicated. But in view of the fact that several members of the committee had gone to Watervale to bring back Harvey Vanover's killers, and Marshall Ashworth had sent word he wasn't coming, those present at the meeting decided to wait until the following day to hold the trial in obedience to their own rule that no one would be tried and hanged without all members of the committee being present.

Moreover, they reasoned, in the interest of expediency, they could try Franey and Massey and the young men accused of the Vanover murder at the same time, and if the suspects were all found guilty, they could all be hanged together—an event that would hopefully make more of an impression on any potential miscreants who may be present than would individual executions.

It was a decision the vigilance committee would later regret.

Just as Pick-Em-Up had no real law, it had no real jail. Men were incarcerated in a structure called "the cage"—a small, windowless rectangular building made of rough wood. So far the cage had served the needs of a town with no laws and no lawmen, but the vigilantes were not taking any chances. They stationed three armed men to guard Franey and Massey, whose body had been so badly battered in his fight with Chambliss that he was unable to resist or try to escape. The guards would take turns staying awake through the night, though no one believed Franey's gang would come so soon. And even if they did, they would not know where he was being held.

***

After Chambliss and the other weary posse members returned to Pick-Em-Up with Franey, Chambliss went to his camp and slept for a couple of hours. Afterward he got up and made a brief attempt at working in his mine, but his heart was not in it. Night came, and he tried to sleep, but though he was physically and emotionally exhausted, his mind was filled with thoughts that kept him awake. He thought about his claim and had no desire to work it anymore. He thought about his cattle and no longer cared about them.

He had a sudden urge to leave this place for good. There was nothing here for him now. He had accomplished his purpose. Jack Franey had been captured, and by now he had surely been tried and hanged. Chambliss had had no desire to be present for those proceedings; he wanted to put the whole episode behind him. All that had occurred since he had left Wisconsin was a bad memory. Jane had been dead for well over two years. Her killers were dead now too. His promise to her, made after her death, had been kept at last. He felt the need to leave this place, with all its bad memories, and never return.

An image came into his mind, and it was an unsettling image under the present circumstances: he clearly saw Tory Shaw's face, and he told himself he was a fool. He should leave. If, having no other reason to remain in this place, he allowed a woman who disliked him to tie him here, he was most definitely a fool.

But when he thought about leaving, he could think of no place he wanted to go to. Nowhere else was there anything that drew him, and so, the pull to remain was as strong as the need to leave. He did not know which would win out, and his sense of discouragement grew.

On an impulse he saddled his horse in the dark and rode over to Tombstone, where he took a room at the Grand Hotel. He was able to sleep a little, and in the morning, he went out and purchased a new set of clothes, from the underwear out. Afterward he returned to the hotel and ordered a bathtub, hot water, soap, and a razor brought up.

After his bath and shave he put on his new clothes and went down and had breakfast. He walked around town for a while, stopping in at a couple of Tombstone's more than one hundred saloons, and later went to Vogan's and watched people bowling at the bowling alley—something he had heard about but had never seen before.

He stayed two days in Tombstone and returned to Pick-Em-Up with nothing resolved in his mind, feeling as empty as when he had left.

It was around two o'clock in the morning, just a few hours after Chambliss left his camp and rode to Tombstone, that Clyde Roth was awakened by shooting. Gunshots were a common occurrence in Pick-Em-Up, but this was different. This was a battle with multiple combatants on each side, and, fearing the worst, he grabbed his Winchester, stuck a pistol in his waistband, and ran out.

The shooting had died out before he got there, and he heard the hoof beats of retreating horses. There were four men on the ground around the makeshift jail, and two of them were dead. One of the dead was Curley Archer, and the other was one of the outlaws that had attacked the men guarding the prisoners. The two wounded men were members of the vigilance committee. Roth did not have to ask what had happened. Jack Franey's friends had come and broken him out.

Roth said, "Where's Massey?"

One of the wounded vigilantes growled, "Inside with his head blowed off."

"Who did that?"

When there was no answer, Roth decided it would be best not to repeat the question.

Men were arriving now, some of them carrying lamps. Doc Stender showed up and started firing off instructions. There was a good deal of shouting, and more than a few questions were thrown around. Roth told a man to go get Chambliss, but the man returned a short time later with the news that Chambliss was not at his camp.

A posse of eighteen men was hastily formed and set on the track of the outlaws. Many members of the posse believed their efforts would be futile; the outlaws would ride straight to Mexico. They certainly would not return to their hideout now that it had been discovered.

The posse returned three days later, tired, dispirited, and empty-handed. Franey and his men had done exactly as expected and were now safe, somewhere south of the border. The question in everyone's mind was, would they return?

Pick-Em-Up settled back into its normal routine, and it was the hope of everyone in the surrounding area that, though none of the outlaws had been captured and brought to justice, they would decide to move on to someplace where they could carry out their nefarious activities with less notoriety. And as the weeks passed with no sign of outlaw activity, it seemed that this may be the case. Pick-Em-Up and all the neighboring towns that had been holding their collective breath now seemed to heave a general sigh of relief.

In May, a letter arrived for George Durfee. Chambliss and Bledsoe and Westmoreland read the letter together. It was from Durfee's fiancée. She spoke of her concern over not having heard from him and said that his mother was very ill and was not expected to live much longer. She ended the letter by saying how much she loved and missed him and wished he would hurry home and would he please write to her. It was a sad moment for the three men, but they were grateful to have a return address. They sent the money to her immediately.

The weeks passed, and summer came in full force. The desert became dry and brown and dusty, the heat a tangible, unrelenting presence. Unlike deserts in other parts of the world where the days are unbearably hot and the nights turn cold, this low southwestern desert offered no such respite. The stifling heat of the breezeless summer nights made them almost as hard to bear as the days. It was only in the early morning hours when the sun had been long enough away from the land that it became cool enough for comfortable sleeping.

Late summer came and with it the storms. Violent dust storms, usually occurring in the late afternoon and evening, swept across the desert, blasting everything in their path with blowing sand, and dust and hot air. Rainstorms sometimes followed the dust, and sometimes they didn't. Always unpredictable, these storms at times sprinkled their water lightly across the desert and at other times poured it down in sheets. The moisture and coolness from the rains was always welcome, but when the sun returned to the desert afterward and began drawing the moisture back into the air, the perspiring desert inhabitants longed for the dry heat they had so recently cursed.

Chambliss was always amazed at how quickly the desert dried out again after a storm. Even the most productive of downpours, which filled the dry stream and river beds and brought the violent flash floods rocketing down the canyons, were only a memory within a couple of days. All water seemed to disappear into the thirsty earth and the hot, dry air.

Everyone in Pick-Em-Up believed the outlaws were gone for good, but in early August, two miners, partners who had sold their claim and were on their way back to their homes in Kansas with their earnings, were robbed and killed. Four days later a freight wagon carrying an assortment of supplies to be sold at Charleston and Fairbank was attacked, the two teamsters killed, and the wagon ransacked. Two days after that, a miner working a claim not far from town was killed and robbed right in his camp. In all three cases, attempts to track the outlaws were unsuccessful.

The citizens of Pick-Em-Up and the surrounding area were frightened. Angry meetings were held, and angry ideas were thrown around, and nothing came of them. A large posse was sent to the outlaws' hideout in the Dragoons, but predictably, the outlaws had not returned there. Men traveled in heavily armed groups, even when going short distances.

Though many newcomers to the area did not know it, there was nothing new in this situation. Attacks by Apaches and outlaws had been chronic in southern Arizona and northern Mexico for centuries. Outlaws like Verdugo, Lencho Bautista, Jack Franey, and their bands were merely perpetuating an old tradition.

It was midafternoon; the sun glowed white and hot in the sky, giving an illusion of nearness. It had rained the night before, and now the humidity was unbearable. The air was still and heavy, and few people were in the streets, both humans and native desert creatures alike having sought shade. Coolness there was none.

Chambliss didn't like to be idle, and during the hottest parts of the day, it was his habit to work his claim, the air inside the mine being cooler than the sun-heated air outside. However, on this day, he had some business to conduct in town. Not wanting to saddle his horse for such a short ride, he took off his work boots and put on his moccasins for the walk.

Later, finished with his business in town, he started back to his claim, passing Shaw's store as a matter of course. He noticed the two down-at-the-heels-looking men sitting under a mesquite at the east end of town opposite Ralph Shaw's wagon yard but paid them little attention; Pick-Em-Up was full of down-at-the-heels types.

Tory Shaw had also seen the two men. They had been there for about two hours. When Chambliss walked by, she saw him turn his head to look inside the store, but she knew he could not see far into the dark interior. After he had passed, she saw the two men exchange a conspiratorial glance and stand up. They looked around and casually walked to their horses.

When they were out of sight, Tory left the store and ran across the road to see where they had gone, hoping her suspicions were unfounded. She caught sight of them mounted on their horses following the trail that led to Chambliss' camp. She squinted her eyes against the brightness of the sun and scanned the desert, hoping to see Chambliss, but he was already out of sight around a bend in the trail.

She ran to the wagon yard. Jess Tatum was talking to her father at the far side of the enclosure. They were squatted down in the shade of a wagon. Tatum's horse was tied just outside the gate, and she ran for it. The animal shied, but she grabbed the reins, untied them, and leaped into the saddle. Tatum was taller than Tory, and the stirrups were too long, but there was no time to adjust them, no time to do anything but ride as fast as she could. And this she did, out of the yard into the dusty street. Neither her father nor Jess Tatum—or anyone else—saw her ride away.

It was only a hundred yards or so to the trail that led to Chambliss' claim, and she took it on the run. She was not dressed for riding, and her undivided cotton dress rode up high as she straddled the horse, scandalously exposing her white legs from the knees down.

And scandal was not all her legs were exposed to: the spiny desert vegetation slapped and scratched them as she flew by. Her hair streamed back from her hatless head, shining golden in the blazing sun, and Jack Franey and his companions, viewing from atop a nearby hill, affirmed categorically and profanely that none of them had ever witnessed such a sight. Franey's face creased into a lecherous smile, and he murmured, more to himself than to those with him, "So he's got himself a woman, has he?"

Tory kicked the horse repeatedly in the flank with her spur-less shoes. She had not as yet caught sight of Chambliss, but she had seen some dust up ahead and hoped he had seen hers. When she thought she was close enough that he may be able to hear her, she began shouting his name.

Suddenly, from the brush on either side of the trail, two riders emerged to intercept her. Abruptly she hauled on the reins, but they were too close. She tried to veer off the trail, but one of them leaned over and jerked the reins from her hands. The other rider moved in and wrapped an arm around her waist. She struggled and tried to scream, but he clamped a hand over her mouth, spurred his horse away, and pulled her out of the saddle.

Chambliss heard the sounds of riders behind him and left the trail, fading into the brush, wondering if they were following him or merely riding this way. These thoughts were interrupted by a woman's voice shouting his name. The shouting was abruptly interrupted and there was a muffled scream, then nothing.

He spun around and started off at a run, back toward town. He heard the windy breathing of a horse just before it rounded a bend in the trail ahead of him. Seeing Chambliss, the rider pulled his pistol. Chambliss fired first and the man fell onto the trail. Chambliss caught the reins of the horse and swung into the saddle, wheeling the horse around.

Tory's struggling had frightened the horse of the outlaw who had taken her, and having his hands full with her, the man was having difficulty controlling the animal. Tory understood that if she let these men carry her away, she was lost. From the trail up ahead came the sound of rapid hoofbeats, and she saw Chambliss riding at full tilt. She saw the gun in his hand and the grim look of angry determination on his face.

Relief swept over her, but it was short-lived. The report of the rifle shot reached her ears just after she saw Chambliss' horse falter. Its front legs buckled and it went down. She watched in horror as Chambliss flew over the horse's bowed neck, landed hard, and lay still. The downed horse did not move.

Chambliss was not unconscious, but when he tried to move, he found that the entire left side of his face and upper body were numb. He pushed himself to his knees with his good arm. Hearing a sound, he looked up. A horse and rider loomed over him, but he paid more attention to the hollow barrel of the .44 that was pointed at his head.

He rose to his feet and watched as several riders emerged from the brush. He was not surprised to see that one of them was Jack Franey. Franey held a rope in his hand and was making a loop. He spurred over to where Chambliss stood and without preamble dropped the loop over his head. He pulled the loop tight, took two turns around the saddle horn, and kicked the horse in the flanks. The animal lunged forward and jerked Chambliss off his feet. Chambliss grasped the rope, trying to get his fingers inside the loop to loosen it, but each time he did, Franey spurred forward.

Chambliss felt himself becoming light-headed; the strength was going out of his muscles. He was barely conscious when Franey stopped and allowed him to loosen the loop. While he struggled to catch his breath, Franey looked down at him, smiling in malignant satisfaction.

Franey called his men over and ordered two of them to hold Chambliss. They stood him on his feet and held his arms while Franey dismounted. He said, "How's breathing feel, Chambliss? Like it? You'd best enjoy it because you ain't got much of it left to do. Remember how you hung me? Do you, Chambliss? I remember it real good, and that's what I'm going to do to you. Only I ain't going to let you down."

He went to his saddlebags, took out a pair of gloves, and put them on. Chambliss knew what was coming and he steeled himself for a beating. As Franey drew near, Chambliss lashed out with his foot, but it was a predictable move, and Franey twisted and caught the brunt of the kick on the outside of his thigh. He struck Chambliss a wicked blow in the face with his right fist and then another with the left, followed by a hard blow to the midsection. This continued until Chambliss no longer felt the pain of the blows but only a distant, deep aching. Finally, with the sharp edge of his fury sated, Franey stepped back, breathing heavily from exertion, and regarded the results of his efforts. At his nod the two men released Chambliss, and he fell to the ground.

He was only half conscious, but the part of his mind that was still functioning told him to lie still. One of the outlaws had been sent to check on the man Chambliss had shot. He came back, and Franey said, "Well?"

"Dead."

One of the men said, "Jack, we better get out of here. We're too close to town."

Franey glanced at him and then back down at Chambliss. He nodded. He gave Chambliss a final kick in the ribs, grinned, and said, "Wake up, Chambliss." He turned to face the others. "Now that we've got a girl involved in this, we'll have to drift fast. They'll have every man in the territory looking for us." He addressed one of the men, a dark-skinned, black-bearded Mexican. "Vicente, you put Chambliss on the girl's horse. Tie him on so he doesn't fall off. The girl rides with you." Then he added with a grin, looking directly at Tory, "But don't get any ideas about her; I'm keepin' this one for myself. She's way too purty for you."

Vicente did not join in the general laughter that followed this comment. He nodded, his face expressionless. He motioned for one of the other men to help him, and they lifted Chambliss onto Jess Tatum's horse and tied his feet beneath the horse's belly.

Chambliss was feeling some of his strength returning, but he did not let it show. He sat in the saddle, feeling sick and weak. One eye was swollen completely shut, the other was open a mere slit, and he was unable to breathe through his nose. The numbness had worn off, and he was starting to feel the throbbing pain of a hundred injuries.

Franey walked over to him and said, "I ain't done with you yet, Chambliss. Ain't even started good. You'll feel that rope around your neck again."

Franey led the way, leading Chambliss' horse. The others followed in single file. Vicente, with Tory mounted behind him, was second from the end. She clung to the back of the saddle, refusing to put her arms around the outlaw. Her clothes were soaked from her own perspiration. The desperate, sickening fear she felt was almost too much to endure. She was afraid for Chambliss, and she was afraid for herself. She counted nine outlaws in all, and they were a savage, malefic-looking group—border trash—reminding her more of animals than humans.

They rode fast, and Vicente turned often in the saddle to check their back trail. She noticed other men doing the same. After they had ridden for two hours they stopped to rest, and Tory was allowed to get down and stretch her legs. Chambliss was not.

She asked for water, and Vicente offered her his canteen. She found the thought of drinking from it repugnant but did so anyway, knowing that in this heat her body required water. She started to walk over to Chambliss, praying they would allow her to give him water, but Franey stopped her, smirking. "You'd just be wastin' it, honey. Shortly, he won't ever be thirsty again."

Franey was standing next to Vicente. The Mexican was scanning the horizon in the direction from which they had come. "See anything?" Franey asked him.

Vicente shook his head. One of the men said, "Jack, let's get it done and get out of here."

Franey nodded. He said in a loud voice, "I'm lookin' for a tree with a good, sturdy branch."

Horrified, Tory looked around at the desert vegetation. There was plenty of it, but for the most part it was short—mostly cacti, chaparral, catclaw, and other brushy plants. There were a few scrubby trees in view, but these were all too short and slender-limbed to hang a man from.

There was a sense of urgency in the group. They had kidnapped a woman. A woman would always be missed. With a man you could wait until he turned up. He may have gone off exploring or hunting or drinking or carousing. Men were that way. But in this wild land, when a woman went missing, the alarm was quickly sounded and the search begun.

Some of the outlaws were starting to complain. One of them voiced their concern. "Jack, there'll be a hundred-man posse comin' after us, and we're wastin' time lookin' for a tree."

Franey exploded, cursing furiously. He strode over to the horse Chambliss was riding, displaying his anger by the forceful motions of his body. He pulled his knife and with a quick movement cut the rope that bound Chambliss' ankles and jerked him off the horse, slamming him hard onto the ground. Vicente rode forward, and it was the first time Tory had heard him speak. His English was understandable despite a strong accent. "We need to go now," he said.

Franey said nothing for a few moments as he looked around. Finally, settling his gaze on the opening to a nearby wash, he said, "All right, let's go. Bring Chambliss."

Chambliss was lifted back onto the horse, and this time his ankles were not tied. Franey led the way up the wash. Presently they came to a place where the wash made a bend, and on the outside of the bend there was a cutbank created by years of flash floods. Franey dismounted and jerked Chambliss off his horse once again. This time it almost felt good to Chambliss to land in the soft, sandy bottom of the wash.

"Stand him up," Franey ordered. Two men lifted Chambliss to his feet. Franey stood in front of him and cursed him. "Chambliss, I can't find a decent hangin' tree for you, but I made a promise you'd choke to death, and you will."

Chambliss spoke, his voice a barely audible croak. "Before you do it, I could use a drink of water."

Franey grinned. "When you get to hell, you can ask the devil for some water."

"I just did."

Franey hit him hard in the stomach, and Chambliss felt the jolt of pain travel clear through his body. He wanted to double over, but the two men holding him wouldn't allow it. He closed his eyes and was unable to breathe.

As his breath came back he felt himself being half dragged and half carried. When he finally opened his eyes, he saw they were approaching the cutbank. He knew what they were going to do, and he couldn't think of a single thing he could do to stop them. He had seen men buried this way, but they had already been dead. It was a quick way of getting a body underground without having to expend the time or effort to dig a grave. They took him to the cutbank, and Franey, smiling, hit him in the face, knocking him down. They laid him up against the base of the bank while Franey held a gun on him. "This'll be a pleasure, Chambliss."

Three men climbed up onto the rim of the wash where there was a large fissure. Chambliss knew what they were doing. He recalled having done it many times as a boy with his Indian friends. A river or stream would erode away the base of a bank, and at some point a fissure would appear at the top, gradually going deeper and deeper as the weight of the separating piece pulled away. He could remember the feeling of power he and his friends had felt when they were able, with their own puny strength, to overbalance the separated chunk and cause tons of earth to go crashing down.

He felt the bank tremble as the men up above pushed with their boots, but Franey held up his hand for them to stop. He approached Chambliss and leaned down, "Before you die, Chambliss, I want you to know I'll take real good care of the girl for you. She'll be my woman until I get tired of her, and then I'll kill her—same way I did Jane. Yes, Chambliss, I remember Jane." He grinned. "Enjoy breathing, Chambliss, you've only got a few seconds of it left." He stepped back, and Chambliss heard the men above grunting from their straining as loose dirt and rocks began falling on him.

He turned his head toward the bank to keep the dirt from falling into his eyes, and he saw the indentation that marked the deepest point of the undercut. He saw something else too, something of significance. With a quick, painful squirming movement that used every muscle in his body, he pulled himself close to the indentation, hugging the bank as tons of earth came down and he was enveloped by darkness and a crushing weight.

From the back of the horse, Tory watched in horror as Chambliss was buried by the mountainous pile of earth. She tried not to scream but could not help herself. Some of the outlaws laughed. Jack Franey stood grinning, gazing at the place beneath which Chambliss was buried. He did not shift his gaze for the space of several minutes. Finally, he gave a grunt of satisfaction and turned to face the expectant group. "Now we'll have to move fast. Vicente, you and Ames and Parish take the girl and go to the spring. The rest of us will go back to camp to get supplies and the packhorses. We'll meet you at the spring late tonight."

He walked over to the horse upon which Tory sat, looked up at her, and put a hand on her leg, stroking it. She flinched and leaned away. He saw the revulsion in her face and smiled a leering grin. "You might never like me, honey, but you're goin' to get to know me real good." Turning to Vicente, he said, "Remember, she's mine. Take good care of her until I get there."

CHAPTER 18

For the first few seconds, Chambliss was unable to breathe because of the weight of the earth that was against him. But with a frenzied strength born of desperation he managed to squirm closer to the indentation and found that this eased some of the pressure. The outlaws had made a mistake in putting him so close to the base of the bank—most of the dirt had fallen farther out. If they had placed him just a few feet out, he would have been instantly crushed to death.

There was a small cavity in front of him, but he knew the air it held wouldn't last long. He had seen a hole, probably an animal burrow, just before the embankment had caved off, and in the total blackness he now tried to worm his way up to it. He was lying on his side with his arms and the front of his body against the embankment. The outlaws had tied his hands in front instead of behind his back—presumably so he could hold on to the saddle horn—and for this he was exceedingly grateful now.

With no small amount of effort, he managed to pull his arms along his body and draw them up past his head where, feeling with his fingers, he located the burrow. He began working to free his legs and managed to draw his left knee up slightly. Now he pulled with both arms and pushed with his toes and moved his entire body a few inches headward. By repeating this action he was able to pull himself to a point where his face was directly opposite the animal burrow and he could feel and taste the fresh air.

He lay there for a few minutes, exhausted and panting. He had never experienced such intense thirst. His mouth was completely dry. The dirt that had gotten in it had not even turned to mud. Every part of his body ached. He thought of how good it would feel to just relax and go to sleep and let death come unnoticed, but the thought of Tory in the hands of outlaws gave him renewed determination.

Having no other plan, he started to enlarge the burrow, digging with his bare hands in the damp earth. At one point something

175

happened that made things easier: in his digging, he unearthed a flat, oblong rock, not terribly sharp but good enough to use as a digging implement.

After a time he decided that further enlarging the burrow was pointless. He considered the situation and decided to try a new tack. He needed to hollow out an area that would enable him get up onto his hands and knees. He realized that he had two firm surfaces to work with: the one on which he was lying and the vertical face of the embankment in front of him. If he could tunnel straight up using the vertical surface as one side of the tunnel, he may be able to push the earth away from it and pack it in such a way that it would not constantly cave in and refill whatever space he hollowed out. But first he had to get on his hands and knees.

This he was able to accomplish in a surprisingly short time by pushing his back against the earth that was pushing against him and compacting it, thus enlarging the hollow space around him. He was grateful for the recent rains that had made the earth damp instead of dry and hard and dusty. Frequently he put his face into the burrow and drew in deep breaths of air.

When he was finally able to pull himself onto his hands and knees, he began to think out the next stage of his plan. He could see no way to tunnel upward that would not result in closing off the burrow and packing dirt around his feet and legs and lower body as he went up. In other words, once he started tunneling upward, he would have to continue as fast as possible until he either ran out of air and died or made it through to the surface. He took a few deep breaths of air from the burrow and began digging, pushing upward with his legs as he did.

The dirt was soft and loose, and the tunneling went quickly, but he soon found himself in a position where there was a great deal of pressure on his back and legs. He was in a half kneeling, half standing position, and his legs were losing their strength and beginning to cramp up.

He knew that by now the burrow was closed, and he felt the weight of the earth all around him. Breathing was becoming more difficult in the hollow he had created for his head; the air was humid and heavy from the damp earth all around him and from his heavy breathing. He started feeling light-headed, and the muscles in his legs felt as if they could no longer support him. His arms would barely move. Still, he dug and clawed like a badger.

And then, in an instant there was light. One of his eyes was swollen shut, the other was closed to keep dirt out, but he could see light through his eyelids—and he could breathe. His head, at least, was in the open.

After a brief rest, he began pushing the dirt away from his upper body and was able to push himself up and straighten his legs. Now he was standing erect, buried to his chest, with his head and shoulders free. He rested again, breathing the fresh air and allowing the strength to come back to his muscles. When his head had cleared and he felt stronger, he began digging a horizontal trench in front of him. As the trench grew longer he had to lean farther and farther forward to dig.

When he could reach no farther, he began reaching down and pulling dirt out from around his body and legs until he had removed enough to be able to move. Now he leaned forward, pushing with his feet and pulling with his hands in the loose soil—almost like swimming in dirt—and he began sliding forward. Soon his feet had a purchase on the bank behind him, and he pushed himself out of the hole and rolled onto his back, conscious of a sense of freedom, intense thirst, incredible fatigue, pain in his entire body, and an overriding need to get to Tory.

He rested now, while he used his teeth to undo the knot in the rope that bound his hands, but he did not rest long. There was no time for it. He untied the rope pieces that had been left on his ankles and took off his moccasins and dumped the dirt out of them. Replacing them, he pulled himself to his feet, walked back to the main trail, and found the tracks of the outlaws' horses.

By the time they got to the spring it was dark. Tory rode the distance silently, behind Vicente, her fear churning inside her like hot liquid. Often, she thought of how Chambliss had died, and she cried softly. How ironic it was, she thought, that now that he was dead, she could finally admit to herself that she loved him, had loved him for a long time.

The spring was dry at this time of year. The outlaws knew it, but they had cached water there earlier in the summer when it was still flowing. There was still some graze for the horses in the valley where the spring was located, and the men began unsaddling the weary animals. Vicente waited for Tory to get down, and he dismounted too. He unsaddled the horse and set the saddle on the ground.

"Stay here," he instructed her. He took some grain from his saddlebag, poured it into his hat, and fed it to the horse. After it had eaten the grain, he rubbed it down and led it a short distance away to where there was a bowl-shaped, man-made depression in the ground, roughly three feet in diameter.

One of the men produced a small tarp and lined the depression with it while Vicente and another outlaw dug out a whiskey keg, which they had buried earlier in the soft, sandy soil nearby. The keg was rolled over to the depression, the bung knocked out, and the water poured into the makeshift trough. The horses were brought to drink and afterward led a short distance away, hobbled and left to graze.

From the same area where the whiskey keg had been buried, the men unearthed a large number of whiskey bottles, which had also been filled with water. Without speaking, Vicente gave one of these to Tory. She accepted it and drank deeply. A fire was built, and supper of beans, jerky, and hard biscuits was prepared. Vicente brought Tory a plate, but she pushed it away, too full of grief and fear to eat.

After the meal the Mexican squatted by the fire, sipping on a cup of coffee, watching her with inscrutable dark eyes. She wondered what was behind those eyes. When the other men looked at her they leered, and it was not difficult to read their thoughts. It wasn't that way with Vicente. Still, she knew she could expect no help from him. He was an outlaw like the others—a thief and a murderer. She was completely alone.

The three men squatted by the fire for a long time, speaking in low voices so that she would not understand what they were saying. The two white men looked often in her direction, laughing at times over some shared joke. Vicente spoke only when spoken to. He never smiled and he never laughed.

Eventually the outlaws seemed to decide by mutual agreement that it was time to get some sleep. There were no bedrolls. The men simply stretched out on the ground, resting their heads on their saddles. Vicente came over to where Tory was sitting, carrying a long stick. He lay down about three feet away from her and placed the stick across her legs, holding one end of it in his hand. She had no doubt that the life he led had conditioned him to be a light sleeper. Any movement of the stick would awaken him.

She had, of course, thought about escape, and intended to do so if the opportunity presented itself, but she had no illusions. She knew she could not survive in this desert. She had decided, however, that she would rather die of heat and thirst than to spend a minute with Jack Franey.

She lay there for a long time, listening to the deep breathing of the outlaws as they slumbered. She heard Vicente's breathing become heavier and knew he was asleep. She had not intended to sleep at all, but it had been a long and difficult day, and against her will she found herself dozing off.

She shifted her position slightly. The stick moved and Vicente awoke. He didn't move or make any sound, but his breathing changed, and in the moonlight she saw his eyes. He glanced at her and closed his eyes again.

She didn't know how long she'd been asleep when she felt the stick move, and she came instantly awake. Her fear returned. Vicente was sitting up. The other men still appeared to be asleep. Quietly Vicente put the stick aside. His pistol was in his hand.

The fire was dead, but the moon was bright. Vicente was listening. He must have heard something, she thought. He turned his head slowly to one side and then the other like an animal sensing danger. He stood up and crept quietly away, past the fire, past the inert forms of the other outlaws.

Vicente was certain he had heard something. It could have been one of the horses, but he didn't think so. He didn't trust Jack Franey. It would be just like the man to ambush them and take their share of the money.

The moon was bright, and he felt exposed. As he moved past a clump of brush, he heard a sound to one side and turned to look. Vicente Ramirez was not fainthearted, but the apparition he saw before him sent a chill through his body and momentarily froze his muscles. It was the ghost of Martin Chambliss. His swollen features were covered with dried blood and dirt. His hair was tangled and matted, his clothing torn and disheveled. The light-colored dirt that covered his entire person gave him an otherworldly aspect. He was clearly a man returned from the grave.

Vicente gave a little cry and swung his pistol around. He didn't feel the heavy mesquite branch crash into the side of his head with all the force Martin Chambliss' tired body could put behind it, nor did he feel his pistol being pulled from his unresisting fingers after he fell.

Tory sat on the ground, Vicente's stick still lying across her lap, her eyes wide in astonishment. She looked at the other two outlaws still lying with their heads propped on their saddles and wondered why they didn't move. Hadn't they heard Vicente cry out?

Abruptly she realized they were both dead.

Chambliss was walking toward her. She stared at him numbly for a moment, her eyes filling with tears. She leaped to her feet and rushed over to him. They clung to each other tightly for a moment as all the suppressed emotions of the day came spilling out of her in torrent. It was uncontrollable, unstoppable, and he sat down and pulled her down beside him and held her for a long time. Presently, when she was composed again, he said in a hoarse whisper, "I'm glad to see you too. Now, can I have some water?"

"Oh," she cried, and springing to her feet, she ran for one of the water bottles and brought it to him. Nothing in his life had ever tasted as good to Chambliss as did that water. He drank deeply again and again.

She said, "You'd better stop before you get sick."

"I know." He lay on his back and poured water over his face. It hurt, but it felt good.

She started crying again and laid her head on his chest. Chambliss was sick and exhausted beyond anything he had ever experienced. Every part of his body ached, and more than anything in the world he wanted to just lie there with his eyes closed and go to sleep. But he knew they had to leave quickly.

He checked Vicente and found that the Mexican was still alive but unconscious. For a moment he considered what to do. He knew he should kill the outlaw, but something stopped him. He rummaged Vicente for weapons and found a sheath knife, which he took. Then he dragged the man into the clearing by the fire, where he could keep an eye on him. He gathered up all the weapons in camp and loaded them on the horses to keep them safely away from Vicente's reach should he wake up.

"Is there any food around here?" he asked Tory.

Without answering, she rushed around and found him some biscuits and jerky. The coffee pot was still on the fire, and the live coals had kept it hot. Chambliss ate ravenously, and as Tory watched him, she found that she too was hungry now. They ate together, chewing in silence. When they were finished, he said, "We have to leave."

She told him about the cache of water, and he said, "We'll take as much as we can load on the horses."

Chambliss rounded up the horses and saddled them while Tory dug up bottles of water and gathered every bit of food that was in the camp, which wasn't a lot.

He and Tory filled the saddlebags with supplies and water-filled bottles. Afterward, they finished emptying the whiskey keg into the makeshift trough and gave the horses a long drink. The animals were still noisily sucking water when Chambliss heard a sound and knew immediately what it was. He looked and in the moonlight saw a line of horsemen streaming over a saddle into the far side of the valley. Tory noticed his quick alertness and the tension in his body and followed his gaze. Nothing needed to be said. They mounted up, and Chambliss took the reins of the extra horse, and they slipped away.

Chambliss decided not to immediately try to ride back to Pick-Em-Up. It would be a predictable move, and the outlaws would quickly pick up their trail. Moreover, at present, he was in no condition to make such a long ride. The food and water had done much to restore strength to his battered body, but he desperately needed rest.

The wind began to blow, and he felt a light sprinkle of rain. Rain would be a blessing. A good storm would wash away their tracks. But the light rainfall lasted less than a minute, and the wind died down shortly thereafter.

He looked at the sky. Half of it was filled with clouds, but the moon still shone brightly through the other half. It was hard to tell if the dark clouds represented a heavy storm in the making or just a false promise. For the next several hours, clouds passed in front of the moon in a steady procession, alternately covering and exposing it.

Chambliss wanted to ride as far as possible tonight because he knew that when daylight came they would be followed. But his fatigue finally overcame him, and, seeing that Tory was in much the same condition, he found a sheltered spot in a small canyon where he tied the horses to a tree, leaving them saddled against the need for a quick getaway. He would have let them graze, but he was too fatigued to hobble or tether them. Besides, he was only planning to rest for about an hour.

They found a soft, sandy place in a dry streambed, and he took another long drink of water, unable to get enough to satisfy his dehydrated body. Tory watched him as he lowered himself to the ground and lay back in the sand. He had been moving around like a man in a daze, and she had an idea of how sick and exhausted he must be. She herself was weary to the bone. She knelt beside him and gently stroked his face. "I love you, Martin," she said. "Thank you." But he was already asleep.

The day dawned overcast and gray. The broken parade of clouds that had crossed the night sky had at some point before dawn become a seamless gray canopy. The air was still and humid and oppressive, but at least the sun was not blazing down on them.

Jack Franey in his rage had allowed his men only two hours of sleep, and after a breakfast of coffee and biscuits, they had begun searching for the trail of the two fugitives. It had been a wasted effort in the dark, but now, in the dawn, they found it. They had ridden into the valley the previous night and found Vicente lying where Chambliss had left him. Half a bottle of water poured on his face roused him, and a couple of shots of whiskey helped clear his head.

At first Vicente did not remember what had happened, then he remembered hearing sounds and getting up and seeing the ghost of Chambliss.

"It wasn't a ghost, you stupid greaser," Franey raged. "It was Chambliss. Somehow he must've managed to dig himself out from under that cutbank."

Franey cursed and ranted savagely. All day and all night, he had carried the image of the girl's white legs and yellow hair in his mind, and now she was gone. He had pushed his tired men and their jaded horses hard in order to make it back to the spring as soon as possible. Now all his anticipation had turned to disappointment. And the triumph he had felt at the death of Chambliss had turned to frustration.

He cursed Chambliss, and he cursed himself for not having shot the man. At least he would have known for sure that he was dead. Next time he would make no such mistake. He would blow

Chambliss' head off; he would cut his heart out. And he would have the girl back. He ran for his horse. "Let's go!" he shouted furiously.

CHAPTER 19

Chambliss awoke with a start. It was daylight. He had overslept. He looked around for Tory and saw her sleeping a few feet away. He sat up and found that the achiness of last night had turned to stiffness and soreness. But the throbbing in his head had lessened considerably, and he felt stronger and more alert. There was a bottle of water nearby. He opened it and downed its contents. He touched Tory on the shoulder. She jerked awake, saw his face, and relaxed and smiled. He smiled back. "You looked beautiful lying there."

"I'm sure I did," she replied, frowning and putting a hand to her hair. "My hair is a mess, my clothes are a wreck, and I'm filthy."

Just then he wanted to kiss her, but he had a pretty good idea how his swollen, bloody face looked and decided against it. "We have to go," he said.

They ate jerky and biscuits in the saddle, washing them down with frugal swallows of water. He regretted the fact that the horses had been left tied while he and Tory slept, but he had been at the limit of his energy last night. Nor had he intended to sleep as long as he had.

The country they were in was not altogether unfamiliar to Chambliss. He had known a man who had prospected here and who had told him a great deal about the region. He had even come here once on one of his long rides of exploration. Now, as he rode, he tried to create a map in his mind, and he scanned the surrounding area, hoping to orient himself in relation to that map. There was a particular place he wanted to find.

To the northeast, behind the mountains in the distance, Chambliss observed a darkening of the sky that might presage a storm. But in this unpredictable desert one could never be sure. He said to Tory, "We may get a soaking before the day is out."

Two hours later, from the top of a hill, he saw the outlaws moving at a determined pace. There were seven of them and four pack animals on lead. He returned to the horses, and in answer to the questioning look on Tory's face, he said, "They're coming."

She nodded. "I want you to promise me something, Martin, and it's a hard thing."

"What?"

"If they catch us, I mean before they catch us, if you see that we won't get away . . ." She looked at him with deep significance in her eyes. "You know what I'm saying. I could face death, and it would be all right if you were the one who did it. But I don't want to die the way Jack Franey would do it."

They sat there for a few moments, looking into each other's eyes, and finally Chambliss said, "You have to trust me, Tory."

She touched his arm. "I do, but just in case, promise me."

"I give you my word."

An hour later the dust storm hit. They saw it coming from a distance: a towering, dark brown cloud carrying dust and dried leaves and sand that could sting like birdshot.

They found shelter in a narrow arroyo that was barely deep enough to shelter the horses. "Do you think they'll find us here?" she asked.

"No. They'll stop and find a place to wait out the storm." He stood for a moment, looking at her pensively, and then glanced back in the direction where they had last seen the outlaws.

"What are you thinking?" she asked.

"That I don't like being hunted."

Jack Franey was not at the head of the group as was his custom. Charlie Renfro, who was one-half Lipan Apache, was the best tracker in the group, and in situations like this he was, by common consent, always given the lead.

A good tracker he may have been. A good leader he was not, and when he saw the dust cloud approaching, Renfro was at a loss as to what to do. He had been told to follow the two fugitives, but now it seemed imperative that the group seek shelter. Franey rode up beside him and said, "Let's find a place to get away from that dust storm."

"Where?"

Franey looked around and pointed. "The best shelter is going to be up there in those canyons."

"That's the direction the storm's coming from. I don't like goin' in there if there's rain behind the dust," asserted Renfro.

"If we hurry we'll get there before the storm does," said Franey, and he spurred his horse into a run. The rest of the group followed.

The canyon in which the gang found shelter was one of many that had their beginnings far up in the mountains. Its sides were nearly vertical—for the most part solid rock—with a few scrubby bushes growing high up, seemingly rooted in the rock. The canyon bottom was gravel and sand, and nothing grew there. From the entrance, the narrow canyon was straight for about a hundred feet, and then it made a sharp bend. Franey led the group of riders around this bend and reined in. "We'll wait here. Shouldn't last too long. Looked to me like there was rain comin' after this dust. We won't hide from the rain. Once it gets here we'll ride out again. Rain never hurt nobody."

Charlie Renfro was acting nervous. He had dismounted and walked over to the canyon wall and was looking up at the high-water mark, which was well above his reach. "We shouldn't be in here, Jack. I say we go someplace else."

There was an almost unanimous grumble at this suggestion.

"Go out into that dust?" said Franey. "No, sir. We'll stay here. We'll leave as soon as the dust quits blowin'. That'll be soon enough."

Renfro was not satisfied. He shook his head but added nothing to what had already been said. They sat and waited patiently, but the horses were acting nervous. Renfro paced back and forth, looking often at the sky. Abruptly, he tilted his head back, testing the air like an animal. He said, "Do you smell it? Do you smell that? It's rain; the rain's comin'. We got to get out of here before we get washed out."

Several of the men voiced their assent. They all knew what a flash flood could do, and none of them had any desire to be in its path. Jack Franey merely grunted and heaved himself to his feet. By the time he got to his horse, Charlie Renfro was already around the bend, heading out of the canyon.

Two other riders were not far behind Renfro. The rest, like Franey, were just mounting up and gathering up the reins of the packhorses when they heard a shot and then another. Within seconds the two riders who had followed Renfro rode back around the bend at a dead run and reined to a hard stop. One of them, a big man named O'keefe, said, "Renfro's dead. Somebody shot him right out of the saddle." He put a hand to his neck and it came away bloody. "He grazed me with that second shot."

"Who?" one man asked.

"Who do you think?" spat Franey, and he cursed Chambliss with savage vehemence.

No further explanation was necessary. There was not a man in the group who failed to understand. Chambliss, instead of seeking shelter, had followed them and had seen them enter this canyon, and now there was no doubt as to his intentions. He would keep them in here until the water came and washed them out onto the desert floor. Anyone who tried to leave would be shot. They had a choice between death by drowning and death by bullet.

All at once it started to rain, and it came down in sheets. Within seconds the men and horses were soaked. The horses were becoming increasingly restive, and some of the men were beginning to panic, their voices increasing in pitch. Two of them decided to scale the canyon wall and then sneak around behind Chambliss. It would be risky, but it could be done if they had time. Franey paced and cursed.

A few minutes later they heard it.

It was a sound like ten locomotives. No further thought or discussion was necessary. They mounted up and dug their spurs into their horse's flanks, and the horses, needing no urging, flew around the bend toward the opening of the canyon. They knew Chambliss could shoot some of them, but he couldn't possibly shoot all of them before they were past.

As they raced past the dead body of Charlie Renfro, they waited for the shots, but none came. From a safe distance they watched the flood. They would later argue about its height, some saying it was thirty feet, and others saying it was a mere fifteen or twenty.

Of the two men who were attempting the ascent of the canyon wall, one was roughly fifty feet up, and the other just beginning to climb when they heard the flood coming. The lower man dropped to the sandy canyon floor and raced for his horse, but the terrified animal pulled free from the bush it was tied to and left its owner to his fate. And that fate was swift and wet and deadly.

The other climber would have been safe, but so unnerved was he by the awesome violence of the flood below him that he tried to climb faster and missed a handhold on the wet rock. He plummeted, screaming, into the rushing water.

Vicente was last among those who made it out alive. As he rode, he looked behind him to see how close the water was and saw the most terrifying sight of his life. The leading edge of the muddy brown flood was traveling faster than any horse could possibly run. He reached the mouth of the canyon and reined hard to one side, achieving high ground just as the water launched out of the canyon mouth like vomitus.

The water flowed less than a mile out onto the desert floor, fanning out into a widening delta, depositing its load of sand and gravel as it lost velocity. The downpour lasted an hour, and it was over. The wind continued for a while, and then it too died down. The muddy torrent of water issuing from the canyon gradually subsided, leaving the bodies of horses and men strewn along its course—dark mounds partly buried in the silt. Among these mounds were two of the four packhorses. Their packs had been ripped off by the force of the water and the supplies scattered. The bodies of the two men who had been drowned by the flood were located and buried. Charlie Renfro's body was not found.

Jack Franey sat on a rock and watched Vicente pile rocks on one of the bodies. He had not ranted and thrown a temper fit as was his custom when angered, and he didn't understand it. He was angrier now than he had ever been in his life.

As Vicente piled on the last of the rocks, Franey said, "I won't leave this desert without Chambliss' carcass. I'll drag it behind my horse until it falls apart piece by piece along the trail or starts stinking so bad I can't stand it anymore. Then I'll leave it for the coyotes and the buzzards. There'll be no rocks piled on him."

When the rain started coming down so hard he was unable to see more than a few feet in front of him, Chambliss went to his horse and returned to the arroyo, where he found Tory stalwartly holding the reins to the other two mounts. The animals were acting frightened because of the storm. Tory was hatless, and her wet hair hung in strings, streams of water dripping from the ends, but she smiled when she saw him, and he experienced a moment of admiration for her.

"I'm glad you're back," she said, and Chambliss saw a welcome in her smile that made him feel warm. He dismounted and walked over to her. She stood looking at him, her head up, her shoulders back, without fear and without embarrassment, and he could tell she knew what he was going to do.

He took her in his arms and kissed her and felt her response in the softness and giving of her lips. They clung to each other tightly for a long time, heedless of the rain. Presently, he said, "We have to go."

They ran the horses until the rain stopped. Chambliss chose to go in a different direction than the one they had been traveling before the storm, hoping this would throw the outlaws off and buy some more time.

At some point during the afternoon, the horse Tory was riding, a chestnut mare, went lame. Chambliss examined the mare's leg and said to Tory, "You'll have to switch horses."

The mare's limp was significantly lessened without a rider, and she was able to keep up, for which Chambliss was grateful. He liked having an extra horse.

They still had a little food left, and because Tory had had the presence of mind to refill their empty bottles during the storm, they had enough water to last several days. Moreover, for a couple of days there would be pools and puddles if one knew where to look. They would drink that, saving their bottles for later. Chambliss had a particular destination in mind, and he believed that if he could find it, they would be safe.

The sun came out again and turned the desert into a steaming nightmare. Their clothes, which had not completely dried from the drenching they had received, were now soaked again with their sweat. Chambliss pushed them hard, allowing only occasional, brief stops to rest. He forced himself to stay alert and constantly vigilant, but his bone-deep fatigue and the monotony of the ride made it difficult.

Tory dozed often in the saddle and more than once nearly fell off the horse before she caught herself. She paid no attention to where they were going, trusting Chambliss to lead the way. He intentionally took them across spots of extremely rocky and difficult terrain in an effort to make it harder for their pursuers to track them.

Dusk was approaching when Chambliss spotted the landmark he was looking for, and it was well after dark when they arrived there. It was a rugged, flat-topped bluff, two or three hundred feet high. On the side from which they approached it, there appeared to be no way to get to the top; however, Chambliss knew of one. He led them around to the opposite side where a series of ridges and canyons ran perpendicular to the bluff.

They rode about a half mile to a point where the first of these small canyons could be crossed. Afterward he took them over a succession of ridges and into a little valley. Here they gratefully dismounted, and Chambliss unsaddled and hobbled the horses. He stored the saddles, two of the saddlebags, and the extra weapons and ammunition at the base of an overhanging boulder where they would not get wet if it rained. He took a rifle, a pistol, and one of the saddlebags and said to Tory. "Do you feel like a little climb?"

"Up there?" She pointed.

"There's a safe place up there. I know you're tired, but . . ."

"I can make it."

He smiled and pulled her near and held her for a while and promised himself he would do everything in his power to get them both out of this desert. He kissed her and said, "Let's go."

It was a steep climb, but not a dangerous one, and within twenty minutes they had reached the top, where he led her to a place where one end of a huge, flat rock had fallen on top of a large boulder and rested at a slant, creating a sheltered space. At some time in the distant past, someone—Indians perhaps—had piled rocks at one end of this sheltered space, effectively creating a cave.

Chambliss struck a match to light his way and put his head inside the shelter to look around. The first thing he saw was the bore of a pistol a few inches away from his face. A quiet voice said, "If you make one move, I'll kill you."

The match went out, but Chambliss knew there was enough moonlight to frame him in the opening of the shelter. If he moved he was dead. In the second or two before the match went out, he had seen the face of the man holding the gun. It was Ricky Shaw.

"Who are you, and what are you doing here?" Ricky Shaw demanded.

"I'm Martin Chambliss, Ricky, and your sister is here with me."

He heard a little gasp behind him as Tory became aware of the situation.

"You're a liar, Chambliss," Ricky said, and Chambliss detected in the timbre of his voice a sense of desperation that made him realize the danger was not over.

Tory moved to stand beside Chambliss. She said, "No, he isn't, Ricky. It's me."

Ricky struck a match, but he didn't put down the gun. Tory was shocked by his appearance. He was gaunt and hollow eyed and bearded and dirty. His face had the furtive look of a trapped rodent.

"What are you doing here with him?" he demanded of Tory. Then, without waiting for an answer, he said to Chambliss, "Did you come hunting me?"

"Put down the gun, Ricky. We're not hunting you," said Tory in a soft voice. "I'm your sister, remember?"

This seemed to calm Ricky, and he lowered the gun just as the match went out. He struck another and lit a candle. He looked at them in the candlelight and asked Chambliss, "What happened to you? You look like somebody took a hatchet to your face."

"That's about the only thing they didn't do to me," said Chambliss grimly.

Tory gazed at her brother in the candlelight and tried to reconcile this feral creature with the boy she had climbed trees and ridden horses with. She didn't know how to feel toward him. He was her brother, but he was also a murderer. She became aware of her fatigue and said, "Ricky, I need to sit down."

Ricky looked at his sister, and there was no warmth in his gaze. She wondered if there was any warmth left in him. "All right," he said. "You can come in, but I hope you have your own food and water because I ain't sharin' mine."

Inside the cave Tory immediately sat down, and Chambliss arranged the saddlebag behind her so she could lay her head on it. It would not be comfortable, but it was the best they had. She smiled at him wanly and said, "Thank you."

Chambliss leaned his rifle against the wall, undid his pistol belt, and rolled it up and set it on the floor. He turned, and without a hint of warning lashed out and slapped Ricky hard on the side of the head and face. At the same time, he moved in quickly and grasped Ricky's right hand just at it closed on the butt of his pistol. A quick punch to the midsection doubled Ricky over and loosed his grip on his pistol, and Chambliss took the gun. Ricky lowered himself to his knees, gasping, cradling his abdomen with both arms.

Chambliss said through clenched teeth, "You useless little skunk." He pointed to Tory on the floor. "That's your sister over there, and she will have whatever you've got that she needs. I want you to tell me you understand that."

Still struggling for breath, Ricky nodded his head. Chambliss put Ricky's pistol in his waistband and set his own weapons at the other end of the cave, as far away from Ricky as possible. Afterward, he began going through Ricky's small stock of supplies. There were two full canteens and one that was half full. There was some jerked beef, some stale biscuits, a little flour, some coffee, and some canned food, which included a can of tomatoes, two of oysters, and one of peaches.

He turned to look at Tory and asked, "Hungry?"

"Starving."

"What's your pleasure? Ricky's hosting."

This elicited a baleful glance from Ricky, who was still kneeling on the floor.

"Peaches sound good to me," she said, "and jerky and some biscuits."

Chambliss cut open the can of peaches with the knife he had taken from Vicente. She ate ravenously and protested when he began pulling his own meager supper out of the saddlebag they had brought.

"I'll eat none of his food," he said, inclining his head toward Ricky, "but he'll share it with you. He already said so. I'll have some of his coffee, though."

Ricky had a small fire going near the back of the cave, and on it was a pot of coffee. There was only one cup, so Chambliss poured it full and handed it to Tory, and they took turns sipping the hot coffee.

Ricky was now sitting at the far end of the cave with his back against the wall, sullen and silent. Chambliss finished the last of his meal, and Tory said, "You didn't have enough, Martin. You should have some of the peaches." But Chambliss shook his head. He asked, "Ricky, how did you come to be out here?"

"Just hidin' out. I guess you heard I'm a wanted man. I'm bein' hunted for somethin' I didn't do."

Chambliss made no comment, but Tory wanted to discuss this matter, which had caused her family so much grief. "Tell us about it, Ricky."

"Not much to tell. Cole killed that miner. I tried to stop him, but I wasn't fast enough. We weren't doin' anything wrong, just a little drinkin'. That miner came back there and started hollerin' insults at us. He was drunk. Cole shouldn't have paid attention to him, but he was a little drunk himself. After Cole killed him, we all got scared and took off. I guess that was a mistake. I should have turned Cole in myself; then I wouldn't be in this mess."

Ricky was lying and Chambliss knew it. He said, "Seems to me like a strange place to hide out, way out here in the desert. Seems like you would have drifted some other place, where nobody knows you and you could find work. Why out here?"

Ricky acted uncomfortable with these questions. "Well, to tell you the truth, Chambliss, it's none of your business. I didn't want to drift somewhere else. I came out here because it's my life and my decision. Whether you understand it or not doesn't matter one bit to me. Anyway, me being here ain't nearly so strange as you being here; the two of you alone in the desert and comin' up here to sleep. Seems to me you've got more explainin' to do than I do."

Tory blushed for a moment, and then her embarrassment was replaced by indignation. She said hotly, "We don't have any explaining to do at all, especially not to you, Ricky Shaw, because we haven't done anything wrong. And even if we had we would owe you no explanation, you who have done nothing but bring shame and dishonor and grief to our family. No one has to justify anything to you."

Her words had a noticeable effect on Ricky, and he reverted to his former sullenness. For a few moments, no one spoke, and Chambliss reviewed the situation in his mind. He was not pleased at having found Ricky here. He neither liked the young man nor trusted him. He was a murderer and a liar, and Chambliss doubted he would be any good in a showdown with the outlaws.

Chambliss had known men like Ricky. They would shoot a man in the back or knife a helpless drunk, but when it came to dangerous situations, they were useless. Moreover, Chambliss knew he would have to watch his own back with Ricky around.

No one spoke for a few minutes until Tory said to Chambliss, "I think he should know."

Chambliss nodded. "All right."

Tory said, "To make a long story short, Ricky, Jack Franey and his gang are hunting us."

Ricky's head jerked up, and he looked at her, wide-eyed. At first,

Chambliss thought he was afraid, but then he realized it wasn't fear he saw in Ricky's face, and it left him feeling unsettled. There were many things about this situation that he didn't like, but for right now he couldn't worry about that. His head was throbbing, and he desperately needed sleep.

But Ricky had questions. He dropped his confrontational manner and Tory, anxious for any sign of the old Ricky, answered his questions. In a short time, she had told him the entire story. Ricky listened intently, interrupting frequently to ask questions, mostly about locations. The sound of Tory's soft voice had a soothing effect on Chambliss' fatigued brain, and he felt himself drifting. In spite of this he was aware that Ricky seemed altogether too interested in the outlaws and where they might be. He added this to his list of things to think about tomorrow.

Before falling asleep, he said in fatigued, slurred words, "Ricky, take the first watch. Wake me in four hours." He was grateful when Ricky agreed without protest. He fell immediately asleep.

Tory lay a few feet away from him, stretched out on her side, propped up on one elbow. She watched his face as he slept, its features still swollen and bruised, and she felt a love of a kind she had never felt before. She remembered that just twenty-four hours before, she had been in the hands of the outlaws, facing a terrible fate. She remembered the unspeakable dread of knowing what awaited her. She reached over and put her hand near his face. She did not touch him for fear of waking him. It was then that she realized she was crying. She glanced at Ricky to see if he had noticed, but he was lost in his thoughts.

While she had narrated the story of their capture and escape from the outlaws, she had seen an eager, attentive look on her brother's face that reminded her of the old Ricky. And she had been able to convince herself that he wasn't a murderer, that he was really telling the truth when he said someone else had knifed the drunk. Now he had reverted to the furtive, feral man who had met them with a gun at the entrance of the cave, and he was a stranger to her. She did not trust him. She wiped away her tears, not wanting him to see them.

As she watched Ricky, his face changed, and a small smile came to his lips, like a man who has just worked out a difficult problem in his mind. He said, "If I'm going to stand lookout, I'll need my pistol."

She shook her head. "No. If you see something, just come and wake us."

Scowling, he rose and stepped out into the darkness. Deeply weary, Tory laid her head back on the lumpy saddlebag and fell asleep.

CHAPTER 20

For the second time in as many days, Chambliss woke to the feeling that he had overslept. He could not remember having slept so deeply in his life as he had the past two nights. He understood the reasons for this—his brain and body were still suffering from the abuse they had taken—but it worried him. He and Tory were in a dangerous situation, and he needed to be more alert. It was still dark outside, but the clock in his head told him he had slept longer than his allotted four hours. Ricky must have fallen asleep on lookout. He pulled himself to his feet, feeling incredibly stiff and sore, and went outside. The moon was down. Ricky was nowhere to be found.

Chambliss wasn't sure what had happened, but he had a bad feeling. Where was Ricky, and why had he gone? He stepped back inside the cave, fumbled around, and found the candle and some matches. Striking one, he lit the candle, held it up, and looked around the cave. Ricky had taken everything except the rifle, the sacks of food, and the saddlebags under Tory's head. Chambliss had been lying near the sacks of food, and he had slept with the rifle beside him. For obvious reasons, Ricky had not attempted to steal these, but with Tory and Chambliss sleeping as soundly as they had been, it had been a simple matter for Ricky to slip in and quietly take the rest. Chambliss was grateful Tory was using the saddlebags—with the water bottles they contained—as a pillow, or her brother would certainly have taken those as well.

He left the cave and hurried down the trail to where he had left the other saddlebags with the extra weapons and supplies he had taken from the outlaws. They were gone, and so were two of the horses. Ricky had left the lame mare.

It was starting to get light now, and on foot Chambliss followed Ricky's trail. It led out of the little valley and around to the north where there was a box canyon, the far end of which held a small basin where some of the water from yesterday's rain had pooled. The signs on the ground showed him that Ricky's horse had been picketed there. It was gone now.

Chambliss was grateful to find the water, however, and so was the thirsty mare when he took her to it. When he got back to the cave, Tory was awake and waiting for him. She, like Chambliss, had taken stock of the situation and had her suspicions. One look at his face confirmed them.

"I'm sorry, Martin," she said.

"If I ever see your brother again, I'll . . ." Then, seeing her unhappiness, he smiled and said, "Oh, don't worry about it, Tory. We're better off without him." Changing the subject and trying to sound cheerful, he said, "Have you had breakfast yet?"

She shook her head.

"Well, at least he left us some food. Let's eat."

"The only reason he left the food was because he couldn't steal it without waking us," she said, and he could hear the grief in her voice.

After a breakfast of biscuits and coffee and leftover canned tomatoes, Tory said, "What will we do?"

"We'd better stay here today. The mare's leg is better this morning, but it's not healed enough to ride her any distance. Anyway, we have food and water, and if the outlaws are still looking for us, the less we move around the better."

Chambliss had a fear that he didn't mention to Tory. It had occurred to him why Ricky was out here in the middle of the desert, and the thought sickened him. Ricky wanted to join the outlaws. He wanted to become one of them. This explained why he had shown such an interest in their whereabouts.

Chambliss didn't really care if Ricky found the outlaws or not. If he did, they would probably kill him, and the world would be better for it. But what concerned him most was that after all his efforts to disguise their trail yesterday, Ricky was probably at this moment leaving a clear trail to them. If Ricky did not tell Franey he had seen Chambliss and Tory, the outlaws might not back-trail him, but Ricky could not be counted on for any kind of loyalty.

They spent most of the day in the relative coolness of the cave, talking and, despite their dire circumstances, enjoying each other's company. They partook sparingly of their supplies, and they rested—something they both needed.

At dusk, Chambliss took the mare around to the box canyon and let her drink. There was less water in the little catch basin, and Chambliss knew that all over the desert the residual water from yesterday's storm was drying up just as this was. He hoped it would rain again soon.

He was to be disappointed in that hope.

He tethered the mare near the basin where she could drink and where there was still some graze. Back at the cave Tory had a small fire going and had prepared some coffee and a meager supper.

After they had eaten, Chambliss said, "We'll leave tomorrow. We don't have enough supplies left to keep staying here. We'll head for Watervale."

"How's the mare's leg?" she asked anxiously.

"Doing better. I think you'll be able to ride her tomorrow. We won't ride double. You can ride and I'll walk."

"We'll take turns riding and walking," Tory said firmly.

"We'll see," replied Chambliss noncommittally.

He checked the Spencer carbine, the only weapon they had left, and experienced a fresh surge of anger toward Ricky Shaw. It was an old seven-shot lever action, and he had used two of the cartridges yesterday when he had killed Charlie Renfro and shot at another of the outlaws.

He stood up, holding the rifle, and said, "I'm going to stand lookout tonight. If I sleep at all, I'll sleep outside."

She smiled at him and nodded in grateful understanding. He was a gentleman. "I love you, Martin."

He pulled her to him and kissed her fiercely, then, without a word, he turned and quickly left the cave.

Chambliss kept watch all night, allowing himself to doze periodically for an hour or so, trying to balance his need for sleep against the need for vigilance. At dawn he checked on Tory, who was sleeping soundly. He went back out and scanned the surrounding area, and his keen eyes immediately caught a movement. It was a man on horseback, several hundred yards away. The man frequently leaned out, looking down at the ground, no doubt following the trail Ricky Shaw had left. Chambliss couldn't be sure, but it looked a lot like the Mexican he had knocked unconscious. Tory had told him the man's name was Vicente.

Ricky's trail followed the natural contours of the land and led directly up to the steep side of the bluff and then curved around to the sloping side. Vicente was approaching the bluff and as yet had no way of knowing about the trail that led up to the cave. And Chambliss didn't want him to know. That was their escape route.

There was only one way to stop the Mexican from following the trail farther, and that was to let him know he had found what he was seeking. Chambliss raised the Spencer, cocked it, took aim, and fired. The distance was far too great for any hope of accuracy, and Chambliss saw a little puff of dust appear a few feet in front of the horse.

Vicente jerked on the reins, wheeled the horse around, and spurred to cover behind a nearby boulder. There were only four shots remaining in the Spencer now, and Chambliss was not willing to waste any more of them. He watched the boulder and could guess what Vicente was thinking. He would be peering around the side, and he would have located Chambliss' position, the latter having made no attempt at concealment. The Mexican was probably debating in his mind whether to remain where he was or make a run for it.

"He'll run for it," thought Chambliss.

He was right. He saw the Mexican spur his horse fiercely out into the open, over a rise and out of sight.

Tory was beside Chambliss now, and he turned to look at her. "I heard the shot," she said.

"Are you afraid?"

"Not as long as I'm with you. Just remember the promise you made me."

"I do," he said, humbled by her faith in him. "We have to go now."

Against the need of a quick departure, Tory and Chambliss had arranged all their supplies in two of the burlap sacks that Ricky had been using for the same purpose. Chambliss carried one of the sacks, the rifle, and the saddlebags over his shoulder. Tory carried the other sack. They descended the trail as fast as they could, and Chambliss left on the run and soon returned leading the mare. He quickly saddled her and tied on the saddlebags while Tory tied the food sacks onto the saddle horn. She climbed into the saddle, and Chambliss took the reins and led off on foot, running.

Chambliss was reasonably certain that Ricky Shaw was dead. Had he been alive the outlaws would have had no need to back-trail in order to locate the bluff. Ricky would have told them where it was and how to get there and anything else they wanted to know. He may or may not have done so willingly, but he would have told them.

Another thing was certain, and that was that there would be no more running away. Two people with limited supplies and one lame horse could not travel very fast or very far. It would be foolish to try to get away now. Safety did not lie in a direct line of escape.

Jack Franey clapped his hands and rubbed them together, a sign he was pleased. The group had been back-trailing the Shaw kid and had stopped to eat a meal and rest the horses. Vicente had said he was going on ahead to scout the area, and shortly thereafter they had heard the shot. Within minutes Vicente had come racing back down the trail with the news that he had located Chambliss.

Franey felt his pulse quicken with anticipation. Where Chambliss was, the girl would be also. Franey had not been sure that Ricky Shaw's trail would lead to Chambliss, but having no other trail to follow, he had taken the chance—and it had paid off. The men mounted quickly, and Vicente led the way. They studied the bluff from a distance and, presently, Franey announced his plan. He described it in detail so there could be no error, and, when finished, he said, "Just remember, I want them both alive. If you have to shoot Chambliss, shoot him in the leg, but I want him alive. And don't hurt the girl."

The outlaws had to get into position without being seen. This was an important part of Franey's plan, and it required moving stealthily and traveling in wide circles rather than going directly to their destinations. Vicente and an outlaw named Stokes made the circle that brought them to the sloping side of the bluff, and they found their way into the little valley where the trail to the top began. They flipped a coin, and the lot fell to Stokes to climb the trail while Vicente covered him from below.

Stokes reached the top without event and waved to Vicente before disappearing into the cave. Shortly thereafter he emerged and waved his hat in a prearranged signal, indicating their quarry was gone.

Disappointed, Vicente made the ascent.

Stokes said, "They've been here. Wasn't too long ago neither."

Vicente crossed to the steep side of the bluff, approached the edge, and looked down. It was a steep climb, though it could be done. But it would be a long way to fall if a man slipped. He was certain they hadn't gone down this way. He took off his sombrero and waved it in the air and received an answering signal from Jack Franey across the wide valley. Afterward he and Stokes descended to their horses and rode out to the end of the bluff. From there it was not hard to pick up the trail of a man on foot wearing moccasins and leading a horse. It was a very fresh trail.

Vicente told Stokes to go back and get Franey while he followed the trail.

Jack Franey watched the top of the bluff through his spyglass. He felt excitement when he saw Vicente appear and disappointment when the Mexican gave the signal that Chambliss and the girl weren't there.

No matter, he told himself. They could not escape this time. They were in the middle of a vast inferno, and the nearest water was miles away. They had little water and less food, while Franey and his men were well supplied. From here there was no place Chambliss could go that he couldn't be tracked.

Chambliss' trail led around the mountain from which the bluff protruded. Vicente followed the trail east to where it rounded the mountain and swung to the west again. This perplexed him. Moreover, it worried him. Up to now he had thought he was following two people who were fleeing, but now that he realized he was being led in a circle he began fearing an ambush.

He decided to wait for the rest of the gang to catch up with him, which they did about an hour later. Franey was angry with him for stopping, but when Vicente explained his reasoning, Franey cooled off, and said, "They can't get far. There's nothing but desert around here."

The outlaws followed the trail past the steep side of the high bluff, cautiously scanning the country around them. Franey occasionally pulled his spyglass out to investigate a particularly suspicious shadow, boulder, or clump of brush.

When they reached the end of the bluff, the tracks merged with all the tracks their horses had made earlier, and it became impossible to distinguish between the different sets of hoofprints. Charlie Renfro could have done it, but Charlie Renfro was dead.

Franey said, "I know what he's tryin' to do. He mixes his tracks up with ours so we can't tell the difference, and we go around in circles till he figures out a way to slip from the main trail without bein' noticed."

Vicente shook his head. He said in his thick accent, "I don' think so. I think he want us to spleet up, to go thees way and go thet way, for so he can amboosh us."

Franey thought about this for a moment, and said, "All right, then, we'll do the opposite of both. We won't split up, but we won't follow his trail, neither. The whole bunch of us will go the opposite direction, and we'll either meet up with him or find out where he left the trail and follow him."

They swung the horses around and started back, Jack Franey leading off at a canter.

Chambliss watched them from above, smiling. It hadn't mattered one way or another to him what they did. He seriously doubted they would think to look for him where he was at this moment. And Tory, he was certain, was even safer than he.

After they had left that morning, they had gone several miles until he found a spot that suited his purposes. It was an area strewn with rocks and boulders. While he led the horse, he explained to Tory what she had to do. She slipped her feet out of the stirrups and perched on the saddle, clinging to the horn for balance. Chambliss led the horse past a tall boulder without stopping. When she was even with the boulder, Tory leaped on top of it, then slid off the back side onto a smaller boulder, and from there she leaped from rock to rock, leaving no trail whatsoever.

In this manner, she made it to a clump of boulders Chambliss had pointed out to her, up against the steep side of the mountain where there was shade and soft sand. She would be hidden there, and she could rest and wait for him to come for her. She had brought with her a bottle of water and some jerky stuffed down the front of her dress.

Chambliss continued on foot for another mile, at which time he swung into the saddle and continued in the wide circle around the mountain and back to the little valley behind the bluff, into and out of which there were now so many sets of tracks that it would be difficult to distinguish his from the others. Here was where the plan got tricky. Could the mare climb the steep trail up the sloping side of the bluff?

Chambliss had come to know her as a sure-footed horse, and he believed she could do it. At first she balked at the steep trail, but at his calm urging, she followed, slipping several times and nearly falling once. They made it to the top, where he led her into the coolness of the cave and tied the reins to a rock. He went down and carefully smoothed out the tracks the mare had left in her climb to the cave so that even if someone came into the valley, they would never suspect there was a horse on top of the bluff. After all, why would anyone in their right mind take a horse up there?

Chambliss watched the group of outlaws going back down the trail they had just followed. He watched until they were out of sight; then, hours later, when they passed the entrance to the little valley, he was on the other side, again watching. They stopped and tried to read the prints going in and out of the valley, but there were too many of them. Only an expert tracker like Charlie Renfro or Chambliss himself would be able to distinguish Chambliss' more recent tracks from those that were a few hours older.

After hours of fruitlessly riding in circles, the disgusted outlaws made camp in a brushy, flat area across the wide valley from the steep side of the bluff, and Chambliss watched them do it. After supper the four men sat and smoked for a while, and, observing them, Chambliss began to feel sleepy. He heard a sound and crossed to the sloping side to look down at the trail. He watched as Tory materialized out of the darkness. When she reached the top, he chided her for her carelessness. "You should have stayed where you were. You were safer there."

"There were snakes."

They sat together in the darkness, watching the camp across the valley. The campfire glow slowly died out. As Chambliss had expected, three of the men went to bed, and one of them, no doubt on orders from Franey, made his way to a small promontory nearby and settled himself on it for lookout duty.

Tory fell asleep leaning against Chambliss. Roughly two hours later, the lookout came back to camp and woke his replacement. Now Chambliss had all the information he needed. The lookout would change about every two hours. Each of the four men would have his turn.

He woke Tory and said, "I'm leaving now. I won't be back until after daylight. Keep out of sight."

"Please be careful, Martin."

Chambliss led the mare out of the cave and began a harrowing descent in the dark. By the time they reached the bottom, he felt like kissing the solid, level ground, and he was willing to bet the mare did too.

As he rode her out of the little valley, he noticed her limp was substantially worse. He dismounted and led her around into the box canyon and hobbled her near the little basin. There was a little water left in it, and she sucked it up thirstily. He left her there and started off on foot.

CHAPTER 21

After two hours of lookout duty, Jack Franey woke Vicente, and Vicente did his two hours, then woke O'Keefe and went back to his bedroll. At dawn he opened his eyes and sat up and looked around. Stokes was asleep, O'Keefe was still on lookout, but Franey was gone. He went over and felt Franey's bedroll. It was cold. No one had started the fire for breakfast either. Vicente sensed something wrong. Was Chambliss around? He doubted it. O'Keefe would have seen him if he was. But where had Franey gone to?

He woke Stokes and said, "Come with me."

As they approached O'Keefe, Vicente became angry and swore softly. O'Keefe was asleep, his head resting on his chest. Vicente strode angrily toward the outlaw, prepared to kick him awake. Then he saw the vacant stare, the slack jaw, the upturned palm.

O'Keefe wasn't asleep. O'Keefe was dead.

So abruptly did Vicente stop that Stokes, walking behind him, nearly ran into him. Vicente closed his eyes and tensed his muscles, expecting at any second to feel the impact of the slug. He had laid enough traps in his life to recognize one when he walked into it, and he knew Martin Chambliss was nearby, watching him and Stokes down the barrel of a rifle. They were out in the open. There was no cover and no place to run. Chambliss had chosen the perfect spot. All these thoughts went through Vicente's mind in a fraction of a second. The only thing left now was for Chambliss to pull the trigger.

And Chambliss would have. He had spent over an hour sneaking up on O'Keefe, and afterward, he had arranged the body to make it look like the man was asleep. Then he had chosen his spot and waited.

He had four bullets left in the Spencer and three outlaws to kill. Vicente and Stokes were out in the open. He couldn't miss. That would leave two bullets for Jack Franey. He should be able to get Franey while he was still struggling out of his blanket. But as he was tightening his finger on the trigger to send a bullet through Vicente's heart, a movement beyond the Mexican caught his eye and his full attention.

Someone, and it could only be Jack Franey, was climbing up the steep face of the bluff, and he was almost to the top. Tory was up there and she was unarmed.

Jack Franey had lain awake a good part of the night, thinking, trying to figure out how Chambliss had tricked him. A man and a horse couldn't just disappear into thin air, and they couldn't ride off into the desert without leaving a trail. Finally, about an hour before dawn, by process of elimination it came to him. He didn't know how Chambliss had done it, but somehow he and the girl and even the horse had returned to the cave at the top of the bluff.

Grudgingly, Franey admired Chambliss' resourcefulness. It made sense. After Vicente and Stokes had searched the cave, it had become one of the safest places for Chambliss and the girl to be. Chambliss would figure the outlaws would not bother looking there again.

Most people would have never gone back there, but Chambliss didn't think like most people. If Franey had learned anything about the man, it was that he was like an Indian. He never did what you expected.

Franey sat up and reached for his boots, turning them over to shake out any unwelcome creatures that may have taken refuge there during the night. As he pulled them on, another thought occurred to him. If Chambliss was in the cave, he had spent the night watching Franey and his men, and he would certainly have planned something for this morning. Dawn was approaching, so whatever the plan was, he was probably already working on it, which meant the girl would be up there alone.

The small animal trail that led up the south face of the bluff was just that: a trail for small animals. It started out easy enough, just a gentle slope. After that it was a harder climb up to a narrow ledge about two-thirds of the way to the top. Franey made it to the ledge and crept along sideways, hugging the mountain, moving slowly, taking each step carefully so as not to step on anything loose that might dislodge and send him plummeting two hundred feet to the rocks below.

The next phase of the climb was a steep slope. There were plenty of good handholds and footholds, but each move had to be chosen carefully. From here on, if he slipped, there would be nothing to break his fall. He found that it wasn't a difficult climb as long as he took his time. He felt very little fear; he was too excited. He was certain the girl was up there, and he was equally certain she was alone.

He could have gone around to the sloping side of the bluff and up the safe trail, but he was sure she would be watching that trail. And, he reasoned, she would have a gun. Chambliss would have made sure of that. He had no way of knowing that between them, Tory and Chambliss now possessed only one firearm—thanks to Ricky.

Franey felt the familiar thrill of anticipation as he thought about the girl. He was even glad it had taken so long to catch her. It made the ending that much more exciting. He only had about ten feet left to go to be at the top of the bluff.

Chambliss had never known greater anguish than in the first few seconds after he spotted Jack Franey on the side of the bluff. There were four shots left in the Spencer, and Franey was far out of accurate rifle range. And what was he to do about the two outlaws standing a stone's throw away, watching him? His moment of indecision lasted a mere two or three seconds. He knew what he had to do.

There was no wind. He would not have to compensate for lateral drift, but he would have to allow for the fact that the bullet would drop significantly below the spot where he was aiming by the time it traveled such a great distance.

He took aim at a point just above Franey's head and squeezed the trigger. A tiny puff of dust appeared several feet below the outlaw's boots. Chambliss swung the barrel of the Spencer to cover Vicente and the other man and barked, "Stay where you are." He was reasonably sure they would not move; they would have too far to run for cover, and they knew he could shoot them before they made it. He levered another cartridge into the chamber and raised the barrel higher. He fired and this time the puff of dust appeared between Franey's boots.

Franey was climbing faster now, dislodging small stones that rolled and rattled down the slope. He knew he was being shot at, and he knew it had to be Chambliss. But he was almost to the top. Once there, he would be safe and he would have the girl. After that, Chambliss would not be able to touch him. The girl would be his hostage.

Chambliss raised the barrel higher this time, aiming almost at the top of the cliff. This one hit slightly to the left of Franey's midsection, and he cursed himself for having fired too quickly. He had one shot left.

Franey had just a few feet left to go when he saw the girl above him—her yellow hair, her fair skin, her blue eyes—leaning out over the edge and gasping in horror when she saw him. She jerked back, and Franey reached down and pulled his pistol just in case she tried to push him off as he eased himself over the top.

Chambliss took careful aim. This was his last chance. He sighted on Franey and then raised the barrel, gauging the distance.

And then he saw Tory.

In order to hit Franey he would have to aim directly at her. He knew the bullet would drop. He knew it would miss her, but squeezing the trigger that last time, with Tory perfectly notched in his sights, was one of the hardest things he had ever done. He felt the rifle kick against his shoulder. He heard its booming voice. The lead slug traveled the distance, and this time there was no puff of dust. Chambliss saw Franey flinch, but the outlaw didn't lose his grip. He stopped climbing. He was clinging to the mountain face like a fly.

Chambliss had scarcely noticed that Vicente and Stokes had pulled their guns. From the corner of his eye he had seen them move, and the fact had caused in him a greater sense of urgency, but he had paid no attention to them after that. Now he was aware that they were coming toward him.

He dropped the empty Spencer and faced them as they approached, their guns leveled at him. He turned to see if Jack Franey had made it to the top.

The outlaw still clung to the face of the bluff, and Tory was standing at the edge, looking down at him. With both hands, she held a large rock she had picked up nearby. She saw that he had dropped his pistol and was no longer climbing, but not knowing he had been shot, she didn't understand why. The look she had seen on his face when she first leaned over the cliff—that look of malicious triumph—had been replaced now by one she could not explain. He seemed . . . terrified. Was he suddenly afraid of the height? It didn't make sense.

"Please," he gasped. "Help me. I can't move my legs."

He was truly afraid, Tory realized. He actually wanted her to help him to the top. And then what? Would they have tea together and talk about old times?

Oddly, the thoughts that came into her mind at that moment were not of herself and Chambliss and all they had endured because of this man, but of the young boy who had died in Doc Stender's office while she held his hand, and of Mrs. Day, who, after fifty two years of making breakfast every morning for her husband, would never do it again.

She dropped the rock.

It struck Franey full in the face. He uttered a cry of anguish and started to slide downward, scrabbling and clawing at the mountain with his hands. He picked up speed rapidly down the steep slope, and when he reached the point where the slope ended, replaced by a vertical wall, he flew out over the edge. His hands continued clawing, though they grasped nothing but air. His legs did not move.

Chambliss and the two outlaws watched, fascinated. When it was over, Chambliss turned to face Vicente, whose pistol was pointed at his head. The Mexican gazed at him for a long moment with unreadable dark eyes. He shot a quick glance at Tory, still standing on the bluff, and turned back to Chambliss, "Jour woman?"

Chambliss couldn't tell if it was a question or a statement, but he nodded. "Yes, she's my woman."

Vicente motioned for Chambliss to step back, and he advanced and picked up the Spencer. He opened the breech, looked at the empty chamber, and dropped the rifle on the ground. Holding out a hand he said, "*Mi cuchillo.*"

Chambliss handed him the knife he had taken that first night after he had knocked Vicente unconscious. The Mexican grunted. He said something in Spanish to Stokes, who apparently understood the language, then holstered his pistol and walked away. Stokes stood there with his pistol in his hand, looking perplexed, his gaze shuttling between Chambliss and the departing outlaw. Presently, he shrugged and said, "Don't try to follow us," and he turned and walked after Vicente.

—➤━━━━━━━●

Across the distance, Chambliss and Tory watched as Vicente and Stokes packed up and rode away. They had not bothered to bury their dead companions, nor did Chambliss intend to burden himself with the task. He would need all his energy and all the water left in his body just to get Tory and himself out of this desert alive. He had retrieved Jack Franey's dropped pistol and found it to be scratched up and with one of the grips broken off, but still serviceable.

They took stock of their provisions. There was enough food for a couple of meals, but the water was almost gone. Ricky had left them very little. It would not be enough. They discussed the situation, and Chambliss asked, "How many whiskey bottles full of water were there at the springs?"

"Hundreds."

"Do you think the outlaws could have carried them all on their packhorses?"

"Not if they had other supplies, too."

"Then chances are," said Chambliss, "they left some there. We've got enough water to get us there, and if they left even a few bottles we can make it to Watervale—if the horse doesn't die."

"We're closer to Watervale right now, though, aren't we?"

"Yes, I wish we could go directly there, but to my knowledge there's no water between here and there." He looked at the sky. "Looks like there's a dust storm coming."

She looked and saw the towering dark brown cloud covering the horizon, and he saw disappointment on her face. He knew she was anxious to leave, and the storm would hold them up.

He went down and tied the horse in a sheltered spot and went back up to the cave to wait for the storm to pass. It lasted over an hour, and when it was over he went down again to check on the mare. She was gone. She had broken free during the storm. He climbed to a nearby promontory and spotted her in the distance, head down, grazing placidly. He set off on foot after her.

He had not lost the habit of vigilance, even though the outlaws were gone, and as he came over a rise he saw in the distance a dark spot against the light-colored desert. A horse and rider were coming toward him. He thought of Vicente and Stokes and knew it couldn't be them. They had ridden in another direction, and there were two of them—with extra horses. He concealed himself in a clump of brush and waited.

As the rider approached, Chambliss recognized Ricky Shaw. Ricky's horse was dying. It plodded along unsteadily with lowered head. Ricky was slumped in the saddle, looking as weary as his mount. Chambliss stepped out from cover and Ricky reined in.

"Chambliss!" his voice was a dry, rasping sound. "I'm glad to see you. Have you seen anything of Franey and his bunch?"

"They're gone."

"They shot me," Ricky said, indicating a blood-stained hip. "I didn't even get close to them and they shot me. I left everything behind, barely got away with my life."

Chambliss stood regarding him with unsympathetic eyes.

"You got any water, Chambliss? I need water real bad."

"No," said Chambliss coldly.

"Where's Tory? Is she still at the cave?"

Chambliss didn't respond.

"You trying to tell me she doesn't have any water? I don't believe it. You just don't want to give me any." Ricky spurred his horse forward a few paces to keep out of Chambliss' reach. "You'd let me die, wouldn't you, Chambliss. You've got water in that cave, and I'm going to have some of it. Tory won't keep it from me."

Chambliss knew that what Ricky was saying was true. Tory would give him water, and he would drink it all before she could stop him, and then there would not be enough for her. She would die in this desert.

Chambliss found himself in a difficult situation. For Tory's sake, he would not harm Ricky, but he knew he would have to protect her from her brother's selfishness. "Ricky," he said. "Let me catch my horse, and we'll ride to the springs, the three of us. The outlaws left water there. It'll be a thirsty ride, but we can make it."

Ricky laughed. "There's no water at the springs. I've just come from there."

Chambliss said, "It's buried. They put it in whiskey bottles and buried it."

Ricky shook his head. "They unburied it all. They took what they could carry and busted the rest. Must be a hundred busted whiskey bottles layin' there. I dug all around and didn't find a single bottle of water. I rode all this way on two swallows full. I guess I'm pretty thirsty, Chambliss. See you back at the cave." And with this he spurred his dying horse.

Chambliss didn't spend any time thinking about what he had to do. Ricky had left him with only one option. He pulled Franey's pistol out of his holster, sprinted alongside the pathetic animal, and shot it in the head. Ricky kicked free of the stirrups as the animal fell and then lay on his back and began to cry.

Chambliss said, "He was dead anyway, Ricky. You killed him riding him across this desert without water."

"Now I'll never get out of here," Ricky sobbed. "Because of you, I'll die here."

Chambliss felt no compassion for the young man. He said harshly, "Come on, let's go. Crying is just a waste of water." He walked away.

But Ricky lay there and sobbed like a child. Chambliss was a good distance away when Ricky's childish self-pity turned to childish anger, and he stood up and pulled his pistol and fired several times. He fired wildly without aiming, and he missed. Chambliss spun around, palming his pistol as Ricky fired another shot. Chambliss felt the air move as this one passed close by.

Ricky thumbed the hammer back again, calmer now, taking careful aim, and once again he left Chambliss only one course of action. And Chambliss didn't miss.

Tory met him at the entrance to the little valley. She had heard the shots and feared for his safety. He was leading the mare, and she saw the body slung over the saddle. She immediately recognized the clothing.

He looked at her and did not know what to say. She looked at him, and she didn't either.

The children were sitting in the shade of a mesquite tree, flipping seedpods at each other and trying to catch ant lions. It was too hot to do anything more strenuous than that. Billy Patterson was the first to see the man coming out of the desert. He was walking slowly, weaving ever so slightly, like a man who knows he has had too much to drink and is determined not to let it show. Fascinated, the children watched the man as he approached. His clothes were ragged and filthy, and he was hatless. He wore moccasins instead of shoes, but he didn't appear to be an Indian. He was burnt by the sun, and it was clear that he had been without water for some time. He reached the main road and turned, walking toward them.

Billy Patterson stood up and said, "Hello, mister."

The man gave a nod.

Billy said, "Mister, we got water."

The man spoke in a cracked voice that was just above a whisper. "You got a horse?"

"Pa took it."

"Can you run fast?"

"Uh-huh"

"Then run as fast as you can and get Marshall Ashworth."

Billy told one of the other children to bring the man some water. He took off at a run, and within minutes, Marshall Ashworth rode up. It took him a moment to recognize Chambliss, and then he exclaimed, "Martin! We thought you were dead."

Chambliss said, "I need a wagon and some canteens."

"What you need is a week in bed."

Chambliss shook his head adamantly, "Tory is still out there."

Ashworth's eyes widened. "Tory? Tory Shaw? Is she alive?"

"She was when I left her."

CHAPTER 22

Martin Chambliss walked up Montezuma Street in Prescott Arizona and wondered why he had come here. It had been a long ride for nothing. There was nothing for him here. The problem was there was nothing for him anywhere. He had lost everything he had ever cared about. Considering how little he had accomplished in his long ride up to the center of Arizona Territory, he may as well have stayed in Pick-Em-Up; at least there he had some friends and he had had his claim to work and his cattle. Not much of a purpose for a man's life, but more than he had here.

Hal Dean, of all people, had started the sequence of events that had brought him here to Prescott. The former Diamond J rider had walked into the Frisco Lady one evening when Chambliss was sitting with Westmoreland and Bledsoe at their usual table. Chambliss saw him come in and watched as Hal scanned the room, his gaze lighting on Chambliss. They each gave a brief nod, and Hal went to the bar and got a drink. Chambliss had a pretty strong hunch that Hal's presence here was no coincidence, and he waited to see what the cowboy would do.

Presently, Hal turned back to look at him, and with a motion of his head, indicated an empty table. Responding to the invitation, Chambliss crossed and sat opposite him.

Hal said, "Been hearin' about you, Chambliss. Word is you killed Jack Franey."

"What can I do for you, Hal?"

Hal held Chambliss' gaze for a few moments, then, with an ironic smile, looked down at his drink. He said, "I don't suppose you have any reason to like me, Chambliss, but I figure I owe you an explanation about something."

"You don't. Let's just forget it."

"Will you let a man talk?"

Chambliss leaned back, folding his arms on his chest.

"That day in Arivaca—the day you killed Lencho Bautista—you thought I told you he was gone so you'd go in the saloon and get yourself killed. You were wrong. I lied to you thinkin' you'd ride away. I figured if you met up with Lencho he would kill you. I was tryin' to keep that from happenin'." His voice dropped, and he looked away. "Just wanted you to know that."

"Didn't know it mattered to you," said Chambliss.

"Hal smiled a little. "It didn't—much. But I can dislike a man without wantin' him dead."

Chambliss smiled a little too. He had a feeling Hal had something else to say, so he waited.

"Listen," said Hal. "I was wrong about you. We all were. That's all I wanted to say." He tossed off the last of his drink and said, "Guess I'll be movin' along. Take care of yourself."

He started to rise, but Chambliss said, "There's something you need to know too."

Hal settled back in the chair.

"I knew Jane before she ever came out here. We were going to be married."

Hal's eyebrows lifted, but he remained silent.

"Shortly before the wedding, she got word her grandfather had died, and she decided we needed to come out here after we were married. We quarreled about it—a bad quarrel. She cancelled the wedding and came alone. Not long after that, I came out to make things right between us. You know the rest."

There was sympathy in Hal's eyes when he said, "I'm sorry, Chambliss. I didn't know."

"No. She wouldn't let me tell anyone. She wanted me to work for her and try to find out who was stealing her cattle."

"Does Whitey know any of this?"

"No."

"You still interested in knowin' where he is?"

Chambliss was thoughtful for a moment, and he said, "Hadn't thought about it in a while."

"He lives in Tucson with his sister. Runs a few head of cattle thereabouts. If you ever get up that way, seems to me he ought to be told."

Chambliss nodded, making no commitment.

There was a break in the conversation, and then Hal said,

"Chambliss, I guess a man who could kill Lencho Bautista and Jack Franey wouldn't lie about outrunning an Apache."

Chambliss almost laughed. "Is that a question?"

Hal seemed to struggle with his answer, but he obviously wanted to know. He finally nodded. "Reckon it is."

Chambliss said, "It was not a lie."

For some time, Chambliss had been planning to leave Pick-Em-Up, having no reason left to stay, but Hal's visit had stirred up old memories in him, and he departed shortly thereafter, hoping to leave some of them behind. But of course it was a false hope. A man carries his ghosts with him wherever he goes.

Tory had been almost dead when they brought her out of the desert. She had been delirious for days, suffering from horrible, lurid nightmares. She had dreamed that Chambliss had murdered Ricky out of spite and then abandoned her in the desert, leaving her to die. In her partially lucid moments, she talked about these things with her parents, and they, having no other information, took them to be true.

Ralph and Myra Shaw were guilt stricken over having brought their family to this violent place. When Tory was brought back to them by the men who had been guided to her by Chambliss, the Shaws immediately made arrangements to move someplace more civilized, and they took Tory away even before she was fully recovered.

Numerous times, Chambliss tried to see her before the Shaws left but was coldly told that if she wanted to see him, they would let him know.

No word ever came.

Though he did not know about her disarranged mental state, he thought he understood how she must feel. He had killed her brother. She probably felt she simply couldn't love the man who had done that, no matter what his reason for doing it.

He had relived that event in his mind a hundred times, asking himself what he could have done differently, and he had concluded every time that he had done what he had to do. Ricky had given him no choice.

He remembered the long trek out of the desert, traveling at night to conserve what little water was left in their dehydrated bodies, the death of the mare, and watching Tory's strength fade until he had decided the only way to save her was to leave her and go on alone to get help.

Leaving her alone had been the hardest thing he had ever done. Harder, even, than putting her in the sights of the Spencer when he had shot Jack Franey.

So many hard things. Life was full of them.

Whitey and his sister lived in a small house on the outskirts of Tucson. It was early evening when Chambliss knocked on the door. He had chosen this time of day hoping to catch Whitey at home. And he did; Whitey answered the door.

There was no welcoming smile on the old man's face, nor had Chambliss expected there would be. Without preamble, he said, "Hal told me where to find you."

"Hal ought to keep his mouth shut."

"There's something he thought I should tell you."

Whitey seemed to ponder this for a moment, then stepped aside and growled, "Come in, then."

Whitey's sister was there, a petite, gray-haired woman. She said, "Dinner's on the table. Would you like to stay, Mr. . . ?"

"Chambliss," supplied Whitey.

Her expression changed, and Chambliss knew Whitey had told her about him. But the invitation had been extended, and he accepted it.

It was the best meal Chambliss had eaten in a very long time, and it made him realize how many things he had been missing in his solitary life. The realization made him think of Tory, and he experienced a deep pang of grief.

After the meal, after he had bestowed his sincere compliments on Whitey's sister, he looked at Whitey and said, "Jane and I were engaged to be married."

Chambliss watched as Whitey's face reddened. "That's a lie," he said hotly. "We found you out in the desert."

"I was coming to marry her when the stage was attacked by Apaches."

Whitey rose from his chair. "You're a liar. Get out."

From his shirt pocket, Chambliss produced the small newspaper clipping he had kept since cutting it out of a fresh newspaper. It was the same one he had showed to Captain Roderick in Skeleton Canyon, the same one he had shown to Sally Ewart on the day he had gone to see Slim.

He handed the clipping to Whitey, who passed it directly to his sister, and Chambliss realized the old man either had bad eyes or did not know how to read.

She read aloud. "Mr. and Mrs. Amos Quilter are pleased to announce the betrothal of their daughter, Miss Jane Alice Quilter to Mr. Martin Chambliss . . ."

She finished reading the piece, and she and Chambliss both watched Whitey's face. The old man sat down again. He seemed lost in thought. Finally, he said, "I though your name was Horace."

Chambliss replied, "That was a little joke between Jane and me—the name of an old boyfriend of hers. Jane wanted to keep our relationship a secret while I tried to figure out who was doing the rustling."

Sounding hurt, Whitey said, "Why didn't she tell me? Didn't she trust me?"

"She trusted you and she loved you. She wanted to tell you, but I made her keep quiet. I was wrong, I know that now, but I didn't know you any better than I knew the others. I didn't know who I could trust and who I couldn't."

Whitey pondered this in silence for a time. When he spoke, it was in an accusatory tone. "You opened that letter and read it."

"The letter to Lester Howard."

"That's right. That was the name."

"Near the place where Jane and I grew up, there's a small meadow with a creek flowing through it. There's an old abandoned cabin there that was built by a man named Lester Howard, who died before either of us was born. The roof has caved in, and it's full of mud, but it's still known as Lester Howard's cabin. It sits next to the creek. We used to go fishing there. That was where I kissed her the first time, and it was where I asked her to marry me."

"Oh," said Whitey's sister, "how precious."

Chambliss continued, "She wanted to tell me some things, and it would have seemed suspicious—and improper—if she had called me to the house every time she needed to talk to me. She knew I would recognize the name and know the letter was for me."

Whitey's sister got up and started removing plates and dishes from the table. For a long time, no one spoke. Finally Whitey said, "I guess Hal was right, Chambliss. I needed to know." He looked at Chambliss. "She was a fine girl. I've missed her."

"I have too."

"I heard it was Lencho Bautista and Jack Franey that killed her and that poor little Josefina."

"It was."

"Couple years back, I heard Bautista was killed. Wish somebody would put a bullet in Jack Franey too."

"Somebody did."

After his visit with Whitey, Chambliss rode north to Phoenix, and again found no reason to remain. After Phoenix he continued north to Prescott, a three-day ride. Before leaving Pick-Em-Up, in saying good-bye to his friends, he had gone to see Doc Stender. Stender asked him where he was going, and Chambliss said, "Don't know, Doc, but I've been missing pine trees and snow."

Stender chuckled and said, "Ever been to Prescott?"

"No."

"Might want to have a look."

Stender had been right. Chambliss liked this place better than any he had seen in Arizona Territory. It was in the Bradshaw Mountains, a cool place with snow in the winter and fresh mountain breezes in the summer—and there were pine trees. But he could think of no reason to remain here, and the realization further depressed him. He was tired of feeling anchorless. He had never wanted to be a drifter. He was the kind of man who needed to put down roots, raise a family, build something.

He reached the hotel and went to his room. He lay back on the bed and tried to understand the emptiness he was feeling. A part of his life had just passed away, he realized. He had fulfilled his promises to Jane and George Durfee. He had made his peace with Hal Dean and Whitey. He had left southern Arizona, the place where it all had happened. It was almost like a death.

He knew there would always be a part of him that would miss

Jane, but she had been dead for almost three years, and a man had to move on with his life. But what life?

There had been a brief time when he had thought that life would be spent with Tory, and he had felt a joyous hope. But that hope had been replaced with more grief and loss.

And he missed Tory. He missed her constantly. She had taught him that he could love again, and love every bit as much as he had loved Jane.

There was a knock on the door. He opened it to find Ralph Shaw standing there.

"Hello, Martin."

Chambliss made no effort to conceal his surprise. "Ralph . . . hello. What are you doing here?"

"I . . ." Ralph didn't seem to know what to say.

Chambliss was not much better off. The suddenness of the situation left him without speech. He finally said, "How are you, Ralph?"

"I'm well, Martin . . . And you?"

"Just fine. Didn't expect to see you here."

"I have a store here." There was a silence, and Ralph said, "Family's here too."

With a casualness he did not feel, Chambliss said, "Oh, and are they well?"

Ralph suddenly found words, "Martin, we need to talk. May I come in?"

"Of course."

Chambliss sat on the bed, and Ralph sat in the room's single chair. He said, "Martin, I don't know exactly how to say what I need to say to you, but . . ." He looked down and took a deep breath, composing his thoughts. After a moment he began again, speaking softly, "Tory was very sick for some time after she came back to us. It wasn't until after we brought her up here to Prescott that she truly got well and was able to tell us the story—the straight story. We know now that you saved her life—more than once. Myra and I are very grateful to you. I know Myra would like to tell you in person."

"Are you sure about that, Ralph? She's never . . ."

"I'm sure," interrupted Ralph. "She saw you on the street yesterday. She told me she had seen you, and we . . . we discussed it. She sent me to get you."

Ralph seemed to become uncomfortable, and after clearing his throat, he said, "Back in Pick-Em-Up, we never told Tory you had been coming around to inquire after her. Her mother and I felt it was . . . better if she didn't know. We were wrong. We were trying to protect our daughter, and at the time we thought we were doing the right thing."

Chambliss could think of no words to say. He was struggling to accommodate his mind and his feelings to all that was happening so suddenly. He remembered Doc Stender's recommendation that he come to Prescott. Stender had acted like he knew something he was not telling. Now Chambliss understood: Stender had attended Tory in her illness. Undoubtedly, the Shaws had told him they were taking her away from Pick-Em-Up. Indeed, they may have done so on his recommendation. And, of course, they would have sworn him to secrecy. His mentioning to Chambliss that Prescott was a nice place had been more than just a casual remark.

Abruptly, Ralph said, "Come with me, Martin. Myra wants to see you."

The Shaw home was an impressive two-story structure with a large and well-tended fenced yard. Ralph had done well in Pick-Em-Up, and now his family was enjoying the fruits of that success.

Myra Shaw was waiting, sitting at a table under a tree. She rose and took Chambliss by the hand and bade him sit down. "I have some tea made," she said. She poured the tea, and they all sipped for a few moments. Chambliss waited.

Presently, Myra said, "Since coming to Prescott, Ralph and I have become aware of some things." She looked at her husband and asked, "Did you tell him?"

"Yes."

She continued, "First, I want to apologize for thinking so ill of you. Tory was delirious and she said some things—awful things— that weren't true. We now know that you didn't kill our son. It is a great comfort to know he died protecting Tory from the bandits."

Chambliss understood why Tory had told them that lie, and he agreed with her having done so. He had no illusions, however, supposing she had done it to save them from pain rather than to keep them from hating him. "Yes, ma'am," he said.

Myra spoke again. "We were wrong to keep you and Tory apart. We let her believe you didn't care enough to come and see her. We have seen the results of that lie. It broke our daughter's heart. After we came up here—when she was finally well enough—we told her the truth, and she wrote you a letter. We paid a man to take it to you in Pick-Em-Up, but he came back with the news that you had left for good without saying where you were going."

Myra looked at Chambliss, and he saw tears in her eyes. She said, "Tory has been inconsolable since then." She pointed to the house. "Mr. Chambliss, if it matters to you, Tory is in there."

He looked at her and said without hesitation, "It matters to me, Mrs. Shaw. It matters very much."

Tory was in her room when her mother came in and said, "Dear, your father wants to see you outside."

Tory went out and said, "Yes, Father?"

He sat at the table, looking at her, saying nothing. She was about to speak again when she felt a touch on her shoulder and turned around.

And for a while, all she could do was cry.

*

OFFICIAL WEBSITE
authorcmcurtis.com

FOLLOW C.M. ON FACEBOOK
facebook.com/authorcmcurtis

Made in the USA
Lexington, KY
18 April 2017